IT'S NOT MY FAVORITE

THE LAKE EFFECT SERIES, BOOK 1

BY RUE

Sittin' On A Goldmine
Productions L.L.C.

Sittin' On A Goldmine Productions, L.L.C.
100 Arbuckle Drive
Sedona, AZ 86336

This is a work of fiction. Names, characters, places and incidents are products of the author's imagination or are used fictitiously and are not to be construed as real. Any resemblance to actual events, locales, organizations, or persons, living or dead, is entirely coincidental.

Rue
It's Not My Favorite : a novel / by Rue, —1st ed.

ISBN: 978-0-9860627-6-6 (Paperback)
1. Sisters—Fiction. 2. Dysfunctional Families—Fiction. 3. Love—Fiction.
4. Self-Discovery—Fiction. 5. Lake Superior (MN)—Fiction.

www.sittinonagoldmine.co

Printed in the United States of America

For Rita, who made it possible for me
to live long enough to see this dream come true.

And to MSG, JAG & MAG – my "go-to" boys!

Prologue

Gwenn saw him shining like a lighthouse on the other side of the business mixer. His close-cropped hair and his crisp white shirt created the perfect frame for his rugged jaw and tantalizing smirk.

Greyson Congdon slowly made his way across the room. He stopped to shake a hand here and grasp a shoulder there, he passed a few cards to eager business owners and of course whispered god-knows-what into several women's ears.

"Good evening, Ms. Hutchinson." Greyson extended his strong, long-fingered hand toward Gwenn.

"I think we are way past handshakes." Gwenn flipped her shoulder-length auburn hair and gave Greyson a little wink.

He leaned in and whispered so softly in Gwenn's ear that she had to tilt her head closer to hear. Greyson's tongue flicked the edge of her earlobe and Gwenn felt a sudden change in the humidity. "My office is only a short skyway jaunt away," she managed.

"Let me just check out with the Mayor, you know—City Manager stuff, and I will be right *behind* you." Greyson let his hand slide along the side of Gwenn's breast as he disengaged. "MmmmmHmmm."

Gwenn was in her office, pacing in front of her small desk, when his shadow spilled around the corner.

Greyson strode into the room, locked the office door and salaciously undressed Gwenn with his eyes.

She shuddered under his gaze.

He descended on her like a wolf, devouring its prey. His hands shoved her skirt up and one hand slipped inside her panties while the other unbuttoned her blouse.

Gwenn was moaning and undulating her hips. She could barely concentrate on removing his belt. The leather slapped against her thigh as she yanked it loose. "Oh…Greyson…I want…"

Greyson was way ahead of her. Panties hit the floor and he was inside of her before she could finish her sentence.

Their bodies blended together and Gwenn felt like Greyson was under her skin. The waves of electricity shot through her, she could feel the tide rising and hear the change in Greyson's breathing.

He pulled her down harder and harder he licked the sweet, salty drops of sweat from her breast.

KNOCK, KNOCK, KNOCK. The knocking on her office door was distracting Gwenn. No, no, no not now! She was so close.

"Gwenn, open up! You've got the chain on. Come on freak, it's time to work out!"

Gwenn felt the tide ebbing and watched Greyson evaporate. Just once she would like to finish that dream!

"Goddamit Rachel! I told you last night I DO NOT want to work out." Gwenn stormed out to the hallway, kicked her sister Rachel's toe out of the sliver of space between the front door and the door jam and slammed it shut. She barely had the chain off when Rachel burst into the apartment.

Rachel's ebony ponytail was bobbing angrily. "What the fuck Gwenny? Did I interrupt something important?"

"As a matter of fact you did. I was about ten seconds away from a very big orgasm!"

"Oh, shit! No way, you've got a guy in there?" Rachel was dumbstruck by the thought that Gwenn may have broken her three-year dry-spell.

"No, freak, it was the Greyson dream." Gwenn blushed like a radish.

"Gwenny you're becoming a scary hermit-woman that only has sex in her dreams."

"Leave me alone Rache. I have a social life. I have weekly lunches with Flora and Thea, and I—"

"Gwenn wake up! Flora and Thea are your employees. You take them out to lunch, you pay and they eat. That's not a fucking social life." Rachel unzipped her jacket, wiggled out of it and threw it on Gwenn's couch. She quickly pulled it back when she noticed the half-empty Chinese take-out box wedged between the cushions. Rachel scanned the room and cringed. "This place is a dump! Isn't that kinda bad for *The Organizer*'s image?"

Gwenn did not respond to the jab at her company.

Rachel spun around to see Gwenn shoving an entire glazed donut into her mouth. "How dare you! Gwenny you know how much I hate donuts. You're just standing there tormenting the fat kid trapped inside these Lycra running pants. Bitch!" Rachel stuck out her lower lip and put her hands on her toned, shapely hips.

"Rache, I'm sorry. I just didn't have time to shop and the donut place was open and...I have more excuses around here somewhere."

"Good luck finding 'em!" Rachel laughed at her own joke and continued, "What the hell happened?"

"It's just me here. I spend everyday organizing other people's shit. I organize them because I can't...since Jasper left I just put everything into work and...this place, this apartment, is just the pod where I recharge my automaton batteries.

Rachel's hands slipped off her hips and she ran to swallow Gwenn in a fierce hug.

Gwenn went limp in Rachel's arms. Their mother never hugged like this, no one hugged like Rachel. Gwenn allowed her gaze to take in the horrible mess that was her home and chuckled at its perfect reflection of her heart. A disaster.

"Rache, I'm not going running with you. It's my only day off this week and I am going to sit here and read magazines and eat donuts. I love you, but I hate running as much as you hate donuts."

"Yeah, well we don't all have your bizarre metabolism. You got all the good genes." Rachel shook her head, "Fine, I'll agree to your couch potato day if you'll go to that weird costume party they have for all the companies in your office building next week," she finished with a huge grin.

"Give it up Rache. I don't have anything to wear and I hate watching all those weird middle-aged guys getting wasted and hitting on anything in a mini-dress. And they are ALL in mini-dresses. It's just a stupid hall pass for all the stuffed shirts and uptight control freaks to get wildly drunk and *forget* that their jobs suck."

"You've gotta go to the office Halloween party this year," bullied Rachel, "and you have to make your employees come, too."

"Have to? What catastrophe will befall me if I skip the party and hole up in my apartment with a bag of candy-coated Sixlets, Rache?"

"You mean more catastrophic than those baggy sweatpants you're wearing—from a college you haven't attended in 11 years?"

Gwenn laughed, "You are such a little bitch!"

One

Gwenn Hutchinson tucked an unruly strand of her copper-brown hair back under her leather flight helmet and stared through the fractals of frost on the window of the downtown office complex community room. The lights of the city flickered through the falling snow, and beyond them was the gaping, black void that was Lake Superior. Some days Gwenn found comfort in the huge waves or the glint of sunshine off the water, but not tonight. The disconsolate, brumal blackness matched her mood perfectly.

She rolled her intense hazel eyes at the plethora of cleavage spilling forth in the room, and beamed inwardly at the sensible costume she had procured by combing through the bins at the second-hand clothing store.

Gwenn normally made polite excuses and skipped the office complex Fall Costume mixer. This year her unrelenting sister, Rachel, had railroaded her into attending. Gwenn, in turn, had prevailed upon her staff to share in her punishment.

"Happy Halloween, Elmer Fudd!" Rachel's laugh filled the room and evaporated into the acoustic ceiling tiles.

Gwenn glanced appraisingly at Rachel's sexy witch costume. Thigh-high, leather boots, fishnet stockings and a short velvety cape were the perfect accents to the tiny, black, bustier dress. Rachel's ebony hair was caught up into a pair of loose braids that emphasized her new dark cherry streaks. Her pointy black hat was festooned with spiders and silver stars. Rachel's costume even smelled new—not a whiff of bargain basement castoff.

"I'm Amelia Earhart, Rache, not Elmer Fudd. What are you? The Wicked Bitch of the West?"

Rachel ignored Gwenn's jibe. "Wow, Amelia Earhart! That should get the guys lining up; or maybe you're changing teams?" Rachel's eyes twinkled as she teased Gwenn.

"Hey, I don't try to push my hetero tendencies on you."

"If I get you drunk, will you dance to this awesome 80s music with me?" Rachel sashayed off to the bar, without waiting for Gwenn's reply. Rachel had been openly gay for over ten years. Well, openly to everyone except her parents. Her mother Shirley's religious fervor just wouldn't allow for a lesbian daughter, so Rachel never bothered to tell her. Of course that was only partially effective, since that left Rachel open for a lot of "date a nice Christian boy" speeches. But Rachel was not as independent as Gwenn, and she still needed the occasional loan from Shirley and Pastor Ed. Rachel was pretty sure they wouldn't loan money to someone who was going to hell.

Gwenn searched the crowd for no one in particular while she waited uncomfortably for Rachel's return. The last thing in the world she wanted to have right now was an awkward conversation with some strange co-tenant.

Rachel reappeared with two Slippery Nipples and insisted that she only ordered them because they taste so good. "The bartender said they're having karaoke later. If I get drunk enough I'll have to throw down some Prince. Show these Minnesotan's their roots!"

"Yeah this looks like a real Prince crowd," Gwenn scanned the room and counted at least four Dorothy variations, several Vikings—both the Norse and the football versions—and no less than three nuns. Yep, total *Little Nikki* sex machine vibe.

"Where are your minions? I mean, it's an office party, shouldn't the girls be gettin' their drink on?" Rachel shouted above the hilarity of the *Chicken Dance*.

Gwenn shook her head and shrugged her shoulders. "They're here somewhere. Flora is dressed as a ghost—shocker, and Thea is spilling out of a naughty nurse costume." Gwenn scanned the crowd and pointed to the petite blonde in the white mini-uniform, surrounded by middle-aged men.

"She...is...oooooh, I wonder if I could recruit her?" Rachel twirled her sparkly black wand and sighed.

"What about Annie?" Gwenn knew that Rachel was having some difficulties with her partner, but the two of them had been together for three years; Gwenn hoped for the best.

"Let's not spoil a perfectly wicked night by bringing up the old ball and chain!" Rachel flicked her wand at Gwenn and chanted, "You're getting thirsty...thirsty...thirsty."

"Come on Witchy Poo, let's get you some more 'Essence of Happiness' at the bar," Gwenn chuckled.

Rachel over-indulged, as was her custom when she was in turmoil, and Gwenn happily lived vicariously through her baby sister's passion for life. Rachel danced with all the wallflowers, guys and gals, spreading the love and causing only one minor scuffle.

"Hey, she's dancing with me!" yelled Jeff the sandwich cart guy, currently a decomposing zombie.

"Wake up moron! That was a pity dance. A chic that hot is gonna go home with me!" Retorted some Viking meathead that Gwenn did not recognize.

Viking meathead advanced on poor Jeff.

"Hey big guy," Gwenn improvised, "I hate to break it to you, but that witch is totally gay. She's not going home with either of you." Gwenn searched her brain for a meathead distraction. "However, I happen to know that the naughty nurse over there is straight AND single."

Meathead Viking paused to process the unbelievable idea that the witchy woman might not be interested in him, but when he caught site of Thea's white back-seamed stockings he forgot all about Jeff.

"Thanks Gwenn. Viking beats Lilliputian zombie every time." Jeff tried to laugh, but the beads of sweat on his upper lip belied his off-handed repartee.

"I had to do something Jeff. I would starve to death without your daily sandwich salvation. I mean, you do know that I never leave my office, right?"

Jeff's shoulder's relaxed and he bashfully accepted the sincere compliment. "Hey, where's Flora?"

"Why Jeff, I had no idea you were a necromancer." Gwenn saw the confusion cloud Jeff's face. "Sorry, bad joke. She's a ghost. I mean literally, sheet with holes, etc. Good luck finding her." Gwen pretended to see someone in the crowd and smiled at Jeff as she rushed away. She turned the corner just in time to see Rachel climbing up on the buffet. "Oh, you gotta be frickin' kidding me." Gwenn made it to the bathroom before Rachel hit the chorus of *Let's Go Crazy*.

Hiding in the bathroom, Gwenn remembered a far more embarrassing Halloween. She was barely ten and had just started fifth grade at a new school, several weeks late in keeping with the Hutchinson family annual relocation tradition.

"Hi, I'm Gwenn." No one at the lunch table acknowledged her existence. "Um, sorry, I didn't want to bug you. I was just wondering if any of you wanted to come to my big Halloween party?" Gwenn smoothly lied.

All heads turned.

"Cool!" Came from several directions.

"Yeah, totally," chimed in a few guys.

"Awesome. What's your costume, Jen?" Sarah Beth asked.

"Oh, it's Gwenn, and my costume is Catwoman." Gwenn embellished.

"Wow. My mom is making me dress like Alice in Wonderland. I can't wait to come to your party." Sarah Beth made room for Gwenn at the table, "Here, sit by me."

Gwenn had rushed home, filled with the excitement of acceptance—finally.

"Hey Trixie, yer home early." Pastor Ed patted Gwenn patronizingly on the head. "Take a seat in the living room. We are havin' a family meeting."

Gwenn felt her stomach churn. Oh crap they were moving again. She just made an actual friend. Why were Ed and Shirley so dead set against her having friends?

"Hi Gwenny!" Rachel beamed.

"Shut up, twerp." Gwenn stuck her tongue out at Rachel.

Shirley took the reins, "Girls the Lord has spoken to us and He has shown us that Halloween is Satan's night. As

good Christians we cannot sin against the Lord by paying tribute to the Devil." She closed her eyes and folded her hands in prayer.

"What'd that mean mommy?" Rachel innocently asked.

"Halloween's canceled idiot! No costumes. No candy." Gwenn stormed out of the room.

Big wet tears rolled down Rachel's chubby cheeks. "No candy!" She wailed.

But the torment was much greater for Gwenn.

Ed and Shirley didn't have the decency to cancel Halloween at the Hutchinson house. Instead, they carved up some pumpkins and turned on the porch lights to lure the unsuspecting children. Gwenn hid on the stairs and watched through the banister as innocent trick-or-treaters came to the door and Shirley shoved little orange tracts in their treat bags and told them Jesus died for their sins.

Sarah Beth did not make room for Gwenn—ever again.

That's when the emotional deformities started. The inability to trust completely, the gnawing nameless guilt and finally that unsettling feeling that someone was judging her every action—and Gwenn always came up short.

She kept telling herself it would change, that someday she would find the key that would unlock the door to her invisible prison and she would be free.

Gwenn jumped when the music stopped. She wiped an unexplained tear from her cheek, exhaled the *yuck* and marched out of the bathroom.

The party was winding down and Rachel had crossed the line between life of the party and annoying drunk; landing clumsily on the pain-in-the-ass side of that line. Gwenn shepherded her sister through the maze of glass and steel skyway corridors connecting the buildings of Duluth's downtown.

They emerged into the bitter cold wind knifing across the harbor and Gwenn tried to hurry the procession to her car. Rachel was already quite numb from the alcohol, so the cold had little effect.

"Rache, come on. I'm freezing. I'll take you back to my place."

"No...home," slurred Rachel, insistently.

"But..."

"Gotta work..."

"You have to open the bakery tomorrow? Rache, how the hell are you gonna—"

"No worries, mate," Rachel spouted off in her best Australian accent.

"Oh, crikey!" Gwenn was keenly aware that in the order of Rachel's sorrow-drowning inebriation, accents preceded vomiting and passing out was just around the corner.

"Fine. I'll take you home, but you have to hurry." Gwenn steered zig-zaggy Rachel to the Jeep and fishtailed out of the icy parking lot in a hasty attempt to arrive at Rachel's loft before phase vomit emerged.

Gwenn beat the odds and managed to get Rachel into her own bed without further incident. She removed the alcohol-stained costume and placed it on Rachel's dry cleaning pile. Gwenn kissed her sister on the forehead, tucked the comforter under Rachel's chin and quietly flicked off the light as she left the loft.

Two

Rachel opened her coffee-brown eyes, rubbed her throbbing temples and pulled herself up on one elbow. She touched the striped, cotton sheets where Annie should've been and pulled the down comforter back up over her head in despair.

The first few months had been like a dream. Everything was perfect and they were so in love. The next year things cooled off a bit, but there was still a nice, warming heat. They went on fabulous trips and bought this loft together. Now, another year had slipped by and they barely spoke. Just discussed bills, deadlines and social calendars—oddly the social calendars were synching up less and less. Annie was spending a lot of time with new people, people that Rachel had never met.

The digital clock beeped noisily and Rachel jumped up to shut it off before Annie could be disturbed in the next room. She wasn't ready to start her day with an argument. Rachel grabbed a clean T-shirt, panties and a sports bra from her bureau, and hurried across the chilly, oak floor to the promise of warmth in a shower. As she locked the bathroom door, she thought back to the days when she would have never even imagined showering alone. Now there was no time for fun, or more likely—fights. Rachel combed her long, claret-streaked, ebony hair and put on a little lip tint. She wasn't a total girlie-girl, but she liked to look good and lip protection wasn't optional when the temperature outside might be sub-arctic.

By the time Rachel got out of the bathroom Annie was up and they passed silently beneath the Italian marble sconces in the hallway. Rachel crammed a Clif bar into the pocket of her cozy, Patagonia jacket and grabbed her keys and wallet, "Bye Annie," she mouthed as she opened the door. She stopped in her tracks when she saw Annie's phone sitting on the granite counter.

The phone was in her hand and her heart was racing. "I shouldn't...I really shouldn't...," but she did.

">u can strum me like ur bass anytime" from someone with the initials TK. Annie didn't even put the full name in her phone. That was super suspicious.

Rachel had gone this far, her stomach was swirling and her heart was pounding. She just had to read the reply.

">my next gig is Friday - wanna cum ;-)" Annie had replied.

Rachel heard the handle twist on the bathroom door. She tapped the screen back to Home, set the phone down as fast as she could and raced out the door.

Straight to her big sister's office.

Gwenn was sitting behind her desk staring blankly at the stack of proposals that Flora had prepared. Maybe she should hire The Organizer to straighten up her own apartment—and life. Her cell phone rang, impatiently. It was Rachel.

"Gwenny," Rachel was struggling to hold back tears, "I need to talk to you right away. You in your office?"

"Yeah Rache, come on over..." Gwenn noticed some movement through the blinds on her office window. "Rachel are you standing outside my office door?"

A single guilty hand reached around the corner and waved.

Gwenn smiled and carefully whispered into the phone, "Um, you may as well come all the way in, freak."

Rachel lurched into the room, still on her cell. She leaned against the door and took a dramatic pause.

"Rachel, first of all hang up your phone and second what is so frickin' urgent that you just barged into my day?" Gwenn was accustomed to Rachel's drama, but today she just didn't have the patience.

"Annie's cheating on me." Rachel barely finished the sentence before the tears spilled out.

Gwenn was filled with the sublime childhood guilt that was triggered every time she attempted to put her own needs ahead of someone else's. As usual, her day could wait. "No—are you sure?" Gwenn did not know what to say, or what to do. She put an arm around Rachel and steered her to a chair. "What happened?"

"I looked at her phone...her texts," Rachel blurted out between sobs.

"What? Rachel, how could you? That's totally inappropriate."

Rachel choked down a sob, "Are you fucking kidding me Gwenn? I tell you my partner is cheating on me and you think reading her text messages is the inappropriate thing?" Rachel buried her face in her hands.

"Rache, I'm sorry. You're right. What are you going to do?"

"I'm gonna go to her fucking gig on Friday and beat the shit out of TK."

"Rache, who is TK?"

"How the fuck do I know? Annie was obviously trying to cover her tracks. She only put the initials in her phone. What if it is someone I know? What if she's been in the bakery?" Rachel's tears resumed.

"It doesn't matter who it is, it matters that it's happening...or is going to happen," Gwenn's 'assess, plan and execute' gears were spinning. "What, exactly did the texts say?"

"Why does that matter?"

"Maybe we can intercept and thwart—"

Rachel laughed through her tears, "Did you actually just use the word 'thwart'?" Rachel wiped haphazardly at her tears. "Just come to the gig with me on Friday. I have to see it with my own eyes and then..."

Gwenn put her arm around Rachel, "OK, I'm there."

Three

The day was easily on the top ten suckiest days list. Gwenn poured a third glass of wine after dinner, but then who needs a reason she thought as she finished the bottle. Night after night of eating take-out in her apartment was growing old. Eating out alone was out of the question—even if she was modern and independent.

She leaned back into her sofa, reached over to move a throw pillow to make room for the remaining pad Thai and sighed, the same sigh, she sighed every day. *Is this really my life?* "To whom much is given, much is expected." Shirley's voice screeched through Gwenn's head. She had heard her mother say this a thousand times. When she was little, Gwenn had wanted to believe it, but now the words just mocked her mediocre, meaningless life. There wasn't even a hot guy in the picture to look forward to at the end of a long day. Hell, who needed hot? At this point Gwenn was willing to settle for moderately attractive with a functional libido. She just couldn't bring herself to make the effort;

relationships were always such a disappointment—the failure so humiliating.

Other people managed to have semi-satisfying relationships. Why couldn't she be like other people? Oh, that's right—

The phone rang and Gwenn flinched. It would be bad, very bad. She hadn't spoken to her mother in three weeks (*a new record*) and this was going to be most unpleasant.

Shirley Hutchinson was old-school Minnesotan. She came from a big family, grew up on a farm and had inherited a pioneer's determination. Despite the many relocations of her apostolic adulthood, her entire childhood had taken place in a single farmhouse on the prairie in the land of 10,000 lakes—and she had the unmistakable accent to prove it. She was not a woman to be ignored.

Best to let the answering machine take the heat.

"Hello Gwendolyn, it's mom. I haven't heard from ya in awhile. I know ya don't want ta talk about Jasper, but I think you would feel better if ya did. I've been prayin' ta God ta bring a nice Christian boy inta yer life, ya know. I know ya feel all alone but God will never leave ya, just look at yer middle finger honey..."

Gwenn involuntarily looked down at her hand and performed the drill: thumb = "god"; index finger = "will"; middle finger = "NEVER"; ring finger = "leave"; pinky finger = "you." She grimaced in disgust and repurposed "NEVER" to flip off the answering machine.

"...So maybe if ya come ta the singles' night at our church ya'd meet a nice boy. Ya used ta date so many church boys when ya were in high school..."

Gwenn smiled, of course who wouldn't want to date the preacher's daughter! She remembered Sam Peterson, he was such a nice Christian boy. Gwenn got goose bumps just thinking about the way his lips felt on her neck. She had been head-over-heels for him, and he was so gorgeous and such a smooth operator—the movies, the dinners, the long walks—all so very Christian. He planned a special night, a bonfire on the beach at Park Point. It was the perfect kind of night for snuggling up by the roaring flames. The waves were huge and the fire was awesome.

"Hey Gwenn, you look kinda cold," Sam turned toward her to attempt a first kiss (*he was a very good Christian boy*).

Gwenn could feel her heart beating excitedly.

His eyes got soft and fell to her mouth.

She leaned in ever so slightly and closed her eyes. She felt the most exquisitely soft, moist lips pressing tentatively on hers. Her heart raced and the melting sensation drifted down through her abdomen.

Sam took her head in one hand and quickly pressed her down to the blanket with the other.

He tasted like wild cherry slushy. Their lips never parted and Gwenn wrapped her arms around him.

Sam pressed his body down onto her.

"Oh Sam," Gwenn let out a soft moan. She felt his tongue explore her lips and gently press into her mouth. She was lost. She kissed him more firmly, more recklessly, when she felt his hand slide down to the waistband of her acid-wash jeans—she froze.

Somewhere in the background the answering machine clicked to a stop and Gwenn jolted out of her reverie. "Yeah mom, nice little Christian boys—right."

Gwenn angrily finished her noodles and stretched back to press erase on the answering machine. She hesitated for just a second and called her sister instead.

"Rachel, it's Gwenn."

"What's up?"

"I had a crazy idea—"

"Oh shocker, what's it this time a seminar, a trip, a new invention, a new job—"

"Shut up!" Gwenn wished her sister's words didn't hurt so much, but it was true. Gwenn was always looking for a way out of running The Organizer but none of them actually worked out. "I want you to save all the messages mom sends you and I'm going to save all mine, too."

"What the hell for?"

"I heard about this woman with a Jewish mom, I think, and she wrote a book about all her mom's crazy advice and even made a CD of the actual messages. She's frickin' rich!" Gwenn tried to sound optimistic.

"Gwenny honestly, mom's nuts—who'd ever want to listen to that crap? I mean ever?"

"Come on Rachel it'll work, just save the messages—I'll do all the rest."

"Whatever, hey what're you watching?"

"Um, nothing...just eating dinner."

"At ten-o-clock? How late did you work?"

"Eight-thirty..."

"You're the most boring person I know," Rachel chuckled. "Did mom tell you the super, awesome news?"

"I kinda zoned out during the endless message...are they trying to set me up with someone?"

"You should be so lucky!" Rachel laughed. "Mom and dad are moving this weekend and they want our help—again."

"How much is a one-way ticket to Siberia?"

"Gwenn, you can't abandon me. Misery loves company, and all that bullshit. I'm taking you down with me. Mom says to be there at 8:00 a.m."

"I gotta go, Rache."

"Sure ya do. Hey, you're still going with me on Friday, right?"

"Only if you promise it is just a spy mission. I don't want to be part of some huge plot you are hatching." Gwenn's resolve was wavering.

"Alright, alright, see ya," Rachel sighed and hung up.

Four

Gwenn woke up in a foul mood. She had just gotten the news that Ed and Shirley were moving for the millionth time and she wasn't looking forward to loading the same hundred boxes in a trailer, again. Blast the moving, it was a disease. She had gone to a different elementary school every year of her life, as her parents followed god across the plains. The worst part was that god didn't seem to know when school started for mortal children, so he always got the "Move" message to her parents about six weeks after school had begun in the new town. Yeah! Awesome! Not just the new girl, but also the new-late-everyone-already-has-friends girl. The eternal outsider.

That was what Gwenn always felt like—the eternal outsider. She never felt like part of her family, she never *clicked* with anyone in school and she never found her soul mate. She had always assumed she was an alien sent to this planet to do research, but the mission never ended. "Oh wise elders, please take me back to Urantia," she intoned.

As usual, nothing happened and she groaned extra loudly as she rolled bitterly out of bed.

The only part of her apartment that Gwenn allowed her organizer disease to touch was her closet. Gwenn's closet was immaculate. Everything was hung by color, from spaghetti-strap white camis to long-sleeved black sweaters, and a rainbow of organization in between. However, Gwenn did have to admit that the section of various-sleeved black tops, blouses and sweaters was growing disproportionately to the rest of the palette.

Gwenn thumbed through the dress slacks and chose an oldie but a goodie—slim, charcoal grey slacks with a hint of a pinstripe. Maybe she was deluding herself, but they just never seemed to go out of fashion and they had just enough stretch to fit at any time of the month. A crisp, white blouse and a grey cashmere wrap completed the ensemble, and she was off—without a bite to eat. Breakfast was not the most important meal of the day. Breakfast was a waste of ten perfectly good minutes that could be spent hitting the snooze button.

The interior of Gwenn's four-wheel-drive Jeep was as disastrous as her home and bone-numbingly cold—one of the great blessings of living in the fog-enshrouded city of Duluth. Oh, sure the hills rivaled those of San Francisco and Lake Superior was magical and had that mysterious *lake effect*, but Duluth also boasted less days of sunshine per year than Alaska—don'tcha know!

Gwenn found a space in the parking garage and grabbed her Michael Kors mules from the passenger seat. As the icy wind bit into her cheeks she was grateful for the warm boots protecting her feet. After navigating the downtown skyway system, Gwenn arrived at her small, quaint office at 9:00 a.m. sharp.

She was a stickler for timeliness and Gwenn had kicked more than one boyfriend to the curb for arrival infractions. In fact, she dumped Michael Schafer via a note left with the hostess at the Top of the Harbor Restaurant after his second 15-minute infraction. Gwenn was particularly proud of that one.

The good girls, Flora and Thea, were already buzzing around the spartan office in a flurry of efficiency. Flora's long, mousy-brown hair was held back with a navy-blue headband that matched her plain navy-blue pantsuit. Flora was not a fashion maven but she was an expert at two things, making peach cobbler and preparing proposals. No matter what Gwenn threw at her, Flora delivered profitable, tabbed, indexed and always priced-to-sell proposals. Flora was a genius.

Thea was the best damn saleswoman Gwenn had ever met. She could sell ketchup popsicles to a woman in white gloves. Clients adored Thea, she had the most gorgeous wheat-blonde bob—layered, shining and never out of place. The hair, combined with her impeccable fashion sense and dazzling smile, made her unstoppable. Men worshiped her and women wanted to be her.

"Where's the Hit List?" Gwenn asked.

"On your desk, with the Linder proposal," Flora smiled.

"Oh crap, is the Linder thing today? I thought I had rescheduled that for next week," Gwenn said.

"Well, you did reschedule, but that was last week...for this week," Flora floundered. "You okay?"

"Yeah, I just didn't sleep well last night. Pastor Ed and Shirley are moving again, and I also had the recurring alien planet dream," sighed Gwenn.

"Moving?" Flora and Thea gasped in unison.

"They've only been in the condo eight months," stammered Flora.

"I know, I know, but ever since they got their big inheritance from Gramma Hutchinson they've lost it! They used to prattle on and on about stacking up rewards in heaven, but it seems like that was just a poor man's dream. Now that they've got a bit of cash—forget heaven, they're stacking up right here on the Devil's playground," fumed Gwenn.

"Where to this time?" Thea asked.

"Some frickin' mini-mansion in East End. Snooty, perfectly-landscaped East End. I mean seriously!"

"Are you helping—" Flora stopped in mid sentence, "I mean...sorry," she stammered.

"Oh but of course, how could they ever get things handled without the great Organizer! These are the days I dream of the mother ship taking me home," Gwenn smiled.

"Maybe you really are from another planet." Thea flipped open her compact and freshened her lipstick. "I mean, you don't look anything like your sister and, honestly, how could your parents have any genetic material in common with you?" Thea batted her huge, blue eyes teasingly and smiled.

Gwenn grinned back shaking her head, and with a final shrug of her athletic shoulders, headed for her office. Of course when she got there she saw the Linder proposal and the grin melted into a pouty frown.

This is the only reason people should move—so they don't have to go and present a proposal to an ex-boyfriend from high school. Dean Linder had been good-looking, tall, lean and intelligent. However, he was currently married, a father of two and still a "good Christian boy."

Gwenn let her fingers trace the letters of his name and she thought back to sitting in his car on Skyline Drive. They had shared a can of beer between them and were both imagining quite a buzz. Dean casually flopped his arm across the back of the seat and played with a strand of Gwenn's honey-brown hair. He leaned in kind of suddenly, but the kiss was soft and intense. Gwenn angled toward him and went back for seconds. Dean dropped the empty beer can and grabbed her shoulder. His lips searched hers while his hand slipped into her V-neck sweater and veered south. Gwenn jerked back and asked to be taken home. Dean chuckled and called her a "typical P.K."

"What?"

"You know, a Preacher's Kid," Dean laughed smugly.

That stung Gwenn worse than any other insult and she launched herself at Dean with a fury. She grabbed his hand and shoved it up under her sweater. Without missing a beat, Dean slid into second. Suddenly the car was filled with the glare of headlights and the muffled sound of a police radio.

Fortunately the cops didn't search the car, but they smelled something on Dean's breath and ask for names. Gwenn gave a false one, of course, and the cops sent them home with a warning and a promise to call their parents.

"Gwenn, it's Rachel on line two," interrupted Flora.

Gwenn flipped the proposal upside down and picked up the phone, "Hey Rache, what's up?"

"Can you meet me for lunch?"

Rachel didn't sound stable. "Sure, but I got the Linder thing at 2:00, so we gotta keep it short."

"Oh my god! Are you seriously going to go to *Dig Deep* Dean's and look him in the eyes?"

"Rache it was like 15 years ago—he probably doesn't even remember. I'm sure he's grabbed plenty of more impressive boobs since then."

"Yeah, you were kind of a carpenter's dream—flat as a board..." Rachel squealed and couldn't even finish the jibe.

"Okay, lunch is off you sadist!" Gwenn retorted.

"Come on, I'm kidding. I gotta talk to somebody. The Annie thing is killing me. I gotta vent."

"Fine, Grandma's at noon. Don't be late Rachel," warned Gwenn.

"10-4 Mr. Organizer, sir," laughed Rachel.

Gwenn wasted the rest of the morning shoving papers back and forth across her desk and doing everything in her power to think *businessy* thoughts about the Linder job.

The eternal morning ended and Gwenn took a taxi to Grandma's Saloon and Grill, located near the picturesque Aerial Lift Bridge, Gwenn laughed to herself. She continued the internal tour guide banter. On March 29, 1930 the tugboat Essayons became the first vessel to pass under the Lift Bridge. This beauty is the gateway to the Duluth Harbor and sole access to the stunning Park Point peninsula.

Gwenn was so busy amusing herself she didn't notice that the taxi had stopped.

"Um, miss...you said Grandma's, right? Did you mean your grandma's," the taxi driver chuckled at his clever quip.

"I meant the restaurant. You must be very proud to have found it all by yourself," Gwenn replied curtly as she handed him the fare, plus a tip. Even when she was slicing away with her rapier wit she just couldn't withhold a tip. That was barbaric.

The dark paneling and the smell of delicious food welcomed Gwenn into the Saloon. Rachel was nestled among the vintage metal signs and the sailboats suspended from the ceiling—waving like a lunatic. Gwenn waved back, to prevent Rachel from injuring herself. As Gwenn approached the table, Rachel stood up.

Rachel made a slight bow with her hands pressed together, palms facing each other in front of her chest, "Namaste." She returned to her seat and continued as though nothing had happened. "I got you a diet Pepsi and the Full Monty," Rachel smiled.

"Um, Rache, are you going to elaborate? Have you changed religions again?" Gwenn mused.

Rachel exhaled patiently, "It's a spiritual practice, not a religion. That was anjali mudra, a Hindu greeting. I've decided to practice some meditations to center myself in this shitty situation."

After a long draw on the diet Pepsi, Gwenn smiled lovingly at Rachel, "OK, duly noted. So what's up with Annie?"

"It's over, it's awful. We don't even speak," moaned Rachel.

"It's just a rough patch, you guys have made it through worse," Gwenn coddled, noting that Rachel's center was already drifting.

"Not really," countered Rachel, "Even during the really scary bit last year we were still sleeping in the same bed. She still came into the bakery to kiss me good-bye. She would run me a hot tub, at night, and wash my hair, and we would talk about our day. Yeah, we had some screaming matches and I threw some shit...but we were still connected.

Now…it's just…empty." A tear leaked out of Rachel's left eye and trickled across her lightly freckled cheek.

"Rache, don't cry." Never make a scene in public—it was one of the Hutchinson cardinal rules. "If it's really over then you gotta have the talk. You can't just be a prisoner of your situation," insisted Gwenn.

"But we bought the place together, it's too much for either of us…on our own," Rachel whined.

"Look, you sell it, you split the profits and you move back into the apartment above the bakery."

"Oh god, Gwenny it hurts…it just hurts so much."

"Sweetie, I know, but you were there for me when things went south with Steven, Jasper…and let's not forget Bruce—and I'll be here for you. If there's one thing we Hutchinson's do better than anyone else, it's move!"

Rachel smiled through bleary eyes and nodded.

The remainder of lunch was spent discussing whether or not Rachel should use the same realtor and other details of the move. Rachel bowed wordlessly, hands in mudra, as she left Gwenn to pay the bill.

When Gwenn got back to the taxi (*different driver, thankfully*) she couldn't help but let her mind slip to thoughts of Bruce.

They had lived together for two years, when she was in her mid-twenties, finally Bruce had popped the question. Of course Gwenn had said yes. Bruce was a successful stockbroker and her parents were furious that she was living in sin. They wouldn't even set foot in Bruce's apartment. They even forbid Rachel to visit Gwenn, but no one could keep a leash on Rachel.

Gwenn knew the wedding would fix everything—that was Hutchinson 101. Cover your tracks as quickly as possible and never speak of the sin again. If you don't talk about it, it never happened. So the wedding would take place, with Pastor Hutchinson presiding. Naturally, no one would ever mention the two years that Gwenn and Bruce had spent living together—in the Devil's service.

Bruce's bachelor party got totally out of hand and he still had a hangover the morning of the wedding. In fact, he threw up in the bushes just outside the church. Gwenn was furious, but ever the perfect daughter, she informed Bruce that the only reason the wedding was going forward was because the invitations had been sent and out-of-town guests had spent money to fly to the event. When Shirley wore a black dress to the wedding, Gwenn pretended it was more amusing than anything else, but the not-so-subtle insult still stung.

Time warp to two years later when Gwenn came home early and found Bruce in bed with his *best friend* Kevin. Gwenn filed for divorce.

Shirley, who didn't know the truth, was so disappointed, "I don't know what yer gonna do Gwendolyn, I've always had a man ta take care a me. You're not gettin' any younger, ya know. Ya may not get another chance."

Gwenn didn't think she wanted another chance to be some closet, gay guy's beard, but Shirley's ominous words rattled around painfully in hear head anyway.

Gwenn could not believe six years had passed since that humiliating afternoon. The only real contender since then, Jasper, had ended up leaving the country three years ago to avoid commitment. She wanted to believe there had been a "once in a lifetime" job in Amsterdam—but the timing was uncanny. Probably just as well, he was a Sagittarius and that almost never works with a Cancer.

Gwenn arrived back at the office in a funk and was dreading the Linder meeting even more than she had been before lunch, if that were possible.

Five

It was 1:30, *dirty sow*, as Pastor Ed would say—the only hint of profanity Gwenn had ever heard him utter. Gwenn grabbed the proposal and walked briskly to the parking garage. En route she called Flora to get the highlights. Gwenn arrived at the Linder's palatial East End estate at 1:55, and chuckled as she thought about Pastor Ed and Shirley living in this environment.

Diane Linder answered the door. Her hair was so bleached that it looked otherworldly and her eye tuck was a little too obvious. The garish pink and black pantsuit was an homage to a forgotten fashion era.

"Good afternoon Mrs. Linder, I'm Gwenn Hutchinson, The Organizer," Gwenn said.

Mrs. Linder giggled and blushed, "Oh yah, we been expectin' ya Gwenny. Can I getcha a pop?" Diane asked.

Gwenn bristled at the overly familiar *Gwenny*, but let it slide—under the heading *the client's always right*. "No thank you Diane, I just came from a lunch meeting. I'd love a glass of water, though," she quickly added as she saw Diane's shoulders droop; truly a feat under the immense shoulder pads.

"Dean? Deeeean?" yelled Diane.

"Yeah?"

"Dean, Gwenny's here. Come on Dean, she doesn't have all day!" added Diane, with an attempted wink in Gwenn's direction.

There was a ceremonious rustling of papers from down the hall, a few clicks of a mouse and Dean emerged. He was a little rounder in places, but still very striking—especially considering the competition in Northern Minnesota.

"Mr. Linder," Gwenn held out her hand.

"Oh, for chrissake Gwenny, call me Dean," he smiled warmly, ignored the hand and gave her a big hug.

Diane flinched, she would have closed her eyes if that were medically possible, and darted from the room to retrieve the glass of water.

"Very well, Dean, can we have a seat in the living room?"

The uncomfortable trio headed into the toy-filled living room and Gwenn smiled; nothing beats a good mess to emphasize the need for organization. Gwenn reviewed the plans with Dean and Diane and moved to close the deal.

"Let's get the project launched next Wednesday," Gwenn suggested.

"Oh yes, let's," giggled Diane.

"Yeah, that's fine," mumbled Dean.

"What's the matter Dean? The plans are great," Diane looked worried, or rather, sounded worried—her brow seemed incapable of creasing.

"Yeah, it's gonna cost me an arm and both legs, though," Dean grumbled.

"Honestly Dean, we can afford it," Diane said with unmasked pride, "we wanted the best," she added.

"Time is money Dean, and the amount of time you spend searching for things is time you could be closing more deals, right?" Gwenn added cheerily.

"Sure, sure—we'll start Wednesday...in my office," Dean finished, suggestively.

"But Dean, I thought we agreed to get the kids toys..." stammered Diane.

"I have to get more efficient, right Diane?"

"Oh, I'm sure you're right honey," cooed Diane.

"Okay, the crew will be here on Wednesday—any questions before that, give me a call." Gwenn got up to leave.

"I'll see you out Gwenny." Dean got up to follow her; Diane fidgeted nervously.

Gwenn turned to say goodbye at the door and found Dean standing uncomfortably close.

"Gwenny...the one that got away, eh kid?" Dean grinned.

"We'll see you next Wednesday," Gwenn said in a slightly threatening, but matter-of-fact tone. She used the plural as a defense. *We*, not just weak little Gwenny, *we* will be here—Gwenn and her army. She turned quickly and walked briskly to the Jeep, careful not to wiggle her ass. As soon as she was out of sight she grabbed her cell and called Rachel.

"Hey sis."

"Oh my god! Rachel, Dean was totally coming on to me. What a pig! In front of his wife—puke!"

"Are you shittin' me? What a man-whore!"

"Rache, what am I gonna do? This is a huge account, I have to handle it personally."

"You need Randy!"

"You're a genius! Rache you are my favorite sister—forever. Oh, I almost forgot, you still planning on helping Ed and Shirley move this weekend?"

"Wouldn't miss it! I plan to make several side trips to nearby dumpsters to lighten the load."

"Rache, you're EVIL!"

"Satan's little helper!" Rachel screeched with laughter.

"Buh bye, and thanks!" Gwenn was thrilled with Rachel's suggestion.

She quickly dialed Randy's number and willed the flamboyant designer to be available for some freelance work.

"Randy, it's Gwenn Hut—"

"Gwenny! My fabulous Gwenny! Did you get the Clark & Mayfield tote I sent you?" gushed Randy.

"Yes, thank you so much. It's perfect."

"Of course it is sweetie, it's from me," Randy's voice was petulant and teasing.

"Randy I need a huge favor..."

"I will not pretend to be your boyfriend just to keep Reverend Eddie and Shirley at bay!"

"No it's worse. I need you to run a job at an ex-boyfriend's house in East End. Pretty please?" Gwenn hated to beg but Randy loved it, so she acquiesced.

"Oh sweetie! I wish I could, you have such good taste in men...kidding! Although Bruce was kinda my type—too busy...too busy...up to my ass in acrobats, as they say."

"You wish!" laughed Gwenn, "I don't think anyone actually says that Randy."

"I do, and I'm the biggest someone you'll ever know Gwendolyn Hutchinson," pouted Randy.

"Sadly, you're probably right Randy," Gwenn sighed, "Thanks anyway, your majesty."

"Anytime, serf." Randy had a fit of giggles and hung up.

Gwenn's shoulders slumped in defeat. Maybe someone on the home planet would send her a solution via mind meld. While she waited for extra-terrestrial inspiration she realized it was Friday...she had to go to the *gig* with Rachel. Oh, super!

Six

Rachel was buzzing around her loft getting ready for the mission. She was torn between a very sexy outfit—to make sure TK saw the competition; and a very *blendy* outfit—to keep her top-secret spy mission...well, secret.

The doorbell rang and interrupted her conundrum.

"Gwenny, you remembered!"

"How could I possibly forget? You called me at least 13 times!" Gwenn exhaled and plopped down on the futon that Rachel had set up in the spare room, which was now Rachel's separate-from-Annie bedroom.

"This one or this one?" Rachel held a red dress with strategic cut-outs in her right hand and a black leather mini-dress in her left.

"Neither." Gwenn shook her head. "Rache, I agreed to go with you to get some intel. I did not agree to referee a cat fight at Flame. Pick out a simple pair of jeans, a dark sweater and some sensible shoes—no pun intended."

"Gwenny," Rachel instantly threw on her pretty-pouty face, "I want that TK bitch to see what she's messing with."

"Rache, put on the jeans or I am off the mission." Gwenn crossed her arms and waited. Rachel could pout, but Gwenn had patience.

Ten seconds later...

"Fine! I'll wear the fuckin' jeans!" Rachel dressed angrily. "There, happy?"

"Ecstatic."

Gwenn and Rachel discussed the strategy several times on the way to Flame.

***

Annie was thrilled to get a gig at Flame. It was Duluth's premiere gay bar and an awesome place to show off her guitar skills. It was not awesome to be her own roadie, but she knew everyone had to pay some dues on the way up.

"Bree, I'm moving the amp over here and plugging the monitors in." Annie was pleased with the temporary stage the owners had installed for tonight's show. There was no opening act, which sort of sucked, but Annie's band, *The Spanking Machine*, didn't go on until 10:00 p.m. so it still felt like a headliner gig.

"Annie I need you to do a quick sound check on mic number one." Bree stood in the DJ booth, behind the mixing board, ready to make adjustments. Her shaved head reflected the kaleidoscope of lights from the dance floor. She made a few minor adjustments to mic number one and raised her ring-ensconced hand to direct Annie to the other mics.

"Bree, it doesn't make any since for me to do the mic checks for Cass and Mika, their voices are totally different."

Annie raked her fingers through her spikey blonde hair, frustrated with Bree's amateur request.

"I'm not a fuckin' idiot Annie. Look around. Do you see Cass or Mika?" Bree raised her hands in frustration and flipped off Annie. "Just check the goddamn mics, we have to clear out in five for the DJ."

Cass and Mika were probably sucking face in the bathroom, so Annie belligerently complied.

***

Flame was packed. The regulars were all there, add *The Spanking Machine's* loyal groupies, and the place was filled to capacity...plus.

Gwenn and Rachel slithered past the doorman by virtue of a hefty tip. Rachel kept her hood up and Gwenn steered them to a table tucked in the far corner of the bar. They could see the stage, if they really tried, but no one on the stage could see them. That's what they kept telling themselves.

The DJ finally announced last song and welcomed *The Spanking Machine* to the stage. The Flame was filled with uproarious applause, whistles and screams.

Rachel was feeling a little jealous. It had been a long time since she watched Annie play and she had forgotten much of her soon-to-be-ex-girlfriend's fame.

"Damn, they really like her," Gwenn shouted in Rachel's direction.

Rachel heard perfectly but refused to acknowledge the situation and instead pointed at her ears in frustration and shrugged.

The band had played three songs and Rachel had seen no sign of the mysterious TK. She tapped her fingers in frustration. "Gwenny, can you get us some drinks? This stakeout bullshit sucks."

Gwenn threaded her way to the bar, her ears ringing from the blaring music. No one grabbed her ass, and she wasn't sure if she should be offended. The guys were mostly gay so that explained half of the situation—but no single lesbians wanted…Gwenn mentally flicked herself on the back of the head. *Get it together Hutchinson. You're not gay, remember?*

She ordered Manhattans, in an attempt to raise Rachel's spirits, and returned to the table in the corner without incident. Again.

"After about five more of these, things will be perfect." Rachel slumped down on her barstool.

"Rache, I think you might want to stand up." Gwenn had noticed Annie moving toward the edge of the stage. She was in the middle of a bass solo and it looked like she was playing for someone special. Not Rachel.

Rachel peered through the strobing lights and caught a glimpse of the bright-blue bangs covering half the girl's face and time slowed down. Rachel looked at Annie's face and saw the seductive smile aimed at blue-bangs, a.k.a. TK she assumed. She wanted to sit down and cover her eyes, but her legs would not bend. Rachel watched in painful horror as TK leaned toward the stage and Annie bent down, still rippin' away on the bass, and planted a big, showy kiss on TK's pierced lips. Then Rachel's knees collapsed.

Gwenn barely caught Rachel, and managed to keep her from falling.

"Gwenn?" Rachel's eyes were wet and filled with heartbreak.

"Rachel, please don't do anything stupid. Annie isn't going to be impressed by you punching—"

"Take me home. Take me home, now." Rachel's shoulders fell and her gaze went to the floor.

Gwenn grabbed Rachel around the waist and started shoving her way to the door. After awhile she got sick of saying excuse me and just plowed ahead.

"Hey, watch it bitch!" or "Where's the goddamn fire?" or "Get some fuckin' manners!" followed in Gwenn's wake. She just ignored the insults and dragged Rachel forward, until one came that she couldn't ignore.

"Hey, Rachel? That you under there?" A tall, skinny brunette was tipping down to peek under Rachel's hood.

"Back off! Her name is Fiona and she's pretty fuckin' sick. So unless you want puke all over your Docs—move." Gwenn had seen a bull dyke or two in action and she gave it her best shot. Tall and skinny backed up and Gwenn and Rachel popped out of the crowd like a waffle from a toaster.

They rode back to Rachel's in complete silence.

Gwenn took Rachel's hand and pulled her out of the car. Rachel stopped at the edge of the seat and looked into Gwenn's eyes.

"What did I do?" The tears Rachel had been holding back came pouring forth.

"You didn't do anything, sweetie. Relationships are fucked up and people can't face the truth so they sabotage things the only way they know how...they do something unforgiveable and then it's over." Gwenn pulled Rachel from the car. "Do you want me to sleep over?"

"I just thought we could fix..." Rachel's voice disappeared into a sob.

"Rache, you knew it was over. You were planning to sell the loft and move, remember?" Gwenn tried to be kind as they walked up to Rachel's room.

"But, it was mutual. Now I know she's got someone else and I am going to be alone. It's not fair! I wanted her to suffer without me. I wanted her to regret leaving me...not this." Rachel flung herself down on the bed and cried.

"You aren't going to be alone forever. And don't worry, the first time blue-bangs drops some acid—because she totally looked like the type Rache—Annie will be wishing she could come back to you." Gwenn made up most of it, but she was desperate to stop Rachel's tears.

Rachel rolled over with a glimmer of hope in her eyes, "Do you think so?"

"I know so." Gwenn breathed a sigh of relief and then something popped into her head that sucked all the air right out of her lungs.

"Oh, for fuck's sake! We have to help mom and dad move tomorrow!"

Seven

Gwenn rolled up to her parents' current house at about 9:00 Saturday morning. Shirley had insisted on 8:00, but this was one place that Gwenn allowed herself to be late—always late to arrive, always early to leave.

Rachel was already hard at work, probably thinking about the help she would need, in a few short weeks, when she moved out of the loft.

Gwenn surveyed the garage and looked at all the familiar old boxes. They were like old friends that had long overstayed their welcome, but were too dense to get the hint.

There was Shirley's old hair salon supplies.

Over there was Ed's copper and brass items from his brief foray into the import/export business.

Ah, the boxes housing Ed's precious National Geographic collection, "Those'll be worth some money someday," Gwenn lectured in her best Pastor Ed voice, cracking herself up.

"What's so funny Miss Tardy?" asked Rachel.

"Don't you feel a horrible sense of déjà vu?" Gwenn grinned.

"I don't know what you're talking about, this is all new to me," responded Rachel with mock innocence.

"In that case, I'd rather be Miss Tardy, than Miss Re-tardy—you freak."

"Bitch," mumbled Rachel.

"Oooh, I'm tellin'—be sure your sin will find you out Miss Rachel!" Gwenn admonished.

They were both laughing uncontrollably when Ed rounded the corner.

"What's so funny, Trixie?" Ed asked Gwenn.

Ed was wearing his official moving attire: ill-fitting denim trousers, work boots and a plaid flannel shirt. Gwenn noticed his paunch had garnered its share of the inheritance boon.

"Dad, why is it always Trixie or kiddo or little missy? You named me Gwendolyn, or have you forgotten," Gwenn said in her typical, irritated-to-be-home voice.

"Now don't go gettin' all wound up Gwenny. I'm yer father and that's just what I do," replied Ed.

Gwenn rolled her eyes so hard she thought she heard something pop, and stalked into the garage.

Rachel walked into the house with Ed, and they made trip after trip to the trailer attached to Ed's truck. Shirley was busy packing up boxes in the house. And Gwenn opened up some of the time capsules in the garage.

Only Ed would keep resumes from the 70s. Wow, that was one funky polyester suit Eddie! Gwenn shuffled through a few more boxes of craft supplies and broken-down, museum-quality, kitchen appliances, and sighed—the *where's the mother ship* sigh. And told herself she'd just open a couple more, to keep from actually lifting anything.

The next box was filled with photographs. There she was in her ridiculous, red baby sweater; the old house that her parents lived in when they first got married; and some crazy neighbors she didn't remember. There was an odd packet of photos of paintings, seemingly by the same artist, all hung in an unfamiliar apartment. Gwenn flipped over the first picture and her mom's handwriting explained the paintings were by Daniel Gregory and the apartment was also his.

There was a photo of her mom next to a painting of a beautiful woman and several photos of Daniel pointing to different elements in other canvases. Gwenn looked at the month and year that Kodak had so helpfully printed on the white border of each photo.

"That can't be right." She felt the garage spinning.

Gwenn slowly counted backward on her fingers, twice. She shoved the packet of pictures and negatives under her shirt, mumbled something about needing her water bottle—in case anyone was watching—and jogged to her car. She secretly transferred the packet to her purse and grabbed her water bottle.

Rachel and Ed were still making trips to the trailer. Rachel made a goofy face as she passed Gwenn, but Gwenn was on another planet. Rachel chuckled to herself and wondered about Gwenn's alien galaxy.

The rest of the day Gwenn was like a machine. She just kept making more and more trips to the trailer. She stacked, packed, corrected, stacked again and again. Rachel was growing concerned; usually Gwenn was a lot more fake packer and a lot less like a moving company professional.

"Hey, Gwenn are ya trying to make me look bad," teased Rachel.

"Rache can you come over after this?"

"Um...yeah, everything okay?" Rachel looked confused.

"Can't talk now. Chinese take out or Swedish meatballs with lingonberry sauce?" asked Gwenn.

"You know my weakness, Trixie," Rachel jibed.

"Oh real funny, kiddo," Gwenn snapped, with a crooked grin.

Later when Rachel offered to drive the truck and trailer over to the new place while Ed and Shirley kept packing, Gwenn knew a dumpster detour was on her sister's route.

Gwenn was reheating the Swedish meatballs when Rachel arrived, glowing with the thrill of her successful missions.

"So how many?" smiled Gwenn.

"I managed to prune about 15 boxes from the monster at large, but I have HUGE news!" Rachel looked as though she may explode into tiny pieces that would each be grinning like the Cheshire Cat.

"Oh no, what did you do?" Gwenn asked cautiously.

"I got rid of the National Geographics!" Rachel yelled triumphantly.

"Raaache—he'll notice that! You freak, he will notice that!" Gwenn was having a meltdown.

"Oh jeez—unclench will ya. I printed out a quote from a well-respected appraiser who valued the collection at about nothing. So I showed him how he could own the entire collection on DVD, for less than nothing! He argued admirably, but once Shirley approved the purchase I was home free."

"You are diabolical," Gwenn smiled approvingly.

"I offered to take them to the dumpster myself so he wouldn't have to deal with it, and finally he agreed."

"He didn't!"

"He did! I drove like a woman possessed and if anyone saw me at the dumpster they must've thought I was a serial killer disposing of bodies. I was maniacal, just sick with joy."

"Well, my news seems blasé now," added Gwenn smugly.

"Oh yeah, what crawled up your butt and died? You were halfway to your home planet this afternoon. I mean you didn't even see the Kick Me sign I taped to Dad's back," Rachel was giggling like a ten-year-old.

"Rachel, you better sit down...seriously," Gwenn said in her best school guidance counselor voice.

"Did he call?" Rachel asked with a mix of fear and... worse fear.

"Wha...he, Oh! God no! Please Rache that ship has sailed. If Jasper ever calls me I will politely thank him for thinking of me and tell him I've moved on—end of story. I'm not going to collapse; I'm not that girl anymore."

"Okay, so what's with the "seriously" crap?"

Gwenn produced the packet of pictures from her purse and handed them to Rachel.

"Nice paintings. Oh look, mom looks so young. She really looks a bit like you Gwenny...no offense. Is this the artist?" Rachel pointed to the handsome stranger in the photo.

"His name is Daniel Gregory and...I actually think he may be more than that Rache."

"Oh, was mom dating this guy or something?"

Gwenn hesitated for a moment, wondering if she should reconsider bringing Rachel into the inner circle. Then Rachel noticed the border.

"I guess she better not have been! This is two years after she married dad." Rachel wanted to laugh, but caught sight of Gwenn's pained expression.

"No frickin' way!" screamed Rachel.

"Way," murmured Gwenn.

Rachel counted on her fingers and looked up at Gwenn with all the hope she could find in her heart, "You don't think he's your...do you?" Rachel squeaked.

"I'm starting to wonder," replied Gwenn softly.

"But that'd mean you're only my half..." Rachel was crying before she could finish the sentence.

"Rache you're my sister, my whole sister. My only sister in the world, from head to toe—wholly sisters," assured Gwenn.

"But maybe you have a halfling somewhere," moaned Rachel.

"A hobbit?" Gwenn puzzled.

"No a half-sister, I mean another half-sister. Oh man, this sucks. People always used to say we didn't look alike... do you think dad knows?" Rachel looked stricken. The color just drained out of her face like a falling thermometer.

"Hey, don't even think about it. Let's just go to the parade and forget about all this crap for a few hours. Okay?" Gwenn suggested.

Gwenn and Rachel were bundled from head to toe: earmuffs, scarves, Patagonia down jackets, Thinsulate-lined mittens, long underwear beneath jeans, and thick wool socks shoved into warm Sorrel boots. Tonight was the Christmas City of the North parade—not to be missed.

The Hermantown High School marching band tramped by as Gwenn and Rachel jockeyed for position along the parade route.

"Look! Look!" Rachel pointed and laughed.

Gwenn was relieved to hear Rachel laugh. She looked in the direction that Rachel's mitten indicated and saw a man working his way into range of the TV cameras, waving a sign that read, "We Love Lutefisk!"

The obligatory waving beauties, wrapped in furs and capes, rode by in convertibles. CLICK! The lights went off. Gwenn looked around and finally saw the fiery approach of the flaming batons. These brave girls were wearing leotards; their arms and legs fully exposed to the nasty effects of the wind chill factor. The wind chill factor was the North's answer to the *dry heat* nonsense of the Southwest. Basically the windchill factor just meant that wind blowing makes it *feel* colder. However, Gwenn was quite sure that once she was freezing her ass off, the *feeling* of the temperature was insignificant—the point is it's cold, freezing frickin' cold. Windchill factor is like worrying about an extra gallon of water going over Niagara Falls.

Gwenn leaned over and slipped Rachel's left earmuff back, "By the end of the parade those poor girls will be using their fiery batons to light themselves on fire, just to keep from freezing to death!"

Rachel laughed and her breath formed little puffs of freezing mist in the air.

The TV lights flooded back on and Gwenn's favorite attraction came barreling down the street. The clown band! They were playing crazy music and dancing everywhere. Sure, their frenetic movement was just to keep themselves warm, but Gwenn was willing to take her entertainment any way she could get it, at this latitude.

"Gwenny, is that...?" Rachel's expression changed rapidly as her eyes tracked something across the street.

Gwenn held up a mittened hand to stop Rachel while she adjusted her earmuffs. Once she had exposed an ear, she nodded for Rachel to proceed.

"Look! Look, it's Annie." Rachel shook her mitten hand at the specter. "Someone's pulling her though the crowd." Rachel was frantic, "Is it Blue-Bangs?"

"I see Annie, but I can't see who is pulling her." Gwenn craned her neck fruitlessly. "Maybe it's her cousin—"

"Are you fucking kidding me Gwenn?" Rachel was furious. "Why would she even come here? She knows this is *our* tradition."

"Rache, it's a parade. Anyone can come. Maybe—"

"Let's go. This is bullshit."

"Yeah, my cheeks are numb anyway," complained Gwenn.

Rachel spun around and added, "Let's really act like we're having a blast in case she saw me."

Gwenn didn't dare argue.

They threaded through the crowd and cheered loudly as they passed the Lutefisk lover, even though neither of them would dream of eating anything that disgusting.

Morning came too soon, Gwenn wasn't anxious to think about work and the prospect of going back to the Linder's on Wednesday. In fact, she was the exact opposite of anxious. However, The Organizer can always come up with a solution—the aphorism "Deep shit is the mother of invention" came to mind.

Eight

First thing Monday morning Gwenn called Flora into her office, "Flora, you know how much I depend on your perfectly prepared proposals," Gwenn paused for effect just like she'd practiced in the Jeep on the way to the office.

Flora ignored the obvious alliteration joke and smiled, a little nervously.

"I'd like to give you some more responsibility, and of course a raise," added Gwenn. She hoped she had put just the right amount of mystery and jackpot in the *raise* part of the sentence.

"That sounds great Gwenn, I'm in the office to help any way I can," smiled Flora, more calmly this time.

"I was thinking we may need to get you out of the office," said Gwenn, tantalizingly.

"You're firing me?" Flora was shocked.

Gwenn chuckled, "God no, never, Flora...I want you to start supervising the crews on certain jobsites. You're a natural, you know the proposals inside and out, plus you already deal with all the subs to get the bids. I think this is the perfect next step for your career. What do you think?" Gwenn smiled her best, magnanimous boss smile.

"How soon would I start?" Flora asked suspiciously.

"Oh, right away. We'll get you on the next project that's a good fit for you," enthused Gwenn.

"Like the Linder project?" Flora asked accusingly.

"Flora it's not like that—oh hell, it's totally like that. I just can't be in that man's house. It's creepy! I'm afraid his Stepford wife might malfunction and try to strangle me!" wailed Gwenn.

"Oh, thanks!" Flora widened her eyes in concern.

"She wouldn't turn on you, Flora. She doesn't have any history with you, besides she was friends with Laura...she might even like you."

At the mention of her dead sister, Flora stiffened and shifted in her chair. Laura had been a child prodigy, she skipped grades, she played instruments and she spoke three languages by the time she was ten. She was only 18 months older than Flora and they looked almost identical...people had always made comparisons. Flora was nice, pretty and cooperative, but she "just doesn't have the spark, like Laura."

When Laura was 13 she began sneaking out of the house on dates, and to parties. One morning Flora woke up to find Laura's bed still empty, and it looked as though it had been that way all night. She immediately got up and messed it up, so it would look like Laura just left early. Flora ran out to the mudroom to see if Laura's backpack was gone, eager to complete the cover-up. As she passed her parents room she noticed their door was open and the bed was empty. Flora's heart was beating too fast before she even saw the note.

"Gone to hospital. Didn't want to wake you. Laura will be OK."

Flora called the neighbor, Mrs. Johnson, and through her sobs begged to be taken to the hospital. When she ran into the waiting room she saw her dad looking stiffly out the window and her mother shaking with silent sobs. Flora fell down on her knees and cried, "No...mommy, please...no."

Her father ran to her and picked her up. He sat her down in a chair away from her mom and tried to calm her down.

"I want to see Laura! Please! I just want to see her..."

"Flora, there was a terrible accident on Skyline Drive. It would be best if you didn't see her like that. The doctor's did everything..."

Blah, blah, blah. Flora's mother was never the same, always a little distracted—always taking pills to help. Flora promised herself that she would just go with the flow. She would be an obedient daughter that never got in trouble and never made mistakes. Flora would always be there for her folks—always. She was a good girl.

"Flora?" Gwenn could see the glazed look in Flora's eyes and she immediately regretted mentioning Laura. "I'm sorry Flora, I know it still hurts, I wasn't trying to be flippant— please just think about the promotion. You would be fantastic and you can earn commission on every job, plus a bonus if it comes in under budget." Gwenn was just spitballing now, but desperate times...and all.

Flora tried to control her face, but she was sure that Gwenn saw the flicker of excitement at the words "under budget."

Gwenn was pleased that she had avoided spending any additional time with Dean Linder—Dig Deep Dean. Rachel was such a hoot. Now that her calendar was cleared of the Linder ordeal, Gwenn could focus on more important tasks—daydreaming about Daniel Gregory.

Nine

"Mr. Gregory, the show starts in five days. We have to finalize the collection today. Please try to focus," Todd finished with exasperation.

"Todd, you worry too much. Everything will work out for the best...it always does. I refuse to be held prisoner in this gallery when a gorgeous day is waiting outside. I mean, Todd, how many gorgeous days do we get in January? In Minneapolis?" Daniel smiled and leaned back in his soft leather chair.

Todd was pacing. Todd was tall and thin, almost reedy, he walked slightly bent forward at an angle so it appeared a mighty wind was pushing him from behind. Todd was always pushing. He was the glue that held the Gregory Gallery together—but at a price.

Contrastingly, Daniel Gregory was serene. He had a bit of distinguished grey at the temples of his otherwise flawless caramel and brown mane. His hair was longer than average, for a man his age, but is was mesmerizingly wavy and he was a famous artist, so no one seemed to mind.

Daniel kept his youthful build with the help of a fanatical personal trainer who preached kickboxing, weight lifting, yoga and a mostly organic diet. Daniel indulged in the occasional dessert, but he always made up for it with an extra 30 minutes of kickboxing or power yoga. Of course the yoga was the main reason he was able to keep his cool when others, especially Todd, would lose theirs.

"Look Todd, I'm going to go out on a limb...you finish selecting the canvases for the show and I'm going to the cabin until Monday," Daniel grinned mischievously and waited.

Todd abruptly stopped pacing across the polished birch floor and looked sternly at Daniel. "Mr. Gregory," his tone was patronizingly sweet, like he was coaxing a small child to eat his vegetables, "we both know how important this show is, I think you owe it to yourself to participate in the selection—"

"Todd, I'll be back Monday night. Handle it," Daniel smiled, rose from his chair and added, "...you'll earn season tickets to the Guthrie," as his long strides took him rapidly from the room.

Daniel had been feeling antsy for weeks. Nothing to do with the show, just a strange feeling that something was off. He had doubled his daily flaxseed oil and even added some ashwagandha—but still there was a tingle in his energy field that he just couldn't explain.

He packed some random clothes, a few books, an old iPod and headed north.

The roads were remarkably clear for this time of year and Daniel took full advantage. He arrived in snow-covered Duluth in record time. Nearing the gray steel of the Aerial

Lift Bridge he suddenly felt hunger pains in his stomach and decided to get a quick salad at Grandma's.

While he waited for his table he noticed a new Sunfish hanging from the ceiling. That must be a full-time job, he imagined, combing through antique stores and flea markets to find signs and trinkets to line the walls of this historic establishment. His daydream was interrupted.

"Oh, hi there. Yah, yer table's ready for ya," said the oddly shaped sweater in his periphery.

Daniel nodded politely and he followed the strange shape to his table. Why did women think that bulky sweaters disguised their girth? It seemed to him that sweaters just clung to the oddities and, if anything, emphasized them. His artistic eye felt compelled to capture the odd spectacle on imaginary canvas, *A Study in Geometric Asymmetry*, he mentally named the tableau. 'Oil on canvas,' he added as he slid into the booth.

He scanned the menu and discovered he would be going off his trainer's meal plan. He justified things by reminding himself that this was a short little getaway weekend—he didn't have to live here.

Ten

Rachel had been dreading the meeting with the realtor for days. Annie was pretty detached about selling the loft, but that hadn't made the decision any easier. They had agreed to move out by the month's end and split the proceeds equally, if there were any, after subtracting Annie's initial down payment. Sounded perfect, but Rachel knew from past experience that Annie could be unpredictable. That wild impulsive side was one of the reasons Rachel had fallen in love with Annie, but it could be deadly when used for spite.

The knock at the door sounded like the starting bell at a boxing match and Rachel wanted to get in the first punch. She raced to the door, sliding the last few feet as her socks searched for purchase on the travertine. She took a deep breath and casually opened the door. At least she hoped it looked casual.

Nancy Johnson was a smart dresser. Even though her ears were pink from the cold, she would never muss her carefully back-combed and hairsprayed bubble of grey-blonde hair with a silly hat. She unwrapped her claret-colored, wool cape and stomped the snow off her fur-lined, three-inch-heeled boots.

"Hello Nancy," Rachel said a bit breathlessly.

"Hi Rachel, I'm very sorry to see you sell this place so soon, but the market is improving. You should make a nice profit." Nancy pasted on her plastic, sunny-at-all-temperatures smile.

"That's great, we just need to get things straight for escrow. Annie and I will be splitting the proceeds, less her initial deposit." Rachel rolled it out like a tear-gas canister and waited for the inevitable stinging.

"Oh, you and Miss Nelson will not be buying a new place?" Nancy was hoping this was true. While she liked Rachel and thought of herself as progressive, Nancy had a problem with the whole lesbian thing...not that there was anything wrong with it.

Annie sauntered in and plopped down in an over-stuffed chair on the other side of the glass coffee table.

"Hi Annie," offered Nancy.

"Yeah," mumbled Annie.

"I was just explaining everything..." Rachel made every effort to keep things under control.

"Oh yeah? Does it need explaining?" Annie's voice dripped with sarcasm.

Nancy felt very uncomfortable, and even considered dropping the listing, but in the end her high moral character and the huge commission convinced her to stay.

"There are just a few papers to sign." Nancy opened her briefcase and extracted several forms with little flags stuck on at just the right spots for signatures.

"Do you want something to drink Nancy?" Rachel asked.

"Little miss hostess," sniped Annie.

"Look Annie, I'm just trying to be polite. Can we get through this? Can you try to be civil?" begged Rachel.

"Civil? You're fucking kicking me out of the house. That seems kinda fucking uncivil. You're always at work—I take care of everything..." Annie was winding up.

"Annie please, we've been through all this. We made a fair deal, you'll be compensated." Rachel regretted it as soon as she said it.

Nancy was frozen like a deer in the headlights. Her hand was halfway between putting the papers on the table and shoving them back into her case and running. The room was swirling with tension.

"Compensated, oh that's rich. Like a high-priced whore?" Annie spat vehemently.

"Annie, I didn't mean it that way—for chrissake can we just sign the papers and move on?" pleaded Rachel.

"Yeah, let's just move on!" Annie put a bit more acid into her response than she actually felt—but Rachel deserved it. She was acting so cold and bitchy, like their three-year relationship meant nothing.

Nancy was pale and beyond uncomfortable, but she was a pro, and when she heard what appeared to be a consensus, she flew into action. She was flipping through pages and handing out pens like the President on a veto binge.

"Okay, that takes care of that," announced Nancy, "I'll put a lock box on the door and we'll begin showing the property as soon as you vacate." Nancy was already gathering up her things and preparing to make her exit.

"We'll be out by the end of the month," confirmed Rachel.

"Or sooner," added Annie, just loud enough for Rachel to hear.

"Thanks for your time Nancy." Rachel stood up and walked to the door.

Nancy hurried after her, "We'll be in touch, ladies." Nancy nearly bolted out the door.

Rachel couldn't hold back a chuckle at the sight of Nancy's rapidly retreating behind.

"Scary lesbian death match," added Annie, catching Rachel's mood.

Rachel just cracked up, sinking to the floor where her laughter quickly transformed into tears.

"I'm sorry Annie, I'm so sorry. I'm just trying to do what's right. I never meant for things to get this f'd up!" Rachel choked out, between sobs. She wanted to throw the TK thing in Annie's face, but all she really saw was one kiss. Bringing up the gig would only piss Annie off—Rachel had been spying. It wasn't worth it. Just sell the place and put this loft and Annie in the rearview mirror.

Annie moved to her side and put her hand under Rachel's chin. Her big green eyes looked deep into Rachel's teary, brown ones, "Me neither. Sorry I lost my shit in front of that panties-in-a-bunch realtor," said Annie.

"Is it even possible for us to try to be friends through this?"

"We can try, don't know if it's possible...but yeah...we can try." Annie leaned down and kissed Rachel on the forehead and wiped the tears from her cheek.

Rachel looked up and smiled. The spell of anger and resentment was broken. So she kissed some fucking TK bitch at a gig, whatever. Annie was just Annie, a human being that was hurting and trying to pick up the pieces. And Rachel was just a single, baker trying to sell a loft. Trying to move on.

Eleven

A long, well-muscled leg poked out from under the heap of blankets and a husky, sleep-filled voice was speaking into a phone, "No Todd, I don't care...it's fine...you'll make the right choice...of course...I do trust you...yes, season tickets...I don't remember saying Orchestra, but if you stop calling me this weekend, I'll consider it," Daniel let out a yawning chuckle, "Okay, thanks Todd."

The cabin looked much the same as always, possibly a little dustier and a little smaller than he remembered. The wonderful crevices of the timber always intrigued him and the massive split rock fireplace was both beautiful and practical. The huge fireplace stood in the center of the cabin; it was at least six feet across and two-stories high, plus the impressive chimney. The beauty of the various exposed rocks was obvious, but the ingenious part was keeping a roaring fire going all day so the rocks would heat up, releasing the passive warmth into the cabin during the night—and keep the occupants from freezing to death.

Daniel had installed a back-up solar heating system when he inherited the cabin after his father's passing, but he rarely used it. He loved the nostalgia of the crackling fire, so much so, that he paid a few local boys to chop and stack wood so that there would always be enough on hand.

The cabin was Daniel's paradise. Built from the reclaimed timbers of a sunken ship, and filled with wonderful memories of ice fishing with his father and snowmobiling with neighborhood boys. There were even some late-night Scrabble games and silent, magical canoe rides—this place was heaven.

Whenever the hectic pace of the Twin Cities got to be too much for him he headed north. Just knowing that this oasis awaited, was enough to soothe his spirit and give him hope.

Daniel looked around appraisingly; even an oasis could use a going over once or twice a century. Over the years Daniel had collected a lot of memorabilia, and other things, and the cabin was looking more like Sanford and Sons' backyard than a peaceful respite. What to do? He knew he wouldn't be tidying up by himself, that was for certain.

He had seen a billboard on the way into town. "The Fixer...no, The Cleaner...oh, come on Daniel get it together," he chided. "You're having a senior moment, better start the ginko. Just see the billboard in your mind and... The Organizer," he yelled triumphantly to the dusty walls and grabbed his phone.

"Good morning, thank you for calling The Organizer," Flora's voice was especially cheerful, even for a Friday.

"Good morning, I need some help organizing my cabin," said Daniel in a still husky, but much less sleepy, voice.

"Oh wonderful, can I set up an appointment with The Organizer for next Thursday?" Flora asked, happily.

"Actually, I'm only in town for the weekend and I live in the Twin City area. I was hoping I could meet with someone today, and pass off the keys...or whatever."

"Oh, gosh that's fast, let me put you on hold Mr....?" Flora paused for the name.

"Gregory, Daniel Gregory," Bond, James Bond—Daniel chuckled at his private joke.

Flora chuckled absently in support of whatever the client thought was funny, "One moment Mr. Gregory."

Flora practically ran to Gwenn's office, half panic half excitement, "Gwenn we've got a live one. He has to meet today, has a cabin that needs organizing and he lives in the Twin Cities—sounds moneyed."

"Flora you know I'm swamped—try Thea."

"No good, Thea left for her brother's last night."

"Okay Flora, you're on."

"I'm on what?"

"Take it. You take it, commission and all. I need you to step up and do this."

"Jeez Gwenn, I've never even taken a meeting, ya know."

"Flora don't flip out." Gwenn smiled reassuringly, "Just look at it like a proposal, make sure all the bits and pieces are there and close the deal. Call him back and let him know you'll be there in an hour."

"He's on hold!" Flora screeched as she spun around and ran to her desk.

"You can do this," called Gwenn, with far more enthusiasm than she felt.

She had dodged a bullet on that Linder project and now Flora was coming to the rescue again. It was good to have people you could count on, even if you had to pay to keep them around.

Maybe that would've worked with Steven. Just the thought of his name sent Gwenn back in time.

They were so much in love, so completely lost in each other and he was her perfect match—a Scorpio. What went so wrong that he would run away? Oh, that's right, Pastor Ed and Shirley.

It didn't seem like 12 years had gone by, the pain was still so fresh and raw. Steven was tall and thin, but muscular, and boy-next-door handsome. He was studying to be a doctor—and he was Jewish. That was the real sticking point for Ol' Ma and Pa Hutchinson.

"The boy belongs to a cult, Gwendolyn," admonished Shirley.

"Those are the people responsible for putting Christ on the cross," chimed in Ed.

Gwenn wanted to say, "Yeah, and if they hadn't he would've died in anonymity and you wouldn't have any reason to sit in judgment over the rest of the world!" but instead she went with a more acceptable response, "Just meet us for dinner at Zona Rosa, okay. We've been dating for almost a year and you guys haven't even met him. It's just dinner," lied Gwenn. Actually, it was an engagement announcement dinner, but Gwenn wanted public witnesses before she dropped that bomb.

The restaurant was good and crowded. Gwenn was pleased, lots of eyewitnesses, that should keep things on a small-catastrophe scale as opposed to a holocaust—ooh bad choice of words. Gwenn mentally kicked herself.

Ed and Shirley were standing uncomfortably in the waiting area. Steven marched right over to them and shook their hands like a pro; not at all like a man on death row. Gwenn was pleased she had avoided any gas chamber analogies.

They followed the hostess to their booth. Steven took the lead, then Ed, Shirley next and Gwenn bringing up the rear in case anyone made a run for the fence. Oh, Gwenn was going to flagellate herself senseless when she got home.

Suddenly Shirley stopped, turned and looked at Gwenn's expensive new dress, "Do ya know what people think when they see a girl like you, dressed like that—with a man like him?" Shirley nearly spat with disgust.

"What?"

"Whore." Shirley spun on a dime and continued to the table.

Gwenn stood stark still, teetering on the edge of sanity. Somehow she managed to stumble to the table. Dinner was a blur. There was the cruel set of Shirley's mouth, and Ed's persistently disapproving look as Steven calmly told them of the marriage plans.

"Well, I won't be a party ta this." Shirley got up and stormed out of the restaurant and Ed obediently followed.

On the drive home Gwenn was fuming with indignation. Her anger seethed and every cell in her body screamed for vindication.

Revenge comes in many forms.

Gwenn slowly rolled her thigh-high stockings down her legs; she flung her shoes into the back seat and hung one stocking over the rearview mirror. Her hand slid meaningfully between Steven's thighs. Steven had the car off the road in 30 seconds. He pushed back his seat and Gwenn turned all her pain and anger into an explosion of passion. Steven definitely did not mind.

A few weeks later when Gwenn's period was late, the pain and anger came flooding back—fueled by a cataclysm of soul-numbing fear.

Gwenn was right in the middle of her college career, her heart was still full of dreams of a future that had to be better than her past. This could not be happening to her, so she had a series of increasingly irrational arguments with Steven.

"I cannot have a child right now, especially not a child out of wedlock."

"Gwenn, relax. You sound like your mom."

"Don't you ever say that," screamed Gwenn.

"Gwenn we can work this out, we have each other—we will find a way to make it work."

"I'm not going to quit college Steven. This is my body, my life...my humiliation. I will not have a bastard child. I am not going to give Pastor Ed and Shirley the ammunition to crucify me," wailed Gwenn. Her eyes were wild; darting back and forth across the faces of her imagined accusers.

"Gwenn, be reasonable. What are you going to do, get an abortion?" said Steven in horror.

"Yes." Gwenn grabbed onto that idea like a mongoose holding a cobra.

"Gwenn!" The shock and fear in Steven's voice was like a knife in her back. But Gwenn's mind was made up and no matter how long they argued, Gwenn's punishment was decided. "Be sure your sin will find you out," Shirley's cruel voice echoed back from childhood, and Gwenn wanted to be sure that no one ever found out about this sin.

There were a couple more arguments, but Gwenn simply withdrew into silence and Steven couldn't reach her. He tried to get her to eat, but she just sat and stared out the window of her dorm room. Finally he gave up and went home.

Another day passed and Gwenn decided to call and make him understand, somehow. Steven's roommate answered and was very quiet.

"Alan, what's up? Is Steven there...Alan?"

"Um Gwenn...uhh...I thought he—"

"Alan, stop goofing around, just spit it out."

"Gwenn he left last night."

Cold, icy blades were stabbing into her chest and Gwenn couldn't breathe.

"On a business trip?" choked Gwenn.

"Gwenn, I'm sorry...he moved back to his sister's in Philadelphia."

Gwenn dropped the phone and felt two things, her heart breaking into a million irreparable pieces and a warm trickle of something running down her inner thigh. She wanted to grab the phone and scream, "False alarm! False alarm! I was just late, nothing more." Instead she just picked up the receiver and dropped it into the cradle with a hollow thud of finality.

Gwenn groped her way to the shower, tears blinding her empty, frightened eyes. She didn't even bother to take off her T-shirt or panties; she just crawled onto the floor of the shower. Shivering under the cold water, she watched the swirls of blood circle the drain. It was gone—everything was gone. Steven was gone, happiness was gone, and the future was gone. Steven was gone. Gwenn's body shook with aching sobs. The thin veil that had allowed her to tolerate Ed and Shirley was gone. Her life was gone. *Steven was gone.*

Gwenn rubbed her temples to erase the painful memory and allowed her shoulders to relax as she played her favorite origin fantasy in her mind.

"Yes Doctor, they were sure. My daughter was in a terrible car accident and I gave blood for a transfusion. They said they couldn't use it because my precious Veronica was A-negative. So, they tested my husband and he didn't have the negative either. We aren't her parents. She must have been switched at birth."

The next part was Gwenn's favorite.

"Well, Mrs. Whiteside, there was only one other baby girl born in this hospital on that day...born to a Mr. and Mrs. Hutchinson. The baby's name was Gwendolyn."

"My God!" the woman always clutched her heart at this point, "That's my mother's name. Where can I find this girl?"

Gwenn didn't need to play the whole movie today. The knowledge that deep down she wasn't the fruit of Pastor Ed and Shirley's crazy loins was enough.

But she was going need some help clearing out the *Steven*.

Twelve

Rachel helped Annie load the last of her things into the moving van. They hugged and smiled at each other.

"Take care of yourself, Annie."

"Yeah you too. I still get free scones at the bakery, right?" Annie smiled that big, inviting grin that reminded Rachel of happier times.

"Hey, if I gave free scones to all my former lovers..." Rachel laughed bravely. "Oh what the heck, sure scones... and maybe an occasional Big Cookie."

"Wow, a Big Cookie, now you're just stickin' it to me." Annie smiled and gave Rachel a friendly punch on the shoulder before she turned to get in the van.

"Bye."

"See ya 'round."

Rachel watched as the van turned the corner and disappeared. That was definitely one of the better endings, Rachel thought, as she turned back to the half-empty loft. She would move her stuff back to the above-bakery apartment next weekend, and it would be like Annie never happened. Except for the numbing little ache in her heart, Rachel thought ruefully.

The loft seemed hollow and dead. When the phone rang Rachel nearly jumped out of her skin.

"Hello."

"Rache it's me, can we have dinner?" Gwenn tried to keep the desperation out of her voice, but it's not easy to fool a sister.

"What happened?"

"I've just been Steven-ed. I could use a distraction."

"Sure, grab some take-out and come over to the loft."

"No, let's go to Superior and get drunk and crazy."

"Seriously, it's Friday night, the real party animals will be crawling the streets. Are you ready for that?"

Gwenn laughed nervously, "Sure, I can handle it, I'm not that old."

"Okay, grab some take-out, come to the loft and I will find you something to wear. You really don't have clubbing clothes in your universe."

Gwenn arrived with a sack full of Thai options. Rachel enveloped her in a big hug, but no *namaste*, Gwenn was quite certain a new philosophy was brewing.

Gwenn felt like an idiot in her L.A.M.B. Tizzy heels, too-short mini-dress and too many bangles.

"Rache, I look like Madonna in the 80s with all these bracelets. Are you sure this is even remotely in?"

"Gwenn you're a knockout, deal with it." Rachel skidded to a stop in front of the Yellow Submarine, one of Superior's less than finest.

"Oh my god, Rache we used to sneak in here in high school. I'll look like a geriatric on a day pass," Gwenn shook her head hopelessly.

"Yeah, remember all the gorgeous guys that used to troll this place."

"Um yeah, but they were looking for jailbait Rache, not cougars." Gwenn stepped out of the car and looked at her reflection in the plate glass window. Okay, even she had to admit she had something close to *it* going on. When she got carded on the way in, her spirits soared.

The music was pumping and the cheesy lights were flashing. Not much had changed. The music, of course, but the cast of characters was like a flashback. The grizzled regulars were sitting along the darkened back wall—all drinking beers and shots. The too-young girls were quickly buying the talisman of sloe gin fizz or seven and seven, assuming that a drink in-hand would add the necessary five to seven years to their appearance.

Gwenn paused and took inventory of the men, a rather fine selection, for Wisconsin: some frat boys from UMD, some young businessmen cutting loose and one anomaly.

Gwenn shifted her stance so she could casually stare at the enigma. Tall, handsome, older—but it was difficult to say how much—his broad shoulders and long hair seemed ageless. Of course, in the blinking lights it was hard to get a fix on much of anything.

"I got you a sloe gin fizz, for old times sake," Rachel yelled over the pounding beat.

"I'll probably puke from the sweetness," Gwenn yelled back.

They downed their drinks and hit the dance floor. Gwenn was feeling warm and tingly; a little bit of relaxation was sneaking into her body.

Rachel had always been a good dancer, something about being comfortable with her body and being just a bit reckless—the perfect combination. The highlights in her black hair flashed under the lights. Heads were turning, uselessly, but nonetheless they were turning. Just about the time Gwenn was reaching her limit of discomfort, a pair of frat boys plucked up their courage and descended on her and Rachel.

Rachel didn't even miss a beat, she just turned to bump and grind with Flat-top; that left Baggy-jeans for Gwenn. He smiled suggestively at Gwenn and moved in super close. He was actually a pretty good dancer, but Gwenn was a little uncomfortable with being humped on the dance floor by a complete stranger.

Baggy-jeans was saying something, but the music was so loud, Gwenn couldn't hear. She raised her hand and cupped her ear to indicate the problem and he moved his face about three inches from Gwenn's and mouthed, "You're hot."

Gwenn smiled and did a little turny move so she could shoot Rachel the "help he's a stalker" look. Within seconds Rachel was grabbing her hand and screaming, "I gotta pee." They waved to the frat boys as they hurried toward the bathroom.

Once inside the comparatively quiet haven of the bathroom, they were able to speak in more civil volumes.

"This is a blast, Flat-top was gorgeous. I almost felt bad that he was wasting his time," Rachel giggled as she dabbed away the sweat on her brow and touched up her lipstick.

"Did you see the Lion King?" Gwenn asked casually.

"Who?"

"The Lion King—older guy with the amazing mane of hair?"

"No, where? How old?"

"He was kinda off to the side, not quite on regular row, but in that area. He might be really old, it was hard to tell in the lights."

Rachel looked at Gwenn with an evil grin, "You wanna dance with him?"

"No, you freak. For one thing, I'm too sober and for another, he looked too fancy for a place like this."

"Too sober, Huh...well, I can fix that." Rachel grabbed Gwenn by the hand and dragged her to the bar.

"Two Manhattans, keep it sweet and pop my cherry." Rachel winked at the bartender.

"What the hell did you say?" Gwenn looked shocked.

"Who knows, I just made it up. I just love it when people have wild drink orders. So I kinda made one up." Rachel was cracking up.

The bartender slid two Manhattans, with long-stemmed maraschino cherries, across the bar. Rachel paid him, tipped him and gave him one more wink for the road.

"Must've made sense to him, this is exactly what I wanted." Rachel shrugged her shoulders and strutted back to the edge of the dance floor to watch the action.

Several Manhattans later, Gwenn was feeling no pain and dancing like a maniac. She noticed Lion King watching her, so she raised her arms and gyrated her hips quite suggestively.

Rachel caught the move out of the corner of her eye. "Reelin' him in are we?"

"What? I'd jus...like thmusic," slurred Gwenn.

"Uh oh, time to go," Rachel said to no one in particular. She put her arm protectively around Gwenn and steered her off the dance floor.

"I'm gonna pee n...puke..." Gwenn said thickly.

Rachel quickly steered her around to the bathroom and rudely cut in front of several angry teens, to get Gwenn an emergency berth.

"He's gor...mm...pretty," Gwenn smiled the blissful grin of the inebriated.

"Who, Lion King? Ya still goin' on about him," teased Rachel.

"So pretty, like a god statue of Greek."

"I think he's old enough to be Zeus," added Rachel, through the stall door. "Come on Gwenn stand up and open the door."

"Can't."

"Sure you can sweetie, just open the door."

"S'open...can't stand. No feet. I love him so much Rachel."

"Okay sweetie, I'll fix you up." Rachel took a matchbook from her purse, tore off the flap and wrote "Gwenn H." and Gwenn's cell number. She opened the stall door, wrenched Gwenn off the toilet and headed out of the bar.

As they passed the Lion King, Rachel handed him the phone number, pointed meaningfully at Gwenn and kept walking.

Daniel looked at the intoxicated woman leaning on the brave woman's shoulder and thought, '*Guardian Angel*, oil on canvas.' He reached out for the slip of paper and they were gone. Beautiful, tragic, but hardly the kind of woman he would date. A little young and irresponsible.

Daniel drove back to the cabin in radio silence. His ears were still ringing from the banging beats at the Yellow Submarine. What a funny name for a divey bar. He would have pictured more hippie and less hip-hop—but then he was pretty out of touch with this generation. He took the matchbook cover out of his pocket and flipped it absently between his fingers. Maybe he would call Gwenn H. just to embarrass her and teach her a lesson about giving her number to strangers.

She was striking, though, that auburn hair, the toned legs, and the hazel eyes. Had he really noticed the eyes? How could he help but notice them? She was wiggling and shaking and staring right at him. Her eyes were twinkly and smart, but they had turned bleary and daft—a party girl—not really his type.

Daniel grabbed his cell phone and dialed.

"Todd, I know you'll get this message in the morning. I want you to clear my schedule after the show. I'm going to come back up to the cabin and get some much-needed R&R. Give me at least two weeks. Thanks." Daniel smiled, there would be some time to get the cabin organized, and if he happened to run into an older version of Gwenn H., well, so be it.

Thirteen

The room was spinning violently and Gwenn's head was throbbing. She was definitely going to puke. She sat up slowly, looked around and got very confused. This was not home. For a split second she froze in terror at the thought of a one-night stand. Rachel's soft voice brought reassurance.

"Gwenny, are you still sick?"

"Mmhmm."

"Okay, Gwenny, let me help you to the bathroom."

It was so strange to have the roles reversed. When Rachel was struggling with her sexuality, at least with the coming out of the closet part. Gwenn had run innumerable rescue missions. She even had to take Rachel to the hospital for alcohol poisoning on one outrageous occasion. It felt strange to have Rachel playing nursemaid. Gwenn felt better after she threw-up. She slept fitfully and wasn't all that interested in food when she awoke.

Gwenn and Rachel sat in the kitchen sipping tea and picking at day-old scones.

"If you have to go, it's okay."

"No, I called William he's got the bakery under control. Nathan comes in at 8:00 to help, so the two of them are holding down the fort."

Rachel seemed so responsible, so organized. Gwenn laughed gingerly, "I guess I got that out of my system for the decade. I must've made quite a geriatric spectacle of myself."

"Oh, I don't know, the Lion King seemed to like what he saw."

Gwenn's foggy brain whirred for a minute before it clicked, "The old guy, he was kinda cute for an old guy. Was he checking me out?"

"Yeah, especially after I gave him your number."

"Oh, ha ha, real funny Rache." Gwenn noticed the devilish twinkle in Rachel's eyes and felt her stomach lurch, "You didn't."

"I did."

"He'll think I'm a drunken hussy!" moaned Gwenn.

"I just wrote 'Gwenn H.' he doesn't really know who you are. He probably won't even call. You said it yourself, he's kinda old," Rachel backpedaled.

"Okay, it's official, I can move to Turkey and join the whirling dervishes. Obviously the mother ship has abandoned me and my alien sisterhood is sitting back on planet Urantia, laughing their asses, or whatever they have, off right now. It sucks to be me." Gwenn let her head flop down onto the table. She squeezed her eyes shut tightly but she could still see her hips gyrating and her eyes twinkling at the Lion King.

Gwenn went into the office Monday still feeling like she was doing the walk of shame. The headache was gone, the queasiness had subsided, but the humiliation was palpable.

"Morning Gwenn," smiled Flora.

"Hey there," mumbled Gwenn.

Flora sensed the mood and decided some good news was just what Gwenn needed.

"Gwenn, guess what?"

"I couldn't begin to imagine," Gwenn said distractedly.

"I closed 'em. I got the job!" Flora beamed.

Gwenn looked up in confusion; the events of Friday were clicking into place like a neat little Rubik's cube in her brain. "Oh, Flora, that's fantastic. Sorry, I'm a little out of it. I made a fool of myself at a bar this weekend and Friday is a little fuzzy. Tell me everything."

"Okay," Flora was as proud as a new mama. "The client is a successful artist from the Twin Cities, he is very well-off and he inherited this Park Point vacation home."

"Mmhmm."

"The property is really nice, timber that was reclaimed from a sunken ship, and a split rock fireplace...oh, and there's a lovely deck."

"Nice."

"Of course, the place is chock full of generations of junk. Some of it worth keeping, some headed for the incinerator and all of it needs organizing."

"Flora, that's great." Gwenn was sort of listening, but most of her was puzzling over the Lion King and what he might be doing with her phone number.

"So, I told him at least two weeks for the job and I e-mailed him a full proposal on Saturday." Flora was positively glowing.

"You're amazing, Flora, Amazing. I can't thank you enough for handling this project."

"Don't thank me, just show me the commission!"

"Absolutely, we'll even have a 'Flora lands the...' oh, what did you land? What's the client's name?" Gwenn smiled.

"Oh, it's Daniel Gregory, he got..."

But Gwenn didn't hear anything else. The room spun, her stomach turned upside down and she ran to the restroom in great haste.

Fourteen

The proposal looked solid and Daniel knew he would enjoy working with Flora. She was as efficient as Todd, but she had a better sense of humor and she was easier on the eyes. His cell phone rang insistently.

"Hello Todd, what's the emergency?"

"No emergency Mr. Gregory, just making sure you'll be back in time for the show tonight." Todd was barely masking the irritation in his voice.

"Already back Todd, I'm on Hennepin, just around the corner from the Gallery. I'll see you in a minute." Daniel pressed end without waiting for a reply. "Jeez Todd, lighten up."

The huge glass windows of the Gallery always seemed welcoming to Daniel. He could see the pin lights pointing out the subtle beauty in his paintings and he smiled in appreciation of Todd's impeccable eye. Maybe season tickets to the Guthrie were not enough.

"Todd it looks magnificent," boomed Daniel as he walked into the Gallery.

Todd scrambled out from behind a floating-wall display area and breathed a huge, audible sigh of relief, "You made it."

"I wouldn't miss my own show, Todd. You're going to go prematurely gray from all the worrying. I should know," Daniel ran his fingers through the hair of his temples and chuckled.

"I'm glad you like it."

"Where's *Angel Wings*, Gouache on canvas?"

"Follow me," said Todd as he wove his way through the Gallery. In the center, suspended from cable and floating in an ethereal pool of light was *Angel Wings*.

Daniel sucked in a long, impressed breath and murmured, "Wow, you do me proud, son." Daniel wiped imaginary tears from his eyes.

Todd rolled his eyes, but his chest swelled with pride. It really did look awesome—there would be a bidding war over this one, Todd could guarantee it.

"We have two hours until showtime Mr. Gregory, can I get you something to eat or drink?"

"I drank enough for the both of us Friday night. I'll just take a mineral water and maybe an apple." Daniel rubbed his head with the memory of Friday. Of course, he hadn't had as much to drink as Gwenn H., but who had.

"You were drinking?" Todd couldn't help but let a little alarm creep into his voice. Several years ago, when Daniel's father had passed away, the drinking had gotten very out of control. Shows were canceled, commissions were lost and the Gallery had been in jeopardy.

"Oh, not that kind of drinking Todd, just a few too many at a dive in Superior. I even got a girl's digits, is that what you kids say?" Daniel teased.

Todd couldn't help but get sucked in. Daniel hadn't dated anyone since his father's funeral.

Daniel's first wife died suddenly, and violently when she was only 28; and Daniel's subsequent drinking binges and depression were legendary. Of course Todd didn't work for him then, but everyone in the art world had whispered about the legend of the wasted artistic genius that had been Daniel Gregory.

Todd had joined the team about two years later, and Daniel's drinking had slowed a bit, but he wouldn't touch a pen or brush. He just kept saying his muse had died. Eventually loneliness led Daniel to more public places to assuage his pain with drink. And naturally, women were drawn to his brooding, good looks and his magnificent hair.

Daniel's rebuffs where cruel and filled with malice. He would just glare or laugh mockingly at these pathetic, hollow excuses for women; these cheap imitations who thought they could replace his wife, his Angeline.

But time wore the edge off of Daniel's pain and one day he found himself having a conversation with a petite, brunette named Natalie. They talked for hours and Natalie went home. Not the typical, desperate barfly—Daniel allowed himself to notice the distinction.

Natalie turned out to be the life preserver Daniel had been waiting for. Her clear, green eyes and her obvious physical assets pulled Daniel out of the depths of his despair. When her gentle, purring encouragement coaxed him back into his studio—art collectors across the globe gave her a standing ovation.

Things were really flowing for Daniel, his work turned a corner and the emotional agony of the previous years fueled some of the most evocative works of his career. He skyrocketed into the spotlight and Natalie basked in his glow.

They decided a long vacation, a change of scenery, would be ideal; escape the wintry Minnesota blahs and sneak off to Fiji for a month or two.

So, it was lying on the beach on the island of Vanua Levu, that Daniel received the news that his father had lost control of his vehicle on an icy road, flipped several times off a bridge and broken through a dark, ice-bound lake. The rescue crews worked fast, but it only takes a few minutes for freezing-cold, passionless waters to swallow your soul.

It was more than Daniel could stand. He immediately returned to the States and attempted to handle his father's affairs, but the pain was like a knife—stabbing through the protective layers he had put over Angeline's death—and the relapse was earth shattering.

Natalie abandoned ship when things got rough, and Daniel found his solace in the bottom of an old-fashioned glass, at least when he bothered to use a glass.

Todd stepped in and kept the Gallery afloat, and in his spare time he kept Daniel afloat. Somehow, the honest friendship that Todd offered was more real than any fantasy, rescue-woman and Daniel agreed to get help.

Todd checked in with Daniel at regular, scheduled intervals and Daniel wrote down the feelings and experiences that were attempting to swallow him whole. After several months, Todd convinced Daniel to publish his story and "The Painter's Son" became a bestseller.

Bolstered by the book's success, Daniel returned to painting and the painful process of rebuilding his life.

However, women were not part of the new architecture. Daniel was always polite and charming at every show, but he just wasn't willing to open the door to his heart a third time.

The "preservation plan" as Daniel called it had been working great for almost four years, but Todd was curious about this girl's *digits*.

Fifteen

Gwenn's mortification was not scheduled to depart anytime soon. If she had a cat-o-nine tails she would already be flagellating herself with it.

She rinsed the puke out of her mouth and grabbed the mouthwash from under the bathroom sink. Rinse, spit. Rinse, spit. Gwenn grabbed her cell phone.

"Rachel, I know you're not answering because you're swamped at the bakery but things have just gone to DEFCON 1 over here and I need a bail, out fast. I'm coming to the bakery, I have to talk to you...oh crap I think I'm going to puke again..."

Gwenn dropped the phone on the counter and spun around, barely making it to the toilet in time. She wiped her mouth with the back of her hand and shakily got to her feet. She was pale and her eyes were darting wildly inside her head. Kind of like balls in a pinball machine, she mused, but thought better of it as her stomach lurched in response.

That's when she noticed the cell phone was still connected. "Oh, shit...sorry Rache, see ya soon."

Rachel was pacing behind the counter like a 1940s father-to-be, waiting outside a delivery room.

"Gwenny, what the hell?"

"Umm, can we go upstairs?"

"Yeah, of course. Guys, I'm out—hold down the fort."

Two semi-bewildered heads nodded robotically.

Gwenn let the door shut before she lost it. "Oh my god Rache, I'm a frickin' living soap opera."

"Gwenny, you got drunk, you danced like a stripper and you gave your phone number to a complete stranger. Sounds like a good time to me." Rachel tried to sound nonchalant, but she was more than a little concerned about Gwenn's meltdown.

"You gave it...you...you gave my number to that man."

"Is that what's bothering you? I'm sorry Gwenny, I was just having some fun."

"No it's not about the stupid bar. It's so much worse!" Gwenn collapsed onto the couch, huge tears sluicing down her pale cheeks.

"Hey, come on its me here, what the hell's going on?"

"Daniel...oh it's so morbid...Daniel Gregory!" Gwenn wailed.

"Oh Gwenn, honestly, they were just some old pictures. Give it a rest. We're sisters, full-blooded sisters. I'm not going to let you slip out of the Ed and Shirley noose that easily, ya freak." Rachel threw out a good-natured laugh but it sounded more like a nervous squeak. Not really the reassurance she was going for.

"He's a client," Gwenn forced through her clenched jaw.

"You met him?"

"No, I was too busy on Friday so I sent Flora and she landed the account."

"Oh, good for her. Go Flora, go Flora," Rachel wiggled her hips, but stopped the victory dance abruptly. "Oh, sorry. Not really the point."

"I just found out this morning. After I threw-up once from the shock, I called you and then—"

"Oh, I got the message."

"Whatever, Rache, it's the principle of the thing. I mean what if he is my dad? What if he's not? He's still my client; I still have to face him. Bottom line I have to ask, I have to know the truth."

"I'll go with you, for moral support."

"Here's the thing Rache, I obviously have no morals to support, and also, that would just be too pathetic, even for me."

"So what's your plan?" Rachel tried to sound matter-of-fact, but she knew it had sounded much more "tell me the juicy tabloid details" than she intended.

"I'm going to have Flora set up a meeting. I'm going to bring the photos and I'm going to cut to the chase. Just throw all my cards on the table and prepare to place the arsenic under my tongue." Gwenn's chin jutted out with resolve.

"Okay perfect. When?"

Gwenn's lip was quivering again.

"Gwenny, just do it. Just call Flora and—"

"Oh, for crying out loud, Flora probably thinks I'm checking into the Betty Ford! She said Daniel Gregory, and I ran out of the room like a nun to confession."

"Just call her, she'll understand. I mean, she'll understand the lie you're going to tell her."

"I don't know Rache."

"Gwenn...seriously, you didn't become a consummate truth bender, after all those years with Ed and Shirley, to turn tail now. You can do this; you were born to do this. No pun intended, really."

Gwenn took out her cell phone and pressed the speed dial for the office.

"Was that Speed Dial 3, whose 2?" Rachel quipped.

"You are of course, you giant brat! Oh, hello, not you Flora...just finishing up a conversation on my end. Sorry... umm...sorry I tossed my cookies. I had some really questionable leftovers this morning, and I guess they just couldn't play nice. I'm honestly thrilled about the Gregory," Gwenn swallowed and took a deep breath, "account, really great work Flora. I'm very pleased."

"Thanks Gwenn, you had me worrying a bit there, you know."

"Yeah sorry. I think that we need to pamper this one a bit. I mean he's a high-profile client. I was thinking I should at least meet with him once, to let him know we're all focused on the best outcome for this project."

"Yeah, sure, he was asking if he would get to meet The Organizer."

Gwenn's resolve wavered and wanted to pack its bags, but she forged ahead.

"Oh, how funny. Well then, can you set up a meeting for me as soon as possible? We want to hit the ground running on this one."

"Okay, I'll take care of it."

"Thanks Flora. I'll be back in the office soon." Gwenn hung up and threw her head back onto the couch. A baleful moan escaped her lips.

"We want to hit the ground running on this one? Who are you *G.I. Jane*?" Rachel said mockingly.

"Okay, I have to get back to the office and smooth things over with Flora. The food poisoning thing is only going to get me so far."

"I'll walk ya down."

"Thanks for the emergency visit, put it on my tab."

"Don't worry Gwenn, I think I still hold the record for most 'code blues' in a lifetime. So, this one's on the house."

Gwenn hugged Rachel and wondered if things would be any different if they turned out to be half-sisters. There was one certainty; things would be different for Shirley. Gwenn smiled, in spite of her internal pandemonium.

Sixteen

"Ed. Ed! Oh, yer as deaf as the day is long." Shirley shook her head in exasperation. "Ed!"

"Well, ya don't have ta yell at me Shirl, I'm right here in the kitchen."

"Ed, what are ya wearing?"

"Oh, I dunno know just some pants and a shirt, I guess."

"Ed, go put on the clothes I laid out fer ya. And hurry up, ya don't want ta be late." Shirley just rolled her eyes heavenward, hoping that her Lord was giving her credit for the infinite patience she bestowed upon this slow-witted creature with whom she had formed a union.

"What are ya so fired up about anyway, you said ya hate chaperoning the singles fer Jesus mixers." Ed struggled to tuck his shirt in properly, hoping to avoid another correction from Shirley.

"Ed, are ya kiddin' me? Ya know that Rachel is catering this pot luck and I would think that even you would know what that means." Shirley just exhaled through her teeth and shook her head.

"She needs ta borrow some money?" Ed chuckled at the little joke he had made. Despite the fact that the women of the family found him to be mentally feeble, he had noticed a distinct pattern in Rachel's baking-for-cash schemes.

"Oh Ed, be serious, this is just God's way of puttin' these nice Christian boys in Rachel's path. We just need ta be there ta make sure she notices God's will."

Seemed like a waste of time he thought. He couldn't remember the last time Rachel had taken notice of boys, nice Christian or otherwise.

The lights were on and the streamers streaming in the multi-purpose room of The Nazarenes' First Covenant Free Church of Christ. Rachel was setting up the buffet table with a tantalizing array of crudités, hors d'oeuvres, mini quiches, mini scones, brownie bites and her pièce de résistance—mini sweet rolls with rum-soaked raisins. She knew that baking probably removed all the alcohol, but it pleased her in a deeply twisted way, nonetheless.

"Rachel! Hellooo!" Shirley's sing-songy, save-it-for-church-gatherings voice came rolling through the room.

Rachel endured the huge, all-for-show hug that ensued, waiting for the inevitable commentary.

"Is that what yer wearing?" Shirley appraised her daughter's black slacks, white blouse, apron and sensible shoes and found the ensemble wanting.

"Yeah mom, I'm catering not debutanting."

"Ya could've at least done somethin' with yer hair."

"This is something mom, it's called a ponytail," Rachel said the last part real slowly, like she was talking to a child.

"Well, it's not my favorite."

Shirley's old refrain poked a couple of holes in Rachel's armor, but she quickly repaired them with hate deflecting sarcasm.

"Ya know mom, I can't really remember when I had a hairdo that was your favorite."

A huge fake smile flung itself across Shirley's face and with the expertise of a ventriloquist; she fired one last missile at Rachel. "We'll just have ta make the best of it." And even someone paying close attention would swear that Shirley's lips never moved.

"Oh, hello Teresa!" Shirley's stage voice filled the multi-purpose room with waves of pretend admiration. The facade was so well built that an amateur like Teresa could not detect the ruse and was immediately sucked into the performance.

"Oh howdy Shirley, whaddya think?" Teresa's wide, innocent eyes eagerly awaited what she imagined was Shirley's genuine response.

"Ya really out did yerself. I don't think I've ever seen so many streamers at singles' night. And the music, well, it defies description dear." Shirley punched up the wattage on her smile facsimile, to seal the deal.

"Oh, thank you Shirley. Ya know how much I value yer opinion."

"Oh, fer cute, of course dear. Now ya get out there and mingle. This night is really fer you." Shirley patted Teresa condescendingly on the arm, although from Teresa's perspective it was a loving touch of encouragement from the pastor's concerned wife.

As Teresa turned to mingle, Rachel unleashed a zinger of her own.

"Let me see if I can translate, Oh poor Teresa, the hideous over-abundance of streamers is a perfect distraction to the boring, pathetic music. And if a plain girl like you can't find a date in a room full of desperate, Christian boys, then that hopeless gleam in your eyes will be there for all eternity." Rachel threw a Julia Roberts-sized smile on to bring it all home.

"Rachel, 'judge not lest ye be judged.' I'm surprised at you." Shirley shook her head, ashamed of Rachel's sins, but never recognizing her own.

"Which part surprises you Shirley, that I can translate so well, or that I dared to say it out loud." Rachel's eyes narrowed to impudent slits.

"I'll pray fer ya dear, I know it's been a while since ya've had a man in yer life. This night must be harder on ya than I imagined." Shirley raised her chin piously and scurried off to circulate. Unfortunately, her clueless male counterpart quickly replaced her.

"Hi honey, I wanted you to meet Brad Peterson. He works over at—"

"Hey Brad, I'm sure you're a nice Christian boy, but my mom and I just had a similar discussion and I'll tell you what I told her, 'I'm working tonight and I don't mean the room. This is a job and I'm not here to hook up or be hooked up.' Thanks anyway and have a wonderful evening." That wasn't exactly what she had told her mom, but she thought Brad looked like a decent guy and he probably didn't deserve the full firepower of her acerbic tongue.

"Would you like a mini sweet roll Pastor?" Rachel asked innocently.

Ed walked away a little shell-shocked, but happily eating his sweet roll, Rachel smirked at her private little rum joke.

The night dragged on like a funeral for a distant great uncle that you are forced to attend. Rachel couldn't wait to get home and give Gwenn the full report.

Gwenn answered the phone, expecting the worst. "So how bad was it?"

"It was pretty awful. My hair is not her favorite! And I got into a pissing contest with mom after only five minutes and I was forced to publicly admonish dad and his 'nice Christian boy.' But the food was a big hit. The sweet rolls were especially beloved by all."

"You mean THE sweet rolls—the rum-soaked raisin sweet rolls?" Gwenn asked with mock surprise.

"Yeah, I just never get tired of that one," admitted Rachel. "Hey, I almost forgot, when's the big meeting with the artist-who-would-be-dad?"

"Thursday, that will be the day I finally die and wind up in hell for the long list of burnable offenses I've committed." Gwenn was dreading the meeting, well mostly dreading. Part of her was so excited by the thought of finally finding her true father that she thought she would explode like a bottle rocket.

"Easy girl, it'll go better than you think. This kinda thing is way more common these days. You might like being the spoiled daughter of a famous artist."

Seventeen

The Gregory Gallery was sparkling like the Hope Diamond and the hopefuls were lined up halfway down the block, shivering in winter's icy clutches, and just praying that their assistants had made the call. This was the party to end all parties. Handsome, wealthy artist makes his post-apocalyptic premiere and farewell.

The movers and shakers of the greater Twin City area and even some handpicked collectors from as far away as Hong Kong, New York, and London were the life-blood of this amazing show.

The invitations had been hand delivered by messenger to several of the upper echelon guests. The card stock was heavy and silky to the touch—the black foil simply read "Just As I Am."

Daniel Gregory - A Soul's Dossier
World-renowned Artist and Author
Final show! Premiere works!

35 pieces emblematic of his recent work
Mixed-media on stone
Oil on canvas
Collodion positive ambrotypes

Primordial works, never to be licensed
for giclee or merchandise.

"A Mini-apple coup..." • "A colossal achievement!"
"Phantasmagoric!"

Hors d'oeuvres and wine tasting

Reservations required
Admittance to wrist-banded attendees only

Monday, January 17 • 8:00 p.m. to midnight

The Gregory Gallery
Hennepin Avenue • Minneapolis, Minnesota

A component will be hand-picked by the artist and
gifted to the Metropolitan Museum of Art

Daniel knew that Todd would have something to say about the "hand-picked by the artist" bit, but Todd always had something to say.

"No, I'm sorry Mr. Evans you are not on the list. If you would like to have Mr. Jacobson call me and add you to the list that would be fine." Todd delivered the news with perfect calm and with the finality of someone who knew two huge bouncers stood right behind him.

"Todd, how long have I known you?"

"Mr. Evans, please step to the side we have to move on." Todd didn't have to work the door. It would have been simple to hire a lackey to handle this, but in all honesty Todd loved the list, and he knew it added to the prestige of the show to turn people away—especially important people.

"Yes, she's on the list. Give her a wristband." Todd smiled.

"Oh, thank you," gushed the shining woman.

It was like handing out food to starving people. Wristbands, just wristbands he reminded himself. There was really something wrong with the perspective of these people. But that skewed perspective was what allowed them to pay hundreds of thousands of dollars for Daniel's canvasses, so Todd tried not to hold it against them.

"Yes, wristband," Todd smiled. The woman who strode past the bouncers was striking. Her flaxen hair was caught in a loose up-do and the graceful curve of her neck was hard to miss. Her aquamarine eyes scanned the crowd and fell into place, like a laser target-locking system, onto Daniel Gregory.

Yvonne checked her sable coat, took one perfectly manicured finger and stopped a server in his tracks. She slipped her elegant hand around the stem of a champagne glass and without so much as a nod to the befuddled waiter she advanced on her target.

"Daniel, darling," a fake kiss was thrown to each side of Daniel's square, sexy jaw. "How long has it been?" her eyes met his and held their ground.

Daniel smiled, his work smile and clasped one of her dainty hands between his long, artistic fingers. "I haven't seen you in a month of Sundays," joked Daniel.

"It's obvious you've been quite busy Daniel. Quite busy. I am astonished with the quantity of pieces at this show. You'll create a glut, what will I do with *Ode to Pain*?" Yvonne slid her hand down Daniel's arm and drew a tantalizing little swirl in his palm.

"This is my last show Yvonne, this is it. So there's no danger of a glut. In fact, if you don't get it now you will never have another chance."

"What?" The surprise in Yvonne's eyes looked almost real. Daniel almost took the bait.

"You know *Ode to Pain* is a classic Yvonne. There are several collectors here tonight who would gladly take it off your hands, if you're really worried," teased Daniel.

"Oh Daniel, I never get tired of your dark sense of humor." This time the slender fingers brushed the edge of Daniel's jaw and lingered on his neck before they were begrudgingly withdrawn.

"You better pick out your favorites Yvonne, the larger pieces are going fast." Daniel smiled encouragingly at Yvonne.

"I'll need to speak to you later Mr. Gregory," said Yvonne as she walked into the crowd, hips undulating ever so slightly in her black, crinkled-silk sheath.

Daniel decided to check on Todd. It always lifted Daniel's spirits to see Todd truly enjoying himself.

"I'm sorry Mr. Lexington, Janet did not call. Your name is not on the list. Step to the side." Todd was mad with power and his smile was almost alarming. Daniel stepped up and reached over the velvet rope to put a hand on Mr. Lexington's shoulder.

"Ted, is that you?"

"Mr. Gregory, I..."

A murmur rushed through the crowd as news of Daniel's appearance spread like a dirty secret at a prayer meeting.

"Hey, call me Daniel. I'm sorry Ted. I took that call from Janet myself and I just plumb forgot to pass the info on to Todd." Daniel steered Ted around the ropes, "Please come over and get a wristband, I'll handle Todd."

Mr. Lexington's face lit up like a child at Christmas and he even forgot to sneer at Todd when he put on his wristband.

"Enjoy yourself in there," shouted Daniel as Ted disappeared into the Gallery.

"Mr. Gregory, you have to go back inside. You're completely killing the mystique by standing out here and pandering to the masses." Todd was slightly miffed at the usurping of his power.

"Todd, I'm going to take a stroll through the masses, just to raise their spirits. Don't worry, I'll let you get back to your fun," and Daniel unclipped the velvet rope and stepped across the threshold. The red carpet was dotted with gas heaters to keep the *beautiful people* from freezing and a flurry of shimmering fake snow was falling on either side of the enchanted queue.

Todd motioned frantically to two security personnel on the perimeter and within seconds Daniel was flanked by what appeared to be identical 6'6" stone statues. The crowd went wild, and Daniel shook hands and even endured a few hugs from some over-zealous female fans.

Once Daniel was back inside, surrounded by the glitterati, he noticed that he felt a little lonely. A strange feeling to experience in a crowded gallery, but still it was there, gnawing at the edges of his perfect life. It was easy for Daniel to tell himself he didn't need anyone, when there was no one to need. But that sexy, drunk college-girl in the bar Friday night...he might actually need to get some of that. Daniel chuckled nastily.

"I'd like to be in on *that* joke," Yvonne cooed in Daniel's ear, or at least as near as her 5'8" frame balanced on 5-inch Miu Miu peep-toes would let her.

Daniel turned in time to inhale the wealth of champagne on Yvonne's breath and see the completely unveiled suggestion in her eyes, and for once in his recent life he said *what the hell.* He slipped his arm around Yvonne's waist—partially to keep her from falling and partially to keep himself from running away.

He downed a few glasses of champagne as he steered Yvonne toward Todd's outpost.

"Todd, I need the car."

"I can just call her a cab, Mr. Gregory. We don't need to tie up the car. I mean she didn't actually buy anything," added Todd, almost discreetly.

"Todd, *we* need the car. *We'll* be at the back exit in about 10 minutes," Daniel paused to let that sink in to Todd's one-track mind.

"But the show...it's only 11 o'clock, what will I tell..."

"Todd—car—now." Daniel nodded his head encouragingly, like he was helping a toddler understand that Cheerios were nummy.

"Certainly, Mr. Gregory. I'll take care of everything." Todd grabbed his cell and made the call. Then, for the first time all day Todd actually stopped to think about Daniel Gregory, the man, not just Daniel Gregory the famous, tortured artist. "Good for you Mr. Gregory," said Todd under his breath.

The morning brought several layers of discomfort. There was the headache, the queasy stomach, the nauseating regret and a very specific lower back pain—from years of disuse. At least there were *certain* muscles that had been ignored.

Yvonne seemed similarly stricken, but that was simply because she never liked men to see her without her push-up bra and movie star make-up. She was actually quite pleased to have bedded Daniel. It had been easier than she'd imagined. Unfortunately, the haze of champagne kept her from remembering if it was actually as good as she'd imagined. For purposes of her story, it would be.

She dressed quickly and threw a series of "darlings" behind her as she made for the exit.

Daniel didn't bother to say anything pathetic like, "thanks for last night" or "I'll call you." He was neither thankful nor interested in pursuing Yvonne. She had been an icebreaker, nothing more. His back was killing him, so he decided to stay in bed and watch TV. I'm too old for this he laughed to himself.

When the phone rang and Todd informed him Yvonne had purchased three paintings, Daniel felt like a cheap whore. "Well, not cheap I guess," he mused as he ended the call, "more like a high-priced call boy." These society women were too much for him, maybe a younger girl...like that college-girl from the bar. Daniel drifted off into a pleasant dream about exactly what he would do with that girl—just as soon as his back stopped having spasms.

Daniel opened his eyes. "Son of a—I have to be in Duluth in three hours for that meeting," he complained to his clock.

He rolled out of bed, slowly, rubbing his lower back and cringing at the confirmation that last night wasn't all a bad dream. Packing was a breeze since his bags had never been unpacked from the weekend getaway. He shoved a few more items into his duffel bag and grabbed a quick shower.

Daniel scrubbed the Yvonne off his body and let the hot water pulsate on his back. After drying off with his favorite over-sized Egyptian cotton towel, he rubbed some arnica on his sore muscles and got dressed. He was feeling more relaxed, and he looked forward to the drive that would return him to his oasis of solitude.

Eighteen

Gwenn was half-buried in a mound of useless clothes. She truly had nothing to wear. There just wasn't a Vogue checklist for what to wear to a meeting with your possible, real dad.

After another half hour of tossing things to the floor in disgust, Gwenn returned to her original charcoal-grey Donna Karan suit with a lovely, pale-lavender, silk blouse. She chose a modest pump with a chunky three-inch heel. Professional and organized. That was the only message Gwenn was comfortable sending. She carefully aligned her makeup brushes and closed all of the drawers of her dresser. Anxiety-induced organizing, she was sure it was a real syndrome, or maybe the moon was in Capricorn. She suffered a spasm of concern for the heap of clothes on the floor, but there was no time to iron and color coordinate everything. Gwenn looked at her cell phone and panicked. If she wasted even one more minute she would officially be late to her meeting with Daniel Gregory.

As Gwenn drove across the Aerial Lift Bridge she rolled her eyes at the stupid stunts she used to let her friends talk her into. Back in high school Gwenn could be dared to do just about anything. She had once hung onto the underside of the lift bridge as it was being raised. Of course, by the time she was ten feet off the ground she had to admit to herself that her arms would never make it all the way up and safely back down. Gwenn had to let go and luckily landed like a cat, not even a scratch, her friends were screaming with glee. Gwenn was queen for a day. And that reward was what sucked her into each and every dare—the aching need for attention. The empty hole that God and all the nice Christian boys never quite filled.

The tires hummed loudly across the bridge, transporting her to the magical land of Park Point. Somewhere on this lovely peninsula was Daniel Gregory. In fact, if Flora's directions were accurate—and they always were—in 0.4 miles, Gwenn would make a right then a quick left, and a right into Mr. Gregory's driveway. Damn that Flora.

Gwenn grabbed the Clark & Mayfield tote, from Randy, and walked to Daniel's door. She felt like the photos were made of lead, and her arm hurt from the weight she carried.

Gwenn ran a finger under each eye to erase any mascara crumbs and squared her shoulders. She pretended not to notice the shaking hand that reached for the doorbell. Deep breaths. Deep breaths. Just breathe and you'll be fine she told herself. Gwenn could see her breath coming out in little clouds, and feel the sense of calm radiating outward from her solar plexus. The door opened.

"Hello, you must be Ms. Hutchinson." Daniel stepped to the side and waved his arm magnanimously to indicate *mi casa es su casa*. But the woman outside his door was as still as a statue.

"I'm sorry, are you not Ms. Hutchinson?" Daniel stared in confusion.

Gwenn knew she should say something, she knew she should walk into the house, but all she could do was stare in horror and try to breathe. Her eyes were sending the message to her brain, "It's him! It's the Lion King!" but her brain was refusing to accept the frantic transmission.

"Miss, are you okay?" Daniel tried to sound concerned, but he was mostly annoyed. Who was this woman? Does she just walk around, knock on doors and go catatonic? I mean, this chick looks too young to be a door-to-door sales—and the rest of the thought vaporized in Daniel's head. She was too young; she almost looked like a college student.

Gwenn was just about to regain control of her motor functions when Daniel gave her a mental taser jolt.

"Hey, didn't I see you at the Yellow Submarine last Friday?" Daniel dug up his friendly but nonchalant smile. When the girl didn't answer his smile swirled into a worried frown and he thought, "Oh shit a stalker." "Excuse me miss, but I have an appointment and I'm letting all the heat out, so I really must say goodbye." Daniel was going to close the door.

"I'm...appointment," was all Gwenn managed to choke out before her stomach was taken over by jumping jacks. Her face turned a pale shade of green and her hazel eyes widened with fear. "Bathroom?" she blurted.

Daniel hesitated, but then thought better of it and opened the door wide. He grabbed the woman's arm and steered her into the bathroom. He flipped on the light and closed the door. From his post outside the door he heard dry heaves followed by *almost* silent tears.

Gwenn was drowning and there was no one to save her. Even in her state of paralyzing fear she knew that Mr. Gregory would overhear any phone call she tried to make. She had to pull herself together. "I tried to pick up my dad at...and I did the sexy dance for him," she mouthed. Gwenn was turning green around the edges, but she swallowed hard, pressed her wrist in the mystical acupressure spot and tried to hold it together.

"Get it together Gwenn," she whispered fiercely to her reflection. She dabbed at her eyes and pinched her cheeks in an attempt to hide the fact that she had been crying. "Okay, you can do this." She blew her nose, dabbed at her eyes again and turned to the door.

Outside the pep-rally for one, Daniel was sure of only one thing; the woman had called herself Gwenn. He stepped back a few paces and waited for Gwenn to emerge.

"Mr. Gregory, please excuse my behavior. May I have a glass of water?" Gwenn was pleased that she had gotten this entire speech out without a tear, well, mini speech, that is.

"Sure, sure." Daniel strode off to get the water, he called back over his shoulder, "Please make yourself comfortable in the living room." Daniel smiled and shook his head at the idea of this Gwenn person having even a remote possibility of being comfortable.

He returned to the living room with the water and when he looked at Gwenn he had a remarkable urge to put his arm around her shoulder and tell her everything would be all right. Fortunately his logical brain took over and he simply handed her the glass of water.

Gwenn took a long drink from the glass. She was thirsty, but mostly she was stalling. "Mr. Gregory I don't know where to begin. Let me just apologize for my brazen sister handing you my phone number on Friday. That is not my normal behavior, although it is hers." She stopped to take a ragged breath and Daniel jumped in.

"Gwenn, it is Gwenn?" Daniel looked at Gwenn and she nodded a begrudging confirmation. "Let me just say, I thought you looked fantastic Friday night, and I was quite flattered that a young woman like you, would give an old fart like me the time of day." Daniel smiled what he thought was a comforting and slightly flirtatious smile. He was quite confused when Gwenn lurched back into the couch and put a hand over her mouth.

"Mr. Gregory I have to get to the point of my visit before either one of us says anything else we'll regret." Gwenn reached down and opened her satchel.

Daniel actually felt more than a little offended by this, apparently, colossal tease.

Gwenn retrieved the packet of photos and slid them across the burlwood coffee table. "Mr. Gregory, my mother took these photos."

Daniel picked up the photos and sweet but painful memories passed across his face. He looked at Gwenn with confusion and loss in his eyes.

Gwenn assumed the pain and loss were for her mother and the confusion was for her. "Mr. Gregory, these photos were taken in your apartment the month I was conceived. I believe you are my father." Gwenn's breath came out in a shaky exhale and her hazel eyes flashed up to look into Daniel's.

Gwenn was prepared to see anger and/or denial; she wasn't prepared to see love and shameless tears. "I'm sorry Mr. Gregory, I know this must be a shock but I didn't want to drag it out. I don't want anything from you. Except well, if you would consent to a DNA test...just for my information...just so I know, I'll never bother you again. I'll never..." Gwenn's words were smothered in the strong, heaving chest of Daniel Gregory as he caught her up in his arms and let small, salty tears trickle onto her head.

Gwenn felt simultaneously uncomfortable and completely safe.

Daniel took a few deep breaths and he loosened his hold on Gwenn. He took a step back, smiled at her gently and encouraged her to have a seat on the couch next to him. Daniel took her small, pale hand in his strong one and exhaled audibly.

"Gwenn, I'm technically, Daniel Gregory *Junior*. Despite the distinguishing grey at the temples," Daniel casually mussed his hair, "I'm only 42. A bit too young to be the man in the pictures." He reached for one of the photos and explained, "These paintings are early works of my father, Daniel Gregory, *Senior*...if he was called *Senior*, which he wasn't...but he was the first Daniel Gregory. If that makes any sense." Daniel smiled apologetically at Gwenn.

She wiped her eyes with her free hand and for a moment processed this new piece of information. She had not tried to pick up her dad at a bar, thankfully. However, it was equally unnerving to think that she was hitting on her brother. Well, not quite as bad. I mean this Daniel Gregory was obviously much younger than she had assumed. She surveyed him. He was definitely younger than she had thought, his hair was thick and lustrous, his skin was healthy and nearly smooth, his shoulders were broad and strong...whoa cowgirl! Let's keep it above the waist. She smiled at her clever joke before gazing up into Daniel's eyes. He was smiling back at her.

His eyes were blue or brown...wait...one was blue and the other was brown. Heterochromia iridium. The strange term from college biology just popped into her head. Whatever, they were Daniel's eyes and they were mesmerizing; Gwenn felt her heart speed up and the color return to her cheeks.

"So, you might be my sister."

The husky voice and the word *sister* brought Gwenn back to the room. Shit, she was falling for her brother. Oh, this Greek tragedy just keeps getting better. "Okay, Gwenn look, this guy is a handsome caring stranger. It is perfectly normal for you to feel attracted. You only found out he might be your brother two minutes ago. You will have to develop a sibling relationship. The attraction will fade." Gwenn finished her internal monologue and forced herself to smile a bland, sisterly smile.

"Yeah, I guess I might be. I guess I'll have to show these photos to Daniel Gregory, *Senior* and see what he remembers."

The same pained expression from before shot across Daniel's face and he looked down at his hands. He absently rubbed the back of Gwenn's small hand.

"My father passed away over four years ago, I'm sorry," Daniel's voice was thick with emotion.

Gwenn felt her last tiny lifeline sink into the black ocean. The mother ship was never coming and her real dad had died before she had ever gotten the chance to have a relationship with him. She was stuck with the hollow, heinous parents she had. Pastor Ed and Shirley were the best she would ever know—the revelation was soul crushing. Her chin banged against her chest and the tears fell, unfettered down her alabaster cheeks.

'*Loss*, watercolor on canvas,' titled Daniel in his mind. It was a hard habit to break. The moment was so poignant, so breathtaking; his first instinct was to capture it on canvas. Fortunately his second instinct was to put his arm around Gwenn and pull her into the comfort of his being.

"I'm sorry," Gwenn stuttered between sobs, "I know I didn't...know...but now...never have...the chance." The sobs grew in intensity, "It must...awful...for you," she moaned.

"It was pretty awful," agreed Daniel. "But at least I got to know him. I'm sorry you won't have that chance." Daniel put his finger under Gwenn's chin and tipped her face upward, "He would have loved you. Honestly, you would have been his dream daughter." As Daniel looked reassuringly into Gwenn's despairing hazel eyes he felt an unwelcome heat flicker in his groin. He tried to disengage and sit back casually, but he knew it felt stiff and awkward. "Don't fall for your new baby sister perv," Daniel told himself.

She felt the loss of Daniel's touch nearly as much as she felt the loss of her fantasy father. "You don't have any sisters?" Gwenn asked.

"No, no siblings at all. I was an only child. I was conceived in the early years of the marriage, before my dad started his philandering."

"You don't have to talk about it." Gwenn didn't really want to sully the perfect picture of her dream dad.

"No, my dad and I were always honest with each other, at least after my mom died, that is. He doubled his efforts to connect with me. We had no secrets, well we had one secret it appears." Daniel smiled at Gwenn.

"I don't think he knew about me. My mother's not open or honest, and she was married at the time. I'm sure she just stopped taking your father's calls and put on a lovely performance for my other dad, to convince him he was a lucky first-time father." Gwenn shook her head disapprovingly.

"Gwenn, I would like to take the DNA test. I know it's too late for you to have a real father, but at least you could have a brother." Daniel tilted his head down toward Gwenn, "Whaddya think?"

"Would you? I mean I do want to know. I've never had a brother." Gwenn looked at Daniel with appreciation and wonder. She couldn't imagine what it must have been like to have a father she could've admired—and a father she could be honest with, now that was a fairytale.

"Look, there's a doc at St. Luke's, Dr. Watkins, an old family friend. I'm sure he would handle the tests for us and he's very discreet."

"Discreet sounds good." Gwenn had never played out this part of the scenario and she wondered why discretion was so important. "Are you famous?" she suddenly worried.

Daniel exhaled with a bit of exasperation, "Yeah, I guess. My assistant, Todd, would assure you that I am the finest thing since sliced bread, but I still have a modicum of modesty."

A giggle escaped unbidden from Gwenn.

"What?"

"A modicum of modesty, it was just funny—I don't know, because it sounded pompous and you were..."

Daniel laughed, "Oh yeah, that is funny."

Daniel stood up and walked into the other room. "I'll call Dr. Watkins and find out if he can see us tomorrow," he called over his shoulder.

"Okay." Gwenn couldn't hear the whole conversation but she heard *fragile*, something about *urgent* and several references to *confidential*.

"Are you free around 10:00 tomorrow?" Daniel asked her.

"Sure, 10:00 is great." Gwenn winced at the thought of needles, but she was bolstered by the fact that Daniel would be there, with her, to help her get through it. Now she would have to figure out a way to resist calling Rachel until after the test. She didn't want anything to jinx the outcome.

Nineteen

The lights were pulsating and the techno was near deafening. Rachel was determined to dance away the memory of Annie kissing TK. Drinking away the memory had been her first choice, but a couple of drunken one-night stands with girls beneath her standards had put the kibosh on Plan A. Sex was her new religion.

Sensuous hands slid down the curves of Rachel's waist and she spun around to find herself face to face with a genuine Norse goddess. Her straight white-blonde hair was caught in a loose ponytail, her eyes were clear blue all the way to the soul and the legs...Rachel got lost in imagining them wrapped around—hot breath in her ear interrupted the image.

"What?"

"Let's get out of here." It wasn't a question.

Rachel allowed herself to be steered off the dance floor and out of the club—she wanted some answers. "Hey, what makes you think I'm gay?"

"I've seen you here before, seen you leave with women who are, umm, how can I say this tactfully? Women who are beneath you."

Rachel smirked at the link-up, there. "What's your name?"

"Danica."

"And what do you want with me, Danica?"

"I want you to take me back to your apartment and make love to me." Danica smiled enticingly.

"I don't even know you!"

"Look, Rachel—"

"How do you know my name?"

"I ask around." Another smirk. "Look Rachel, I can tell you're getting over someone and I'm not available for a long-term thing. So I thought you might be interested in something purely physical, with no strings attached. If you're not..." Danica paused tantalizingly.

Rachel grabbed Danica's hand and pulled her into a taxi.

Danica was anxious to get things started; the taxi driver was going to get more than a tip on this fare. She licked her fingers and slid her hand under the waistband of Rachel's mini-skirt, past the thong and into heaven.

"Danica, I think we should wait—oh shit that feels good." Rachel's protestations were lost in her suppressed moans.

Danica breathed into Rachel's neck, "You are already so wet. I can't wait to ta—" The cab swerved dangerously and jostled the busy couple. Danica was unperturbed.

Rachel came in the cab, before they even got close to her apartment. Danica was just such a turn on. However, Danica's next sentence gave Rachel a moment of hesitation.

Danica was kissing Rachel's neck and whispered, "My husband doesn't know I'm *bi*. I think he would try to make me bring someone home, so he could watch. But this," Danica pushed several fingers inside of Rachel, "this is just for me."

Rachel wanted to protest, but good lord this woman had magic fingers.

"Our little secret, no strings, just this..."

The taxi jerked to a stop, the driver's eyes were glued to the rearview mirror. He mumbled something about the fare.

Danica threw a wad of bills at him and grabbed Rachel's hand. "Come."

Rachel didn't need a second invitation. She planned on obeying Danica's every command.

As the first streaks of light peeked through the blinds Rachel willed her eyes to open, she rolled over and found herself alone in her bed. The impression of Danica's head was still etched into the pillow and Rachel rolled a little further to drink in the scent.

Her nipples immediately hardened as flashes of the previous night romped through her head. The lips, soft and firm. The skin, smooth as silk. The legs, Rachel moaned. It had been so much better than she'd imagined.

Ooooh. Maybe a quick shower would help wash away the sticky, sweet memories of last night.

Things took a turn for the worse in the shower and Rachel was forced to use the detachable showerhead for more than just cleanup. The pulsating setting seemed especially helpful.

Rachel drifted out to the kitchen for some coffee and discovered a note on the table.

My daydreams will be filled with
the perfection of last night.
Call me if you like—no strings.
Danica (555-3261)

Rachel repeated the words aloud, like a little prayer, closed her eyes and smiled. This was the perfect solution to her Annie problem. In fact, she could barely remember that there was a problem. "See, it is working already," she told herself.

Rachel grabbed her phone and called Gwenn—no answer. Voicemail, weird.

"Hey Gwenny, it's me. I have to tell you about last night. She was amazing! Call me as soon as you get this."

Rachel tapped *End,* and immediately let her mind drift back to replaying scenes from last night's erotic rendezvous. She was sure Gwenn would call back any minute.

Twenty

Dr. Watkins' office was sterile and professional. The walls were covered with the necessary number of framed degrees and certificates, as well as two unusually beautiful paintings. They were quite different, but somehow Gwenn could sense a link between them.

"You must be Gwenn," Dr. Watkins extended his hand, greeted Gwenn and motioned for her to take a seat.

"Thank you," was all Gwenn could manage. Today the moon was *void of course*—not a good time, astrologically, to start something new. She pushed that uneasiness from her mind.

"Thanks Bernard, I really appreciate the favor. I know my dad would've wanted you in the loop on this one." Daniel shook Dr. Watkins hand and gave him a brief guy-hug with his free arm.

"These are lovely, paintings," Gwenn offered, too nervous to think of anything else to say.

"Well, it looks like good taste runs in the family," joked Dr. Watkins.

What was he so cavalier about, Gwenn wondered.

"My father painted that one about 30 years ago and I painted that one," Daniel pointed to the opposite wall, "about 12 years ago. I believe dad's paid for some medical bills, but the doc got mine at one of my early shows." He smiled at Dr. Watkins, "He always encouraged my artistic talents."

Gwenn marveled at the idea of being encouraged to follow a bohemian lifestyle. These Gregory men led charmed lives.

"Yes, Marjorie, Daniel's mother, was sick for a long time before she passed. Daniel's father was just hitting his stride in the art community and I knew the painting would be a good investment. Of course, now I couldn't possibly part with it." Dr. Watkins fiddled with the I.D. badge on his white coat, cleared his throat uncomfortably and gave Daniel a sympathetic nod.

"Thanks Doc," Daniel nodded back.

"Did Daniel explain the test procedure to you Gwenn?" Dr. Watkins was back to business.

"No, sir." Gwenn was always overly formal under pressure.

"It's fairly simple, I'll just swab the inside of your cheek with this," Dr. Watkins brandished a long, plastic stick with a foam tip, "I'll take them down to the lab and we should have results in a couple of hours."

"No needles?" Gwenn blurted out, without thinking.

"No needles." Dr. Watkins reassured.

"So, you don't like needles, eh?" Daniel teased.

"Not particularly." Gwenn thought Daniel was acting much more like a pesky older brother today.

Daniel suggested an early lunch while they waited for the test results.

The knotty pine and wrought iron Colonial Inn was the perfect escape. There was no waiting and very few patrons. The menu consisted of Midwestern staples like pot roast, liver and onions, and mashed potatoes.

Gwenn and Daniel bravely ordered the meatloaf and mashed potatoes, although there was a tempting hot dish on the specialties page.

"Gwenn, no matter what happens today, I want to be in your life. More than fate brought us together. I want to get to know you, whether you're my sister or not."

Gwenn flinched at the "not." All her hopes were riding on a positive match with this DNA test. She just couldn't face the fact that Pastor Ed was it. "I'm glad you feel that way Daniel, but honestly I'm really hoping for a positive. My whole life I felt like an outsider, like an alien visiting an earthling family. The idea that I had another father out there, well that filled me with a real sense of hope."

"I understand."

"With all due respect, Daniel, I don't think you do understand. It sounds to me like you had a lot of encouragement from your dad. You had things in common, like the painting, and he was proud of you—to me that's like a fairytale. My parents are religious fanatics, they take every available opportunity to cut me down and indicate their profound disappointment. In fact, my mother is so practiced at dispatching backhanded compliments that it sometimes takes days before I realize how deeply she's insulted me."

"At least you have a mother, Gwenn." Daniel's pain was visible.

"I'm sorry about your mother Daniel, but I have to disagree with you. Having a hateful, judgmental, manipulating mother is not better than no mother all."

"It has to be."

"Well, I can assure you it is not."

Daniel let the silence linger between them as he struggled to make sense out of what Gwenn was saying. He honestly couldn't imagine a mother like the one Gwenn described. Even when he allowed himself a brief image he had to wonder, what would his father have been doing with a hateful woman like that. "You know Gwenn, my dad had affairs, but from what he told me, most of the women were young, gushing admirers. They pursued him. Your mother just doesn't fit the profile."

"She wasn't always a wolf struggling to hide in a tattered sheepskin."

"Whaddya mean?"

"She was a very gorgeous, young woman. Homecoming queen, lots of boyfriends, you know the type."

"Yeah, I think I do," Daniel grinned slyly.

"No, no not that type. Shirley, that's my mom's name, was also a virgin when she got married and never drank or smoked."

Daniel just burst out laughing. "Apparently after she got married all bets were off, eh."

"That's just wicked." Gwenn couldn't help but laugh along with Daniel. It felt good to move away from the pink elephant in the room, just for a few minutes.

"Wait a minute, did you say Shirley? Shirley Carlson?" Daniel inquired.

"Yeah, you know something?" Gwenn leaned forward eagerly. Ever since she had seen *Back to the Future* she had dreamed of the moment her mother's perfect, virgin cover story would be blown away.

"My dad always said, 'Shirley Carlson was the one that got away.' I don't think he knew she was married, or maybe things were going on before she was married, or—no that doesn't make sense." Daniel got a faraway look in his eye.

"Daniel, did your dad ever mention having a physical relationship with Shirley?"

"You know, he never really talked about that part of his affairs, and I was pretty okay with that."

"I understand, it was a stupid—"

"No, no. In this case it was hard to shut him up. Mostly wishful thinking, I think. A guy thing I suppose. Anyway, it stuck with me, my mom had passed and I used to fantasize that this Shirley woman would come back and make my dad happy again, and I would have a mom." Daniel looked down at his meatloaf and poked it aimlessly with his fork.

"Trust me Daniel, you're very lucky that didn't happen."

"But you said she wasn't always..."

"She was great, before Billy Graham got to her. She was an activist, an esthetician, went to Earth, Wind & Fire concerts, had wild asymmetrical hairdo's, displayed the occasional body painting and even used an Ouija board—but then old Billy gave his altar call and Shirley sought salvation like a watering hole in the desert." Gwenn finished with a flourish of her hand.

"Do you really think you're my sister?"

"I do," Gwenn said firmly.

"Let's play a little 'What If,' okay?" Daniel offered.

"Okay, I guess."

"In less than one hour we're going to get the results of the DNA test. I want you to know I plan to be part of your life regardless of the results. So let's look at some scenarios. What if the test results are positive?" Daniel smiled encouragingly at Gwenn.

"If the test is positive, I will be ecstatic. I have always known I didn't belong in my family and I will finally be able to confront Shirley on her hypocrisy."

"A positive for me, means I'm not alone in the world." Daniel looked at Gwenn with warm brotherly love. "I have a sister."

Gwenn squirmed under the intensity of his gaze. A shiver ran up her spine and her nether regions were responding in a most un-sisterly fashion. "Shit this is going to take some getting used to," she thought.

Daniel continued, "What if the test is totally negative, no match."

"That's not an option for me. Ever since I was six-years-old I knew there had to be a mistake at the hospital, something better. I remember hiding under the kitchen table with an old tape recorder. I was recording Shirley and Gramma Carlson as they discussed the preacher's sermon. They were talking about all the people who should've heard it. Saying things like, "Oh, I wish Elaine would've been there, yeah ya know she has such a problem with alcohol," or "That Bernice waddled off ta the restroom and completely missed the bit about gluttony, what a shame," and on and on. When I finally came out of my hiding place and played the tape for them, they both cried and repented and said, 'Out of the mouths of babes,' and other ridiculous scriptural crap. Of course, they were back at it a couple of days later." Gwenn shook her head hopelessly. "The mother ship isn't coming back for me, my only hope is that Daniel Gregory, Senior is my biological father."

"Gwenn, it's not your only hope. You are a wonderful, beautiful, inte—"

"If you say intelligent I will punch you in the face." Gwenn's eyes narrowed to slits.

'*Seething*, oil on canvas' popped into Daniel's head before he could stop it. "It was a compliment," insisted Daniel.

"My intelligence has been used to manipulate me all my life; "To whom much is given much is expected," that was the mantra Pastor Ed and Shirley crammed down my throat whenever they wanted to force me to do their bidding. It was like the intelligence was a secret weapon that I didn't know how to use, like only they could direct me. How ridiculous! I was running mental circles around them by the time I was 13. So no, 'intelligent' isn't a compliment in my world."

"I think if I ever have the displeasure of meeting Pastor Ed and Shirley, I may have to punch them in the face." Daniel tried to lighten the mood with some of his so-called wit, but he couldn't help feeling that he'd dodged a bullet in the whole Shirley area.

"Okay now it's my turn." Daniel blurted.

"Hmmm?" Gwenn looked confused.

"It's my turn to answer the 'what if it's negative' scenario."

"Oh, right."

"If the test is negative I'll be bummed. I think you would be a great sister and I would've loved to take you to visit Grandma Gregory. However, I decided that if you are not my sister, I will just have to be your best friend," Daniel grinned like a schoolboy.

"Best friend?" Gwenn shook her head disapprovingly.

"Yeah, best friend. I mean fate brought us together Gwenn, whether we're related or not, there's a reason we have ended up in each other's lives. So if the test is negative, and you puke all over Dr. Watkins and run off in hysterics, I'll hunt you down and I'll be there for you until you really do punch me in the face."

Gwenn cracked up in spite of the tension. "Puke all over Dr. Watkins? Is that what you think of me?"

"You have to admit you have quite a gag reflex when it comes to unpleasant situations," teased Daniel.

"You're not even an official big brother and you're already picking on me. How rude!" Gwenn pretended to pout.

Daniel placed his beautiful, strong hand on Gwenn's and looked deeply into her hazel eyes, "I feel a connection to you Gwenn, and I don't want to lose that regardless of the DNA. You're part of my life now and I want to be part of yours."

Gwenn felt herself lean forward toward Daniel's full, perfect lips and jerk to a stop. This probably wasn't the kind of covenant she should seal with a kiss. "Okay, after the puking and stuff we'll be friends; but that's not going to happen since the test will be positive." A superior smile crept across Gwenn's face.

"Time to face the music." Daniel twisted the watch on his wrist to show Gwenn the time.

Gwenn and Daniel sat in Dr. Watkins' office, holding hands for moral support. Dr. Watkins walked in with the chart and his expression was unreadable.

"Do you want any details or statistics or do you just want the results?" Dr. Watkins asked.

"The results." Gwenn and Daniel said in unison.

"Negative, no match. There is no way the two of you are related. You would need at least one allele in common to prove, conclusively, that you had one parent in common. The test is very accurate. You are not siblings."

Daniel felt Gwenn's hand go limp in his. He turned to look at her face and he saw the tears welling up in her beautiful eyes. "Gwenn...," He moved to put his arm around her shoulders but she pulled away and hurtled herself from the room.

Daniel could hear the click clack of her heels running rapidly, the sound grew faint and was gone. He imagined her throwing herself into an elevator. He looked at Dr. Watkins in despair, "Is there any chance?"

"I'm sorry Daniel, the test is very accurate." Dr. Watkins could only imagine what it would've meant to Daniel to find a sister, a link to his father. He was sorry he wasn't able to deliver that gift to Daniel.

"What should I do?" Daniel looked helplessly at Dr. Watkins.

"Give her a few days to process all of this. Then you should call her and try to talk about things. She needs to talk about this, she needs to know she's not alone." Dr. Watkins stood up and walked over to Daniel. He patted Daniel lovingly on the shoulder, "You're not alone either, Daniel. I'm sorry the test was negative. If there's anything else I can do..."

"Thanks Bernard, I'll let you know."

Daniel stood up slowly and wandered out of the hospital. He half-hoped Gwenn would be sitting on the hood of his car, waiting to punch him in the face. He smiled at the memory of her fiery determination. The hood of his car was empty and so was his heart.

The drive back to the cabin was uneventful, no calls, no Gwenn sightings and no bright ideas. He sat down on the couch and picked up the packet of photos Gwenn had left behind.

His father's early work had always intrigued Daniel. The color choices were so bold and the strokes were strong and defiant. Daniel let his mind wander back through time, he saw his father as a dashing young man in his twenties, wearing the beatnik glasses Daniel had seen in so many old family photos. His father was painting one of the canvases from Gwenn's stack of pictures.

The floor was covered with tarps; there were three or four easels and a stack of canvases leaning against a wall. A soft, northern light illuminated the room, and Daniel Gregory, the elder, was lost in a creative passion.

"Danny, are you busy?" Shirley Carlson was a knockout, gorgeous brown hair in an asymmetrical bob, tight miniskirt and shapely legs tucked into go-go boots.

"Never for you baby." Danny put down his brush and swept Shirley into his arms. The kiss was passionate and suggestive.

"Oh my god, Danny it's so far out." Shirley caught sight of the painting over Danny's shoulder.

"It's you baby. Pretty out of sight, right."

The canvas boasted a strikingly beautiful woman, lost in the bold strokes of her wild, streaks of hair.

"I'm beautiful," Shirley breathed the words with awe.

"You're more than beauty baby, you're my muse," Danny cooed.

"Right on!" Shirley smiled.

But when Daniel looked into the face in the daydream, the eyes were the gentle, hazel windows to Gwenn's soul and the face he saw was Gwenn's. He looked up from the old photograph and closed his eyes. He felt Gwenn's delicate hand in his and knew he had to find her.

Twenty-one

Gwenn was all cried out. Her mascara was streaked down her cheeks and her eyes were dry and red. Her breath was still coming in ragged gasps, but she would not shed any more tears. Instead she would pack.

She was wildly throwing clothes into her suitcases. Screw the airlines! She would bring as many bags as she damn well pleased—even if she did have to pay some ridiculous fee for each and every one of them.

Gwenn had felt the undeniable connection between herself and Daniel. But she had no interest in another heartbreak. A brother had been a blessing; a boyfriend was just another curse in her long lineage of relationship hexes.

She knew he would try to find her, and she knew she had to escape before he was successful.

Flora and Thea had been notified, by e-mail, that Gwenn would be taking a sabbatical. The accountant and the bank had been given the necessary information. Gwenn's cell phone had been thrown into the trash and she was off. She would grab a quick flight from Duluth to St. Paul, where she could play a little airline ticket roulette.

The Minneapolis-St. Paul terminal was bustling with travelers. Gwenn imagined they were all staring at her and laughing behind her back. Another of Shirley's wonderful gifts, the thought that other people were always judging her, and what other people thought of her was far more important than the truth.

Gwenn approached the ticket counter and purchased a one-way to LAX. From there she planned to get to the Bradley International terminal and be out of the country by midnight. She reached for her phone, to check the time. "No phone idiot," she scolded herself.

Leaving the phone had been tough, but she knew she would be too tempted to answer. Yes tempted, Satan himself would be taunting her with phone calls from people who supposedly gave a shit about her.

LAX was enormous. No one looked at her. No one smiled. A sea of angry, isolated beings flowing through the terminals.

Gwenn had to ask for directions to the International terminal, but she was immediately sorry.

"Do I look like Google maps, bitch?" Rap artist wannabe just shoved past her and kept walking.

Gwenn finally saw a man in charge of the taxi queue and decided to try again.

"Ya jus' keep walkin'. Ya'll see it. Ya'll see it." The man pointed down the sidewalk and sort of to the left.

Gwenn just pulled her luggage cart and kept moving. The first sign she saw read New Zealand Air, and her decision was made. She would get far, far away from all the people and problems, maybe for good.

Twenty-two

Daniel knew he had to find Gwenn. He remembered her face when they had played 'What If.' A negative test result would not fit into her perfectly organized life. He understood her attachment to the belief in a fantasy family. Daniel himself had always dreamed that he had a brother out there somewhere. He had believed that one of his father's affairs had produced the perfect, cool brother that would go camping with Daniel and punch him playfully on the shoulder. Those images kept a lonely kid from going crazy. Daniel could only imagine the despair and emptiness that Gwenn must be feeling as she watched her last hope for parental normalcy and acceptance sink like the Titanic.

He grabbed his cell and headed out the door.

"Flora? It's Daniel Gregory, I need to speak to Gwenn."

There was a pause, the pause turned into a silence and the silence made Daniel bold.

"Flora, I know everything. I don't know how much you know, but this is important. I must speak to Gwenn," Daniel's voice was firm.

"Mr. Gregory, I'm sorry, Gwenn has taken an extended leave."

"When? When did she leave?" Daniel's voice cracked.

"Last night, sir."

"Where did she go? Flora this is quite serious, and she's not answering her cell." Daniel's mind was racing, he would need Todd's help, of that he was certain.

Flora paused, "You have her cell number?" This confused Flora a bit; Gwenn never gave out her cell number. Everything came through the office. Even the most important clients went through Flora to get to Gwenn. Strange.

"Yes Flora, she gave it to me at the hospital yesterday. But she's not answering her cell and I have to find her," Daniel was getting angry. "This is a matter of life and death, I can't explain—please tell me something," Daniel's voice softened.

Flora could not imagine why Daniel and Gwenn had been at the hospital. But then Flora had never seen Gwenn take so much as a week off since she opened The Organizer, so obviously something had changed. "Just a moment Mr. Gregory."

Flora logged-on to Gwenn's bank account and saw the airline ticket purchases. When she read North by Northwest Air she got back on the phone. "Mr. Gregory, she got two tickets this morning one that would have taken her to St. Paul and from there she purchased a ticket from North by Northwest Air. I don't know where she went, she did not leave an itinerary—which is unusual," Flora was puzzled.

"Thank you. Please keep checking and call me if you find any other clues." Daniel knew Todd could run with this information. "Oh, and Flora, we'll have to put my project on hold until I find Gwenn. I hope you understand. Thanks, buh-bye."

Flora most certainly did not understand, but something was very wrong and she was going to get to the bottom of it. Mr. Gregory seemed genuinely concerned.

Daniel was loading the car as he called Todd. "Todd, cancel everything. We have a Priority One. Find out everything you can about Gwendolyn Hutchinson and every major city served by North by Northwest Air. I'm loading the car now, call me when you have something and I'll explain the details on the drive."

"Done, Mr. Gregory."

Daniel dropped his phone and smiled. That was why Todd was the highest-paid gallery director/personal assistant in the Mini-apple.

Daniel took one last look at the cabin, squealed the tires out of the driveway and sped across the Aerial Lift Bridge.

"Mr. Gregory I've got something." Todd was pleased with himself.

"Go."

"North by Northwest serves several major cities west of the Mississippi. I calculated Los Angeles as the most likely jumping off point for an international escape. You said Priority One, so I assumed Ms. Hutchinson would be running far and fast."

"Right you are, what else?" Daniel was impressed.

"I pretended to be Ms. Hutchinson's personal assistant and discovered she purchased a ticket—"

"Hold on, Flora is calling on the other line." Daniel pressed a button, "Flora what's the news?"

"She just bought a ticket on New Zealand Air, I don't know where to but it's a start," Flora was hopeful.

"Great work. I'm going to have my assistant, Todd, coordinate efforts with you. Don't worry Flora, we'll find her."

The line went dead. Until that moment, Flora hadn't been worried. Who was Todd, and how could he help?

"Todd, you there?"

"Yes Mr. Gregory, as I was saying, she purchased a ticket—"

"I know, on New Zealand Air, Flora just told me. I need you to find out the destination."

"Then you're in luck, Mr. Gregory. As I was saying, Ms. Hutchinson purchased a ticket to Auckland with a four-hour layover in the Nadi International Airport in Fiji." The smugness was culpable in Todd's voice.

"Perfect, book it."

"Book what?"

"Get me to Auckland, Todd, as soon as possible. Call Flora, Gwenn's assistant, and coordinate my arrangements with any updates she gets from Gwenn's credit and debit card purchases." Daniel paused as he calculated the time necessary to pack, get to the Minneapolis-St. Paul International Airport, on to LAX and finally Auckland. He wished for the millionth time that more technology from Star Trek was available in the present day. The flip phone *communicators* were cool, but it was time for much more.

"Mr. Gregory, are you going to tell me what's going on?" the impatience in Todd's voice was barely disguised.

"You betcha Todd. Hang on to your hat."

Todd noted, with some annoyance, that he had never worn a hat in his life.

So Daniel spilled it all, the photos, the uncomfortable attraction, the DNA test, the lunch and the test results. Daniel even tried to make Todd understand the pain that Gwenn was suffering, the loss of her last hope.

Todd was not unmoved, but as the oldest of four children and having had two working parents, Todd had never had the luxury of fantasy or self-pity. However, Todd was keenly aware of loneliness. The reason he was so good at his job, was because it was his only companion. He had never found a girl who could understand his devotion to Mr. Gregory. Todd could easily imagine what Gwenn must be feeling at the loss of her imagined connection to Mr. Gregory—she must be devastated.

Twenty-three

Gwenn wandered around the Nadi International Airport. She had loaded up on motion sickness pills on the plane and slept fitfully most of the way. Her seatmate was apparently desiccating at an alarming rate; the woman applied lotion almost incessantly for 11 hours. The sickening smell of rose and lanolin was still thick in Gwenn's nostrils.

Gwenn bought a coffee at the Republic of Cappuccino and barely noticed the gorgeous Fijian man smiling from behind the counter. She did see the sign for internet access, but she resisted the urge to check her e-mail.

Her mind wandered back to Minnesota, back to Daniel. He wasn't her brother, she didn't have a fabulous, artistic father and her bitter hag of a mother didn't have an affair. The careful house of cards she had built with her dreams and fantasies had crumbled with one sentence, "the test results are negative."

Even before Gwenn found the photos, she had imagined elaborate scenarios where she had been switched at birth. Shirley had gone into labor and Ed had been out of town. Shirley had to catch a cab to the hospital, as the cab pulled up there was another pregnant woman being wheeled into the hospital ahead of Shirley. Shirley and the mystery woman both had baby girls. The nurses took the babies to the nursery and someone filled out name cards to tuck in the bassinets. One of the nurses spilled her coffee on the desk and the other nurse quickly grabbed the cards out of the way. In the confusion the nurses mixed up the name cards and Gwenn was sent home with Shirley and Ed. Some scenarios involved a janitor moving the bassinets before the nurses came with the name cards or an intern taking the babies for tests and putting them back in the wrong bassinets. The one constant was that Gwenn always ended up going home with the wrong parents, Shirley and Ed.

Her life would've been so different with her real parents—or at least with any parents that didn't live like nomads.

In the third grade, Gwenn had experimented with cigarettes and kissed a friend's brother behind their house. Two months later Ed and Shirley announced a god-directed move to Oklahoma.

It took Gwenn a few months to find the wrong crowd, but by fifth grade, she was smoking in the park across from the school and kissing John Eller whenever she got the chance. Soon after god called Ed and Shirley to a remote town in northern Minnesota. A place so isolated and desolate that sin itself could not reproduce.

So Gwenn brought her own supply. By the time she was in seventh grade she had found the wrong crowd. There were slumber parties with alcohol and spin the bottle—but no boys. A girl like Gwenn needed boys to make her feel good about herself. However, in seventh grade boys expected breasts and if you didn't have any you were singled out.

"Hey Gwenn, you're a carpenter's dream!" Nameless Jock would say.

"Yeah, flat as a board and never been nailed!" Nameless Jock's friend would yell. Guffaws and suggestive, lewd gestures would follow.

When breasts finally came Gwenn thought her problems would be solved, but the taunts turned to accusations of bra stuffing and the seventh grade ended in disgrace.

Her real parents would've loved her and given her stability and self-confidence—not guilt, shame and the swirling emptiness of having no roots. Maybe the aliens...

Gwenn's stomach growled loudly and ended her depressing walk down memory lane. It had been at least a day since she had anything to eat. She had slept through the airline food, probably a blessing.

Gwenn wandered into the airport terminal restaurant and ordered several samosas and a bottle of water. The humor of the *locally bottled* water that cost as much in Fiji, as it cost after it was imported into the U.S was not completely lost on her.

Gwenn strolled back through security and rolled her eyes as she placed her quart-sized bag in a security bin. If only she could compartmentalize her life like she did her toiletries. She knew that a thousand quart-size bags would not hold the emotional sludge of the last few days.

"Passport please miss." The lovely Fijian security officer flashed his beautiful smile at Gwenn.

"Umm, yeah, here it is?" Gwenn smiled nervously. She always imagined the worst when she had to deal with law enforcement officers. She would have been a total failure as a drug mule.

"Ga-when-do-leen?" The disarming smile caught Gwenn off balance.

"What?"

"Ga-when-do-leen Hoot—" the guard smiled again.

"Oh, my name. Gwendolyn Hutchinson, my friends call me Gwenn or Gwenny. Actually pretty much everyone calls me Gwenn. Only my mom calls me Gwendolyn, and I think that's mainly because she can put more condescension into a longer word and..." Gwenn stopped and grinned nervously.

"Thank you Miss Ga-when." The officer smiled again and handed Gwenn her passport.

"Thanks." Gwenn took the passport and turned to walk away as quickly as she could, without arousing suspicion.

"My friends call me Gwenn! Like he gives a shit."

Gwenn's mumbling caught the attention of a pretty Indian girl in a Proud's gift shop uniform.

"Duty-free, Miss?" huge smile.

"No, thank you," Gwenn attempted a smile but her mind was already sinking back into the sludge.

Gwenn grabbed a seat in the International Lounge, near an Indian family. The father was holding a small boy in his lap and the boys deep-brown eyes were transfixed by Gwenn's skin. The mother and grandmother wore flowing, colorful saris and little matching slippers. Gwenn thought they looked very exotic. As she looked around at all the brown and black faces in the lounge she noticed that she was, in fact, the rare animal at the zoo.

Suddenly all heads turned, as a large group of Amazonian-sized women came up the escalator. It took Gwenn about 30 seconds to deduce that the group was a professional women's volleyball team from Australia. Strikingly tall, tan and mostly blond; the gregarious group of Aussies dominated the room.

Gwenn took out her book, on the stages of grief, and pretended to read diligently.

Why did she find the packet of pictures? She'd helped Ed and Shirley move tons of times before. Why this time? This Daniel Gregory person, why was he so keen on being in her life? He was probably just being nice, Gwenn was sure she would have said something equally lame if their roles had been reversed. He hadn't actually made good on his promise, he hadn't made any attempt to get together or even call, "Because you threw your phone away, idiot!" Gwenn reminded herself.

"Sorry? I didn't quite catch that." A young British man had taken a seat next to Gwenn while she had been berating herself.

"Oops, just talking to myself. Didn't mean to say it out loud." Gwenn redoubled her reading efforts.

"Oh, splendid. Well then, I'm Henry and I must say you hardly seem the idiot type." Henry put out his hand in greeting and chuckled at his own wit.

"You heard that? Nice to meet you Henry, I'm Gwenn the Idiot," Gwenn smiled, "I'm escaping my life and wallowing in self-pity," she added. Gwenn absently shook his outstretched hand, although she couldn't imagine why she was telling a perfect stranger these details.

"Sounds like a brilliant holiday."

"Oh you betcha. I'm going to sulk my way around New Zealand drinking myself into a nightly stupor and crying over my eggs every morning," Gwenn actually laughed.

"You may want to consider the obvious self-destructive benefit of wanton sex with strangers, just a suggestion mind you." Henry smiled and winked.

"Random, but point taken," Gwenn winked back. It was official she had lost her mind and was now picking up strangers in strange airports like some kind of globetrotting tramp.

"Where will your debauchery be taking you in New Zealand, Miss the Idiot?"

"I've never been there. Do they have a Navy? I could start with the Navy," Gwenn grinned lasciviously.

"I, myself, am headed for Auckland as the jumping off point for a whirlwind tour of the North Island before I head off to Indonesia. I attempt to take in at least three countries I've never set foot in each time I'm on holiday."

"Can you recommend any place to stay in Auckland?" Gwenn inquired innocently.

Henry turned to look at Gwenn, and she actually noticed him, drank in the details. His short-cropped dark hair and beautiful brown eyes set off his rugged jaw. He was slim, but athletic, —and young. God, he was young. The accent had completely altered her perception. In her mind she had been exchanging banter with a harmless middle-aged Brit. This dashing, twenty-something Lothario could do some serious harm.

"I'd highly recommend the *Hotel My Place*." Henry said it like the name of an actual hotel rather than a bold invitation into his bed.

"Sounds kind of pricey, I'm traveling on a budget." Feint and parry; Gwenn was pleased with her response.

"I'd be a right wanker if I didn't pay my half." Henry's smile was so inviting. "Besides, Gwenn, I think you need a chap like me to help you forget why you threw your phone away."

Gwenn looked at Henry's face and instantly wished she hadn't. His eyes were filled with sincerity and his smile was kind and disarming. She blinked back the surge of emotion, swallowed hard and proceeded to break all of her carefully catalogued rules. Almost.

"When were you born, just month and day?"

Henry smiled inquisitively, "June 19, why?"

"You're a Gemini. That's not a bad fit...I'm Cancer... theoretically a neutral match." Gwenn noticed Henry's concern, "It's just a thing I do."

"I had other *things* in mind," Henry smiled broadly. "Will you join me?"

"I accept your invitation Mr....? No, no last names. I accept, Henry, but I must warn you that I'm a free spirit and I'm absolutely only interested in the sea, the sights and the sex. Agreed?" Gwenn smiled with far more confidence than she felt.

"We have an accord Miss Gwenn. Wild passion south of the equator, no pun intended, and no strings attached," Henry held out his hand to seal the agreement.

Gwenn leaned over to shake Henry's hand and found herself on the receiving end of a deeply passionate and playful kiss. Just the right mix, and it lingered just long enough to beg an encore.

Twenty-four

Rachel was one of those people who actually looked prettier when she pouted. Her full lips curved outward, her long lashes draped sexily over her chocolate eyes and her perfect, apple-bottom tipped impertinently outward. Unfortunately, there was no one to drink in the beautiful elixir. Rachel was all alone, feeling sorry for herself because Gwenn had not returned any of her increasingly desperate messages.

So when the phone did ring, she carelessly answered without checking caller ID.

"It's about fucking time, Gwenn. I mean I've left you about a thousand fucking—"

"Sorry...excuse me...Rachel, Rachel it's Flora." The last word was mostly a yell to staunch the flow of obscenities. Flora wasn't fond of trucker talk.

Rachel laughed easily, "Sorry Flora. I've been calling Gwenn all morning so I just kind of assumed..."

"Miss Hutchinson is missing." Flora chose the direct approach; she'd never been a huge fan of Gwenn's baby sister's egocentric approach to life.

"Missing what? What did she lose?"

"No Rachel...*Miss Hutchinson* is missing. She told me she was taking a sabbatical, yesterday on the phone. She made arrangements with the bank and the accountant, but—"

Rachel was impatient with Flora's no-stone-unturned report. "Flora, I realize it's unusual, but it sounds like she just went on vacation. Ya know, like a normal person."

"Yesterday I would've agreed with you Rachel," Flora refused to say Miss Hutchinson; she reserved that title for the woman she respected and admired.

"So what's changed?"

"This morning I received a call from a very concerned Mr. Gregory. He said something had happened, he couldn't explain...but he said it was a matter of life and death, so I—"

"Holy shit! She must've...shit...I'll get my pendulum and see if I can divine her location. I'll need a map..." Rachel was scurrying around; thrilled to have an opportunity to use her newly discovered skill and was completely ignoring Flora. "Flora I'm going to need that guy's number ASAP. He's not going to find Gwenn on his own." Rachel's mind was racing; this may actually be a life and death thing.

"He is not on his own Rachel, he has an assistant, Todd, and I have been helping out, too," Flora said, with a touch of irritation.

"So what have you and Todd discovered?"

"Miss Hutchinson is on her way to New Zealand." Flora didn't mean to sound triumphant, but this Rachel woman just rubbed her the wrong way.

"New Zealand? She's never even been to Mexico. Shit, this is bad. Flora I need Daniel Gregory's number and that Todd guy's, too." Rachel's heartbeat was picking up speed; she had to talk to Daniel. She hung up on Flora with saying goodbye and hastily dialed Daniel.

"Hello, Mr. Gregory?"

"Gwenn, is that you? I was—"

"No, Daniel it's Rachel, her sister, I got your number—"

"You sounded like her, at first, I'm so worried…I just…is she with you?" Daniel tried to focus.

"No, she left without even calling me," the hurt was evident in Rachel's voice. "She's never done that before."

"She was…umm, how much do you know?"

"I thought I knew everything, but she didn't call me after she met you…so…are you her dad?" Rachel blurted out.

"Rachel, it's a very long story. Here are the Cliff Notes: my father, who was also Daniel Gregory, passed away four years ago…"

Rachel heard the emotion in his voice as he spoke of his father and the frustration as he explained the DNA test results.

"…so you can see why I'm so worried," Daniel finished.

"Oh, sure, sure." Rachel could see why she should be worried about Gwenn, but she really didn't understand why this total stranger—who didn't know or love Gwenn—should be worried. Unless… "You instantly fell in love with her, in a day?" She had recently learned that even love spells didn't work that fast.

The accusatory sound of the question hung in the air while Daniel searched for an answer.

"I think...I can't explain it, but...when I thought she was my sister I tried to turn it into something else...but when Dr. Watkins said *negative*—"

"You love her?" Rachel's tone was scornful and full of Shirley-style judgment. "You don't even know her. Are you insane?"

"Rachel it's hard to explain, but we shared some very personal secrets with each other, we connected somehow. It was just that Gwenn had all her hopes set on this alternate family thing, she couldn't deal with any other outcome."

"She doesn't need another family. She doesn't need you!" Rachel was becoming indignant.

"I just want to be in her life. She doesn't have to fall madly in love with me; I just want to be her friend. I want to find her, make sure she's okay and bring her home." Daniel exhaled in frustration, "She was so upset."

Rachel didn't have any personal experience to draw from, but this guy sounded pretty sincere. They both wanted Gwenny home safe. She decided to help him out, for now.

"She'll e-mail me at some point, I'll get as much information as I can—once she's safely back we'll sort out the details." Rachel paused to think about how she wouldn't be able to tell Gwenn about Danica, for who knew how long. "And Daniel, thanks."

"Thanks for understanding Rachel, I'm looking forward to meeting you when we get back."

Daniel put his phone in the bin with the rest of his personal items, took off his shoes and waited to be waved through the magical, terrorist-detection archway.

The flight to New Zealand was long, but the accommodations in first class were more than adequate. The melatonin tablets weren't making him drowsy so he resorted to an old standby. Champagne took the edge off and Daniel slept during most of the flight. His dreams were filled with images of his father's old paintings and the woman who was sometimes Shirley and sometimes Gwenn. The painting his father was working on changed to something new...the Shirley/Gwenn woman was carrying something in her hand. No matter how hard Daniel tried, he could not see what was in that hand. The dream turned dark and Gwenn's plane crashed on an uncharted island. Gwenn and another man were the only survivors. Daniel saw himself growing old and gray, completely gray, searching for Gwenn as she fell deeper and deeper in love with her castaway. He awoke in a cold sweat and was glad for the reassurance of the hot towel handed to him by the flight attendant.

Daniel couldn't shake the feeling that somehow his father had sent him Gwenn. This was not going to be the one that got away. Daniel had to know more about this mystery woman that danced her way into his life, vomited in his cabin and disappeared. It was time to rejoin the living, and actually live. He didn't need to be saved this time. For once he might actually be the one bringing more to the table.

The view from the window was spectacular—the blue-green waters, the lush hillsides and the hope that somewhere down there...

Twenty-five

The *Hotel My Place* was perfect; warm wood trim, thick carpets and huge four-poster beds. The Kiwi people were friendly and generous. The lovely woman at the check-in desk happily changed Henry's accommodation and sent up extra pillows and towels.

The bathroom was exquisite. Gwenn admired the corner Jacuzzi tub and the towel warming racks. The toilet even had two buttons for flushing—a half flush and a full flush for more serious offenses.

There was an electric kettle and an ample supply of tea in the breakfast nook. Henry had already put the kettle on when Gwenn emerged from the bathroom.

"Henry, I've never...I mean I don't usually—"

"Nor have I my sweet, I usually ply women with dinner and cocktails, before I invite them back to my flat," chuckled Henry. "I've never asked a woman to move in with me after a bottle of water and some nibbly."

Gwenn laughed nervously, "This place is beautiful, though. I guess I'm just jet-lagged and starting to think of all the shit I left behind."

"It's *shite* love, *shite* sounds much more continental," Henry smiled. "Why don't you have a wash-up and I'll arrange for some food to be sent up. Then, of course, I'll make good on my promise to help you forget all the shite back in the colonies."

"That sounds lovely." Gwenn grabbed her quart-sized bag and some fresh clothes and made a beeline for the tub.

When she emerged 45 minutes later, she felt like a new woman.

Henry let out a slow exhale and nodded approvingly, "By jove I think she's got it."

Gwenn obliged with her best British accent, "The rain in Spain falls mainly on the plain," finishing with a curtsy.

"You do clean up rather nicely." Henry moved to Gwenn's side and ran his finger appreciatively down the curve of her back, his warm breath made the hairs on her neck jump up and the lingering kiss forced several other things to perk up, as well.

"Would you like to start with dinner, or would you like to be dinner?" Henry spun her around, swept her hair to the side and sunk his teeth playfully into the nape of her neck.

Gwenn's stomach was growling, but there seemed to be a more urgent message pounding up from somewhere below the stomach. "I'd like to be dinner," she giggled.

"Ah, the house specialty." Henry scooped Gwenn up in his arms and, with little effort, tossed her onto the lush feather-top bed and pinned her arms beneath his much stronger ones.

He kissed Gwenn's lips, her neck and her décolletage as he pulled her arms up over her head. Her shirt rode up and exposed her stomach. He slid his hand down past her breast and gently pulled the shirt up over Gwenn's head. He kissed every inch of her stomach. His tongue drew hot circles on her flesh.

Henry pulled his own shirt off and Gwenn marveled at the perfection of his chest. She reached up to run her hands across the plains of his torso, but Henry caught her hands in his, kissed them gently and pushed them back over her head.

Gwenn could feel herself getting lost in the moment and when Henry slid her pants off and threw them to the floor she wriggled in anticipation. It was at that moment that her left-brain threw a giant wrench into the operation, "Oh shit, I mean shite, do you have any, well...ummm...protection?"

Henry ran his tongue up her neck and whispered hotly in her ear, "You mean, like a gun?"

Gwenn giggled helplessly, "No, like a condom."

Henry rolled off the bed and out of his pants, like a magician, he reached into his suitcase and produced a box of condoms. "How many would you be expecting to need madam?" Henry gave a little bow as he proffered the box.

"Lots," smiled, Gwenn greedily.

"Brilliant," and Henry was back on top of Gwenn, slipping her bra strap off her shoulder and kissing her neck.

The pre-show was so mesmerizing and arousing that Gwenn hoped the main event would be indefinitely delayed. However, when Henry threw her bra across the room and removed her panties with his teeth, she was begging for the main event.

"Please, now...please." Gwenn was pressing her pelvis into him.

"All good things come to those who wait."

The way he emphasized *come* nearly did the trick for Gwenn right then and there. But she waited and the good things did come. In fact her patience was rewarded several times.

Henry was gentle, but so inventive. Gwenn forgot she was a fugitive from a collapsed fantasy and found herself taking mental notes as Henry unfolded her body and found new and unbelievably arousing ways of bringing her satisfaction. His skin was moist with sweat and she could tell he shaved with a straight razor...the smoothness of his jaw against her inner thigh was delicious. His smell was wildly intoxicating...

The incessant growling of her stomach finally forced Gwenn out of the warm cocoon of Henry's arms. He mumbled something as she extricated herself, but he turned and drifted back to sleep.

Gwenn lifted the little covers off the plates as quietly as she could. There was some cold chicken with red sauce and a salad that was only a bit wilted. As the food filled the hole in her stomach, she was pleased to feel completely satisfied.

The satisfaction quickly gave way to worry. She should've called Rachel. She should've simply stayed in a hotel in The Twin Cities. Should she have left a message for Daniel? There was just so much shite.

How did she feel about Daniel? She had never dreamed of a brother and she had to admit her feelings had trouble finding a sisterly tone. Gwenn thought back to the crazy night out with Rachel. She couldn't blame everything on alcohol. She had to admit that she had been flirting with the mystery man, half hidden in the shadows, long before the serious inebriation had taken hold.

Daniel was handsome, accomplished and wealthy—that didn't sound bad on paper, but Gwenn didn't want a knight in shining armor. Gwenn wanted vindication. She wanted to know, once and for all, that she had come from something better than Ed and Shirley. Gwenn indulged herself in another of her endless alternate-reality daydreams.

"Mom, dad, I've decided to change my major to theater arts. What do you think?"

"Oh sweetie, that sounds fantastic. I can't wait to watch your performances," Dream Mom gushes.

"You let me know if you need any money, Princess," Dream Dad generously offers.

In reality, things had gone quite a bit differently.

"That's a sinful profession Gwendolyn. All those actresses just sleep their way ta the top. It would be disgraceful. Remember, God's watching you. Is that what ya want him ta see?" Shirley had admonished.

"I can't see paying fer that Gwenn. If ya change yer major ya'll have ta pay yer own way. Ya've got the brains, why not be a doctor or lawyer?" Ed had hammered another nail in the coffin holding her dreams.

There was no alternate family to make existence more bearable. Gwenn was going to have to face the cold, harsh reality of her parentage and get on with her life.

Tomorrow.

Twenty-six

Daniel's plane touched down at Auckland International, he still felt a bit groggy but he made his way through the jetway. He called Todd for an update and found none.

"What do you mean Todd? She must've rented a car or bought a meal..." Daniel was exasperated.

"Mr. Gregory it may take 24 hours or more for foreign charges to show up on her account. Flora is checking things at hourly intervals. We'll let you know as soon as something shows up."

"Great. Fantastic. I'm here and I can't do anything." Daniel's spirits were sinking fast. "Hey, Todd, get me a picture of Gwenn...e-mail it to me. I'll print it out and check with the car rental places."

"On it."

The line went dead and Daniel slumped into a chair in the food court. His eyes scanned for a sign advertising WiFi access. Bingo. A kiosk with WiFi access. Daniel grabbed his bags and headed over to a cafe to grab some breakfast, or "brekkie" as he soon discovered. He would give Todd 30 minutes.

The wide central aisle between the shops was filled with tourists, business commuters and native New Zealanders. Daniel searched his memory, "Maoris," he said at last. The woman at the next table looked up in confusion and Daniel just smiled pleasantly and hid behind his coffee. Daniel remembered reading about the Maoris when he was doing research on tribal art. It seemed they got shafted, similar to the Native American Indians. The white man landed on Aotearoa and began taking land and killing natives. It always bothered Daniel that history was written by the victors. He imagined the Maori version of New Zealand's history was slightly different from the popular British Empire version. In some ways though, the Maori seemed to be making headway, getting slightly better reparations than their northern hemisphere counterparts.

The Maori had a significant amount of tribal lands, in some very beautiful areas. The tribal land was passed on from generation to generation and every Maori citizen was guaranteed some piece of land. Slightly more autonomous and empowering than the stark government housing on a reservation, he mused. There were also some very nice trade schools where Maori youths learned the arts of green stone cutting, woodcarving and textiles. Daniel thought about taking Gwenn to the Whakarearea tribal lands in Rotorua. He checked his watch, 25 minutes, close enough.

The kiosk was simple to operate and printed a fairly decent copy of the photo sent by Todd. Daniel snatched the slip of paper and rushed to the rental counters.

"Hello, do you recognize this woman? Have you seen her today, or maybe yesterday?" Daniel forced a casual, nonchalant tone.

"Sorey pale," the large Maori said at the first counter. The welcoming, melodic accent lost its charm on the anxious Daniel.

"Theet's nawt famillya," the next counter said.

A couple more "sorey pales" and some head shakes and Daniel was about to give up. Two counters left, local outfits. He had assumed Gwenn would lean toward a name she recognized.

"Excuse me," Daniel laid the picture on the counter, "did this woman rent a car recently?"

"No, sorey pale."

Daniel turned to walk away.

"But, her mate deed."

Daniel, hopeful but confused, "What? Mate? This woman was traveling alone...an American."

"Shear, shear, American...umm Jean, Wendee, no, no, Gween...that's it Gween. She was weeth a British guy."

"Are you sure? Do you remember the man's name?" Daniel was growing concerned.

"I'll look eet up." The man typed a few things into the computer, smiled and said, "Heenry Wilkeen, that's eet."

"Thanks, thanks a lot." Daniel forced a smile and turned to find a chair. He pulled out his phone and found his fingers were shaking a bit as he tapped the speed dial.

"Todd, find out everything you can on a Henry Wilkin... a British tourist. Apparently Gwenn was with him or at least got a ride in his rental car."

"Right away Mr. Gregory." Todd kept his tone professional but he did not like the way this was turning out. This Gwenn woman was beginning to sound like a typical low-life groupie, with no morals and a penchant for drama. The long-lost father angle was new, but this trampy behavior was all-too-familiar.

Twenty-seven

Henry told Gwenn to pack up and get ready for adventure. Today's itinerary included a helicopter ride over Huka Falls.

The drive was beautiful. They meandered along a winding, two-lane road playing hide and seek with the coast, and finally cutting inland through lush, emerald green hills.

Gwenn was in love with New Zealand. Maybe if she couldn't have a fantasy family, she could move to New Zealand and start a completely new reality. It was the opposite end of the world from Minnesota. Ed and Shirley would never come here. It would be nirvana.

Gwenn had to down a couple of motion sickness pills before the helicopter adventure, but it was worth it. The countryside was green and alive. The water was bright, aqua blue; it didn't even look real. Huka Falls churned and spewed the most gorgeous blue water...like a super-powered jacuzzi. Gwenn could see tiny rafts, and imagined they must be filled with insane people, bumping and thrashing like tiny bobbers fighting to stay afloat while some too-large fish pulled them mercilessly to their doom. A helicopter tour seemed quite sensible in light of the rafting option.

Her mind drifted off to questions about her sensible cautious life. She had been trained to please others first, to let other people's opinions carry far more weight than her own. When she looked back at her life, she knew she had been set up, plain and simple. That day in July, the day she was born, her exuberant Gramma Carlson had initiated the clever ruse. Gwendolyn was lying in the hospital bassinet, innocently unaware. Outside the glass Gramma Carlson was convincing Ed that his new, baby girl was a genius.

"Look at her Ed. Look, she's lookin' right at me. She knows who I am. Ya look at those little dark eyes and ya'll see. She recognizes me Ed. She's a smart little corker!"

"She's prolly just lookin' at yer bright red coat, Ethol," Ed offered.

"Okay then, you're talkin' nonsense. She knows Ed. Ya just look, that there's one special baby girl," Gramma Carlson enthused.

It would occur to Gwendolyn many years later, after hearing the story repeatedly throughout her childhood, that being the first granddaughter conceived *in* wedlock might have been the reason Gramma Carlson was so hell-bent on making her special. But she wasn't special; she was completely ordinary and always had been.

And right there in the middle of all that breathtaking beauty, Gwenn cried. Silent tears trickled down her cheeks and her shoulders shook.

Henry's strong arm slipped around her and he whispered in her ear, "Must be time for your medicine."

He leaned in and nibbled her ear lobe, just in case she was confused about his inference.

Henry asked the pilot to take them down. He bought some sandwiches, crisps and drinks and they drove out to Lake Taupo. He took some towels from the boot and guided Gwenn to the sandy, secluded beach.

"Care for a kiss before lunch?" Henry winked.

Gwenn smiled and nodded.

Henry leaned down, brushed a tear from her cheek, and kissed her soft lips.

Tingles of last night washed over Gwenn and pulled her back into the magical, mind-numbing beauty of New Zealand.

"If you could bottle that, you could put the makers of Abilify out of business," Gwenn grinned.

"And Viagra," added Henry, with a chuckle.

Twenty-eight

Three days. It had been three days since Rachel had spoken to Gwenn. In the whole of Rachel's memory she could not think of another time when three days had passed without talking to Gwenn. Something was very wrong. Rachel was strongly considering casting a spell to make Gwenn call her. Her foray into the Wiccan arts was filling her with imagined power.

Rachel had left about 30 messages on Gwenn's phone, until the reality of no callback was sinking in. Even the torrid affair with Danica could not completely take Rachel's mind off the problem of her missing sister. Rachel did the math, one day ahead and five hours earlier. So, if it was one o'clock...yeah, it was time to call Daniel.

"Hey, it's Rachel. Just calling for my daily fix. Any news?"

"Sort of, maybe you can explain—would Gwenn befriend a stranger?" Daniel's voice indicated more than a simple curiosity.

"That's not her normal comfort zone, but I'm afraid were in a 'hey the world of Gwenn is flat...no wait...it's round' scenario. Why? What's going on?"

"Todd e-mailed a photo yesterday and I ask around the rental counters. One clerk claims that Gwenn was with a guy who rented a—"

"A guy? With a guy? Did he mean they were together? Maybe she was just behind the guy in line and struck up a conversation." Rachel tried to hide her concern.

"Yeah, I thought of that, but Gwenn didn't rent a car," Daniel paused and swallowed. "She also never checked into a hotel. Flora's monitoring the cards."

"Just how upset was she?" Rachel's tone was somewhat accusatory.

"When I tried to console her, after the test results...she pulled away from me like I had the plague. She just ran out of the hospital." Daniel's heart pained at the memory.

"Shit, I never knew she was so unhappy." Rachel reflected on their childhood. "Gwenn always towed the line—took care of me, defended me against the fat jokes at school, quoted the Bible verses at church and kept curfew for our parents. All of this sadness and disappointment, maybe even hatred, it was just building up inside her..."

"Like a time bomb," Daniel finished.

"Like a time bomb," Rachel weakly echoed. "Daniel, I don't think we can use the 'old Gwenn' to predict new Gwenn's behavior. This is a totally *exploded* Gwenn. You've gotta find her. Do you have anything?"

"The guy that rented the car was a Brit named Henry Wilkin, Todd's checking him out. I should know more today."

"Maybe she'll contact me. This is the longest we've ever not spoken. It's weird...and empty," Rachel's voice trailed off.

"I'll find her, I have to," Daniel was resolute.

"What are you gonna do?" Rachel asked.

"Until Todd turns up something concrete, I'm just going to keep moving. There's a museum in Hamilton...I thought I'd check that out. I'll keep you posted...bye Rachel."

"Bye Daniel, good luck." Rachel hung up the phone and cried. Mostly it was because she missed Gwenn, but a few of the tears were selfish. If Gwenn didn't turn up soon, Rachel was going to have to tell Ed and Shirley—that was a nightmare scenario Rachel refused to imagine.

Twenty-nine

"You in the mood for a museum?" Henry traced little patterns on Gwenn's naked back.

"Sure." The delicious moment of waking up to Henry's touch was soon consumed by the guilt Gwenn could not keep at bay. Activity was the only solution. "Let's go. I'm ready for anything," Gwenn's valiant tone wasn't fooling anyone.

"It's a bit of backtracking, but worth it," Henry called to Gwenn as she brushed her teeth in the bathroom. "The museum is in Hamilton, we can take in the museum today and spend tomorrow at the Botanical Gardens. It's a beautiful little town, a river runs through it..." Henry's last few words were lost in his shirt as he pulled it over his head. He didn't hear Gwenn approaching.

Gwenn slipped her arms around his taut stomach and as his head popped out of the shirt she planted a deeply insistent kiss on his smooth, firm lips. "As long as I get my medicine, I'll follow you anywhere," she giggled.

"Why you little junkie," Henry teased, and kissed Gwenn's earlobe. "Let's get some brekkie, as they say here, and let the adventure begin."

Breakfast was not to be rushed at the Heli Cafe, so Gwenn and Henry passed the time by making up helicopter inspired names for breakfast menu selections.

"I'll have the Heli stack with copter links," Gwenn joked.

"I'd like two choppers over-easy with a cup of rotor grease...to go," laughed Henry. "I think you'll enjoy Hamilton, college town, lots of shopping and lovely restaurants," he added.

"How do you know so much about New Zealand?" Gwenn probed.

"Good question. I do suppose you might like to know a bit more about your host." Henry continued, "I write for a travel guide, I'm here to do a quick check for new hotels, changes in restaurant ownership, new attractions and the like."

"Wow, that sounds exciting."

"Of course I'll have to add an entire chapter about the dangers of loose women traveling alone," smirked Henry.

Gwenn blushed and laughed at the thought of anyone referring to her as a *loose* woman. She had never acknowledged how tightly she'd been wound...

"Gwendolyn don't ever go near Uncle Jack's dogs by yerself. Uncle Jack has trained those dogs ta kill."

Who tells that to a four-year-old, Gwenn suddenly wondered? Oh yes, that's right, Shirley. Her theoretical mother, who insisted that Gwenn was "so mature for her age," that even at four she was treated more like a friend and confidant than a daughter that needed protecting.

"Uncle Jack jumps trains ta get around and the dogs are trained ta protect him. He says they won't hurt us, but that black one there, he bit a hole in a man's stomach once. So ya just gotta be careful."

And so Gwenn became careful, keeping her fear and pain secret; letting the *joie de* drain right out of her *vivre*—until Dr. Watkins pulled the cord and spun her out of control. The truth had been revealed and Gwenn was going to have to find a way to deal with her new reality.

The drive to Hamilton was scenic and peaceful; deep green forest areas and magnificent bucolic hills. Acres of sheep pastures and several roadside goats.

"Look there's another one. What is the point of tying a goat to the outside of the fence?"

"They eat the grass, and such, in the verges and the shepherds move them down a post or two and before long, they've cleaned up the whole roadside," explained Henry.

"Like a lawnmower, without the maintenance issues. They're goat mowers," pronounced Gwenn.

They were lucky to find a parking spot on the street near the museum. The walk felt good after being cooped up in a car.

"Ah, there it is," Henry pointed to the museum

***

Daniel was about 15 minutes outside of Hamilton when he got the call from Todd.

"They're in Taupo, about an hour and a half south of Hamilton, on Highway 1."

"How do you do it, Todd?"

"I found out Henry writes for Solo Earth, some travel guide, so I called. I told them Gwenn was my bipolar sister who had skipped the country without her medication, etc.," Todd paused for effect. Praise was not showered upon him, so he continued. "The details aren't important, they're going to get a message to Henry. You really need to find her before that happens. I can't imagine she'll be too thrilled with my fabrication. Brilliant as it was," he finished, smugly.

"So how big is Taupo, where do I start?"

"They were on a helicopter tour of the Huka Falls area... doesn't sound real huge. I'm getting a picture of Henry and I'll forward it to you. Try to find WiFi access somewhere."

"Yeah, okay, keep me posted...and thanks, Todd."

Daniel sped through Hamilton on the east side of the river, focused on reaching Taupo before the trail ran cold.

***

On the west side of the river Gwenn marveled at the full-size war canoe in the Hamilton Museum. To think that this was carved by hand, it was amazing.

"What are these?" Gwenn pointed to some shimmering inlays in the prow of the craft.

"That's paua shell, much like abalone. The Maori would place the shells into the eyes of the carvings so the ancient spirits could see the enemies and watch over the warriors." Henry enjoyed seeing everything anew through Gwenn's eyes.

"Are these like totem poles?" Gwenn asked, about the serpentine carvings that stretched from the museum floor to the ceiling.

"Yes, quite similar. These carvings depict the lineage. Each face represents a specific ancestor in the tribe, the whole series is a genealogy." Henry put his arm around Gwenn. "Do you find this interesting or are you just indulging a silly Brit?"

"I bloody love it! You wanker!" Gwenn grinned

"I'm afraid that's far more vulgar than you might think." Henry shook his finger disapprovingly at Gwenn, but his eyes twinkled with mirth.

***

Daniel soon discovered that there was no WiFi access in Taupo, at the moment. There wasn't much of anything at the Heli Cafe. The helicopter tour people remembered Gwenn and confirmed that she had been with a British man, but no one had any idea where they had gone.

"Most folks continue south, to Wellington," indicated the tour guide.

"Might heeve gone to Rotorua," offered a Maori waitress. "There's WiFi there," she added.

Wellington looked to be about four hours away and Rotorua about 45 minutes. Daniel chose the lesser of two evils and hoped it would pay off.

***

The museum had been wonderful. Henry was a wealth of information, and dinner was splendid.

"How is the lamb?" inquired Henry.

"It's delicious, good call." Gwenn didn't usually talk with her mouth full, but she felt unabashedly comfortable with Henry.

"Would you like to stay in Hamilton tonight? If you are not keen on the Botanical Gardens—"

"I'd love to stay. So far everything you have suggested has been fantastic. I wouldn't miss the Botanical Gardens, or anything else," Gwenn nodded approvingly at Henry's masterful guiding skills. Her expression grew serious and her eyes clouded with worry. "I really should call my sister," Gwenn's tone was apologetic.

"Of course, of course. I'll arrange it as soon as we've finished our meal." Henry nodded, adding in a more serious tone, "You're not a hostage Gwenn, you can go your own way whenever you like."

Gwenn's hand shot across the table and grabbed Henry's strong fingers. Her eyes filled with mock panic, "But how will I survive without my medicine?" They both laughed and Henry purred wickedly.

The phone woke Rachel from a deep sleep, her hand felt for Danica, but the space next to her was already empty.

"This better be good," Rachel's sleepy voice was gruff.

"Sorry to wake you Rache, it's Gwenn."

Rachel was instantly alert. "Gwenny? Where are you? Shit, I was going crazy. Are you okay? I thought..." Rachel was crying.

Gwenn managed another "I'm sorry," and she was crying, too. Just hearing Rachel's shaky breathing and listening to her blow her nose warmed Gwenn's aching heart.

"I miss you Rache. I just couldn't handle it."

"I know, I know."

"I met with that Daniel guy—"

"It's okay, I know, you don't have to talk about it," Rachel reassured her.

The words filtered through Gwenn's tears. "What do you mean 'you know'? What do you know?" Gwenn's tears stopped abruptly.

"Daniel was worried, you were so upset, he just didn't think you should be alone. He's only trying to help," pleaded Rachel.

Gwenn didn't think it was the right time to inform Rachel that she wasn't alone. "How exactly is Daniel helping?" Gwenn's voice was stern.

Rachel explained the calls, explained how Flora and Todd were working together and explained how Daniel had flown to New Zealand to find Gwenn.

"He's in New Zealand?" If Henry had stayed in the hotel room, the panic in Gwenn's voice would've sent him racing to her side. But he was in the hotel bar tucked into a pint of ale and some nibbles.

"Gwenn, calm down. He thinks he loves you," the words were out before Rachel could stop them.

"That's just sick Rachel. He loves his sister." Gwenn spat the words at Rachel.

"Gwenn, sweetie...you know you're not his sister." Rachel stated the obvious with as much tenderness as she could muster.

"I know," Gwenn's voice was a whisper and the sobs that followed shook Gwenn's body for several minutes.

"Gwenny, I love you," Rachel's voice cracked with emotion.

"Thanks, Rache, I don't deserve you." Gwenn took a few raspy breaths. "I hope you understand I wasn't trying to replace you. I was trying to get rid of Ed and Shirley."

"We've both wished for better parental units, Gwenny. I guess I just never understood how seriously you took your wishing."

"Yeah, I'm a bit of a nutter," laughed Gwenn.

"A what?"

"Oh, it's just a...it means crazy person," Gwenn quickly finished.

"I can't believe you're in a foreign country all alone, Gwenn. How are you managing?" Rachel hoped the ploy would work.

"I'm not all alone." Gwenn winced at the confession.

"I'm gonna need details Gwenny," teased Rachel.

Gwenn tried to explain her newfound freedom and the fun, no-strings attached agreement she had with Henry, but Rachel was skeptical.

"Gwenn, you're an emotional war zone. You're not thinkin' things through with your normal clear head."

"I know, it's great. I'm just living in the moment. We barely even plan one day in advance. I mean tomorrow we're going to the Botanical Gardens, but after that who knows," gushed Gwenn.

"When are you coming home?"

"I don't know, maybe never. I might just stay in New Zealand for ever," Gwenn's voice was wistful.

"Gwenny, I know you're in pain. Escape is okay for a while, but you can't just abandon me—I'm not the same when you're away. I mean I'm having an affair with a married woman...I'm a wreck."

"Rachel you slut! Tell me everything."

As Rachel recounted the details of her goddess-guided tour on the wild side, Gwenn felt herself relax. The comfortable rhythm of Rachel's voice and Gwenn's consummate role as sounding board put things in perspective. Daniel wasn't her brother. The loss Gwenn felt was for the loss of the dream life she would've had with her fantasy family. Nothing was stopping her from creating that life on her own. Actually one thing was stopping her... Old Gwenn.

"...so basically I'm whipped. It's a disaster," moaned Rachel.

"Rache you and Annie just split up, this Danica woman has been a great rebound girl. Now you have to move on... you have to end it with Danica."

"But Gwenny—"

"You're strong enough. You are the toughest bitch I know. End it and get back in the game. You'll never find the right partner if you're wasting all your time with the wrong one." Gwenn tried to ignore her own words, but it was so obvious—Old Gwenn was the wrong partner. That fact could no longer be ignored.

"Thanks Gwenn. This is why you gotta come back, you're my moral compass, I'm adrift at sea without you. I tried to do a spell to get some clarity, but it didn't work."

"I'll be back soon Rache, I just have to work through a few things. Wait, a spell? Are you a witch now?"

"It's Wicca, Gwenny. And yeah, I like all the aspects of trusting yourself and being in tune with nature. We can talk about it when you get home. What about Daniel? He sounds nice." Rachel didn't really know Daniel, but she gave him an "A" for effort.

"Daniel is probably fantastic, but I met him as my father, thought he might be my brother...found out the whole thing was a dream. A dream that didn't come true. I don't know if I can recategorize him...he said best friends...maybe I could manage that." Gwenn's mind wandered back to the Colonial Inn. There had been sparks, at the time she assured herself it was the excitement of the looming test results, and the misplaced feelings would need to be reinterpreted as she got to know her brother.

He wasn't her brother...no reinterpretation required. Hmmm, that almost made sense.

"Gwenny I've gotta get some sleep. I love you, come home soon."

"I love you too, Rache. I'll keep you posted...e-mails here on in...these calls cost a fortune," chuckled Gwenn.

Rachel hung up the phone and paced nervously around the room. Gwenn is usually right about these things...but maybe...no, no she just couldn't.

It was the second hardest phone call Rachel ever had to make.

Daniel lay in bed pondering his options when the phone rang and Rachel gave him the information he needed. Now that he had a solid lead he doubted himself. What if Gwenn didn't feel the same way? What if she hated him for following her halfway around the world? Then came the toughest question. Why had he followed her halfway around the world? Yes, there had been a connection, yes some inexplicable attraction—Daniel closed his eyes. Immediately he saw Gwenn's hazel eyes twinkling back at him. He could get lost in those eyes...when he looked at Gwenn he only saw Gwenn. For the first time since Angeline, his wife, had passed away he was able to look at a woman and not see Angeline staring back.

Even when he had been with Natalie, he had constantly compared her to Angeline. Natalie had helped him move on, but Natalie had not helped him heal. Every time he had looked at Natalie he had ached for Angeline.

Daniel admitted to himself that Gwenn had consumed him. Gwenn had flooded into places that had been locked off since Angeline's death. Gwenn was the future, pure and untainted.

"Man up, Daniel," he told himself. Maybe he would need to get a B12 shot or find some saw palmetto. He would take the information Rachel had just given him and he would go to the Botanical Gardens and convince Gwenn to come back to the States and give him a chance. Best friends, for starters. Daniel had his sights set on far more than friendship, but it was a great place to start. The image of *sexy Gwenn* from the bar flitted into his head and Daniel fell asleep with a salacious grin softening his chiseled jaw.

Thirty

The sun was bright and golden when Gwenn awoke.

"Tea?" Henry asked from the breakfast nook.

"I'm starving! You're working me like a dog."

"Yes, that was, perhaps, one of our more interesting poses," teased Henry.

"Henry!" Gwenn squealed. She had never felt this uninhibited with anyone, since Steven, the freedom was refreshing. She felt like this might be a new chapter in her life—maybe a new book.

"Wash up and we'll hunt down some brekkie," suggested Henry.

"Done." Gwenn jumped out of bed, abandoning modesty, and marched to the bathroom in all her nubile glory.

Henry nodded appreciatively and raised his teacup in a toast to Gwenn's brazen display.

At breakfast Gwenn mentioned that she would need to find an internet cafe after the Gardens, to update Rachel.

Henry nodded and tapped his temple knowingly with his finger.

Gwenn insisted on buying breakfast, and after a small tussle Henry admitted defeat and allowed Gwenn her moment of victory.

Henry suggested a lazy stroll along the river. The sun was warm and inviting and the trees along the river provided occasional shady respite.

Gwenn was completely relaxed. She reflected on the transitory nature of her adventure with Henry and she found herself accepting, rather than panicking. Perhaps Old Gwenn could be defeated.

Henry casually took Gwenn's hand as they walked. Gwenn turned to look at him and smiled, relaxation spilling out of the corners of her grin. This would be a hard one to leave behind he mused. Even though his wife had grown to accept his tawdry "guide book affairs," Henry felt this one was something more. Admittedly he had sold his self-respect a long time ago, for the price of his wife's inheritance, but maybe he didn't need the money—right, and the Queen didn't need the Crown Jewels. No, he had made his deal with the devil, Delilah Wentworth, and the devil paid quite well.

**

Daniel had stupidly made a wrong turn and ended up in Tauranga, before he discovered his mistake. By the time he turned around and got back to Hamilton the sun was low on the horizon. He arrived at the Botanical Gardens without any further snafus. The full moon was already high in the sky, chasing the sun from its throne. Daniel's painterly eye noted the mix of ebbing golds and oranges woven into the subtle, silvery glow. '*Shimmering Memory*, watercolor on canvas.'

He showed the photos at the ticket window and the young man confirmed that a couple, matching Gwenn and Henry's description, had indeed entered the Gardens a few hours earlier. Daniel took offense to the term couple, and picked up his pace.

The Gardens were quite breathtaking and Daniel wished he had more time. The lambent moonlight was growing stronger and everything took on an ethereal glow. He rounded the corner near the reflecting pool and froze. There on the bridge, crossing the pool, was Gwenn.

***

Henry had his arm around Gwenn's waist and she was stroking her finger along the placket of his shirt. Her head was tilted intimately toward him.

"Gwenn, the past few days...well, it's a bit hard to explain."

"I know, I just feel so relaxed with you...so free." Gwenn rubbed her nose playfully on Henry's.

"I guess I didn't expect to feel this way about you, so I didn't think it would matter." Henry's voice caught in his throat, in what he hoped was a convincingly emotional moment. This time was harder than the others, but he had a lot of practice and the key was to rip it off quickly, like a plaster. No lingering, no regrets.

"Henry we said, 'no strings attached.' Are you going back on your word?" Gwenn pretended to pout, but kissed Henry on the lips instead.

***

Daniel had seen enough, the tender embrace, the lovers' whispers, and the gentle kiss. 'Tryst, silver gelatin print.' This image would be imprinted in Daniel's mind forever. He turned and stalked out of the Gardens. Equal parts pain and anger tearing at the fragile constructs of his heart.

Had he stayed but a moment longer he would have seen a very different tableau.

***

Gwenn was momentarily distracted by what she thought were footsteps, but Henry's next words brought her full attention back to the moonlit bridge.

"Gwenn, I'm married." Henry steeled himself for what inevitably came next.

Gwenn reared back, pulling loose from Henry's embrace and prepared to slap him senseless. Instead, her barely mended world collapsed and she sunk down to the rough boards of the bridge and quietly sobbed.

He waited for the slap that never came, opened his eyes and for a moment wondered if Gwenn had been an apparition all along. Then he heard the sound of crying, ghosts didn't cry.

The parting was messy, uncomfortable and altogether too slow for Gwenn's liking. She got her things and got a taxi to an inn on the other side of town. Henry had offered to drive her back to the airport, but Gwenn had no intention of giving him the satisfaction. She wasn't going to tuck her tail between her legs and run back to the colonies. Fat chance. She came to New Zealand to find herself, and now that she was alone and heartbroken she could get back to her primary objective.

Currently, that objective was to find an internet cafe and pour out some of the pain into an e-mail to Rachel. Why in the hell had she thrown her damn phone away?

From: Gwenn.theorganizer@hotmail.com
To: mybakedalaska@gmail.com

Dear Rache,

I guess I should take my own fxxking
advice.
Henry, the young sex machine is MARRIED.
I knew it was too good to be true. Things
were going too good. I mean things never
go this good for me with men…I ignored
all the red flags.
— handsome
— young
— good in bed (so, so good) :(
— funny
— intelligent
— wealthy (I think…)
What was I thinking! I don't get men like
that. I'm just going to be a cranky, old
maid living alone with 40 cats and
knitting afghans. I hate my life!
For a minute I hoped Daniel would find me
and rescue me. Fxxk that! I'm going to
rescue my damn self and all men can get
bent! Is there a lesbian training
program? I don't think I am…but maybe…I'm
obviously a horrible FAILURE with men!

I miss you…a lot. Write soon.
Love,
Your pathetic sister—Gwenn

PS I rented a Vodafone for emergencies,
here's the number 011-64-555-4118

Thirty-one

Daniel drove straight to the airport in Auckland. He purchased a ticket on the next plane to Los Angeles and marched straight to the bar, to wait for the boarding call. He handed the bartender $100 and said, "Make sure I'm on flight 842."

The bartender nodded and responded in his deeply musical accent, "Shear mate, no worries."

"Maker's Mark, straight up and bring me the bottle."

Daniel woke up somewhere over the Pacific Ocean, with a pounding headache and no memory of boarding the plane.

The flight attendant rushed to his side. "Do you need anything Mr. Gregory?"

"Water." Daniel's mouth felt cottony and tasted stale. He reached up to twist off the fans that were blowing a steady whir of air into his arid eyes.

"Certainly sir." She was back in seconds with a bottle of Voss.

Daniel gratefully accepted the bottle and took several slow practiced sips. No point in shocking the delicate stomach lining.

"Would you care for chilled chicken Wellington or cheese filled pasta shells?"

"Coffee, please."

"We proudly offer Starbucks coffee. Do you take cream?"

"Black, like my men." Daniel tried to joke, but the effort was painful for both of them. The attendant scuttled off to retrieve the coffee.

Daniel brought his seatback up a little and the cabin stopped spinning. Slivers of last night were seeping through his sodden brain. Was Gwenn in love with that Henry prat? Was it just a fling? How could she have gotten so close in such a short time? Maybe they knew each other before...maybe she had planned to meet Henry in New Zealand.

Daniel's stomach was greatly displeased by this last rumination and jumped up and down in protest. He quickly made his way to the first class crapper and allowed reverse peristalsis to relieve him of some Maker's.

The remaining flight was uneventful, but interminably swirly. A bad bit of turbulence nearly did him in.

At LAX Daniel called Todd and ask him to get the first flight back to Minneapolis—direct.

"Just one ticket Mr. Gregory?" Todd was worried.

"Just one. Don't ask." Daniel's tone was icy.

Todd could almost smell the Maker's through the phone, but he shoved the concern aside and his fingers flew over the keyboard. "There is a 2:00 p.m. flight on North by Northwest. Will you be through customs in time?"

"I'll be there."

The line went dead and Todd, atheist that he was, crossed himself against the storm that would soon be coming eastward.

Daniel paid off another bartender/babysitter and got straight to work. He unhappily awoke sometime later, several thousand feet above Iowa. He immediately ordered a drink.

The flight attendant informed him that they would be landing in less than 20 minutes, so she wasn't permitted to offer beverage services.

Daniel informed her of a few things she could do with her regulations and flung his seat backward, as far as it would go. He continued to curse the FAA under his breath as he stewed in his own juices; or perhaps, pickled.

The passengers deplaned, and Daniel walked a crooked line through the terminal. He stopped at an airport bar and grabbed one for the road.

For at least the third time that day, the bartender was glad he was not on that road.

As Daniel emerged from the escalators, Todd swooped in. Todd came personally. Hiring a limo driver to hold the sign would only have served to alert passersby to the identity of the drunken idiot stumbling out of the Minneapolis-St. Paul International.

"The mini bar'sempty," slurred hurricane Daniel, loudly.

"We are in the BMW, Mr. Gregory, not a limo," replied Todd patiently.

"S'where's the booze?"

"Sorry, Mr. Gregory no booze." Todd held his breath. A fist smashed down on the console as hurricane Daniel swirled forward. A gust of stale Maker's-scented wind violated Todd's nostrils.

"That's dee-rickulus! Un'merican!" roared the storm.

Todd attempted several distractionary tactics, but each new topic was met with a louder version of, "I'll drink t'that, if ya ge'some booze," from Daniel.

Mercifully, Daniel passed out and Todd could plan his battle strategy.

Step 1. Call Dawn, the trustworthy housekeeper, and tell her to get her overpaid, designer-jean clad ass to the house, toot sweet. Mission: dispose of all alcohol and lock the wine cellar.

Step 2. Call former UFC contender Frankie the Big Bang Anderson, Daniel's trainer; tell him to meet them at the house. Daniel needed to be sobered up and Todd could not tame the hurricane alone.

Step 3. Hopefully, get to the bottom of the New Zealand debacle. Todd had to know the exact origins of the storm if he was to successfully defuse it and comfortably downgrade things to a tropical depression. Minneapolis was hardly tropical but Todd was a stickler for analogies.

Step 4. Slip Daniel a *mickey*—water laced with Ambien—and throw him in bed. This would buy Todd some time to come up with additional steps, if needed. Todd quickly reminded himself that Step 4 was a long way off, and only possible if Steps 1 through 3 came off without a hitch. Battle stations. Todd could almost hear the warning sirens wailing.

"Dawn, it's Todd...yes, that Todd...I have a Priority One situation...yes, you'll be paid double, I said its Priority One...go to the house immediately...no, not after Wheel of Fortune. You should be on your way now...I think you can talk and put on your shoes Dawn...yes I'll hold while you tie the bows." Todd's eyes rolled so far back he imagined he saw brain matter. "Double bows are just great...your keys are on the table by the front door...because that's where they always are, Dawn...are you ready for the assignment...no getting to the house is just the beginning." Todd risked a hasty glance at Daniel, still out cold—good. "Lock the wine cellar and take the key with you. Retrieve the spare key from the drawer in Daniel's bedside table." Daniel didn't know Todd had noticed the invoice from the locksmith; once Todd had knowledge of the breach, finding the key was a piece of cake.

"Next empty out the liquor cabinet, pour everything down the drain, rinse the bottles and put them in the trash barrels in the garage...yes, you can take the Grey Goose and the Peach Schnapps, just have it out of the house in the next 40 minutes...no that is not it. There will be one bottle of Maker's Mark and one Absolute Citron in the back of the subzero...second shelf, all the way to the back...yes, down the drain, etc. Any questions?...yes Dawn, it's serious...I'm sorry too. I'll drop the money off tomorrow...I'll call first. Thank you, Dawn."

Dawn had never broken a confidence and that was the only reason Todd continued to tolerate her schoolgirl chattiness. Step 2 would be much easier. Frankie the Big Bang was a pro.

"Frankie, it's Todd."

"Sweet, what can I do ya for?" Frankie's folksy words were lost on Todd.

"I need you at the house ASAP. Wear swim trunks."

"Dude, I'm on it." Frankie was no rocket scientist but Todd's urgency, and the mention of swim trunks, was a clearly discernible code to a man of Frankie's experience. A bouncer of several years, he had known his share of drunks.

And as a magnanimous friend he had helped sober up more than his share. In Frankie's world there were only two emergencies that required swim trunks—an impromptu, hot tub party with strippers or a friend that needed the "shake and wake."

Frankie was on his way to Daniel's before Todd had deconstructed Step 3.

***

Rachel read the e-mail three more times. The only part she was having trouble with was the "hoping Daniel would find me" line. So, Daniel didn't find her? Maybe the e-mail was written before Daniel found her, or maybe Henry broke the news before the Botanical Gardens and Daniel had waited all day for nothing. Rachel needed answers.

***

Todd jumped as Daniel's phone rang, but he deftly grabbed it and answered before the second ring.

"Daniel, it's Rachel."

"Rachel Hutchinson? This is Todd, answering for Mr. Gregory."

"Oh, I thought he went to New Zealand alone." Rachel was getting even more confused.

"Mr. Gregory is back in the States as of this morning. We are on our way back from the airport." Todd knew what was coming and he had no answer to give.

"Did he find my sister? Is she there? Can I say hi?" Rachel was worried or excited; it was a toss up.

"I'm sorry Miss Hutchinson, it would appear that he returned alone. I will call you after I learn anything further." Todd put on his extra-professional pants.

"Can't ya just ask him now?" Rachel was impatient and a tad sarcastic.

"Unfortunately, Mr. Gregory is indisposed. He does not enjoy long flights." Todd smiled at his clever lie.

"Is he drunk?" Rachel was practiced at cooking up perfect lies and she wasn't one to pull any punches when she smelled one simmering.

Todd ignored the pointed question. "I will call you as soon as I have more information. Good day, Miss Hutchinson."

Rachel tapped *End* on her phone and typed a reply to Gwenn's e-mail.

```
From: mybakedalaska@gmail.com
To: Gwenn.theorganizer@hotmail.com

what the F, sis? daniel is back
apparently drunk off his ass. his snarky
assistant todd wouldn't even let me talk
to daniel.
did u turn him down? did u slap his face?
did Henry punch him out?
i gotta know…i'm freaked!
love ya - rache
```

Thirty-two

Gwenn was struggling to organize the disasters. There were certain feelings that belonged in the drawers of the fantasy family failure bureau. There were feelings that belonged in the Henry is a bloody wanker incinerator and there were feelings about Daniel that didn't belong anywhere. Life wasn't organized, and that didn't sit well with Gwenn. She opted for the screw-this-I'll-get-a-cup-of-coffee solution.

The internet access sign beckoned Gwenn like a loving grandparent. There, in her inbox was the connection she craved. Unfortunately, the e-mail from Rachel wasn't consoling or comforting it was frickin' confusing. She typed a curt response.

From: Gwenn.theorganizer@hotmail.com
To: mybakedalaska@gmail.com

Never saw Daniel. Not coming home.

```
Henry the bloody wanker not ruining my pity
party/vacation.
Be back soon. Gotta get things organized in
my mind—leaving heart in state of chaos for
time being.

See ya soon,
Gwenn (PS drop the Daniel thing—freak!)
```

Gwenn looked at a map of the North Island, over her spinach and mushroom omelette. Wellington seemed too far, Bay of Islands too dangerous and Rotorua was rumored to be quite stinky. In the end *dangerous* won out over *stinky* and *far*. Gwenn packed up her rental car and drove north.

The hills seemed a more lush, verdant hue and the sky was a clearer azure, now that Henry the bloody wanker was gone.

Gwenn made it as far as Warkworth, when her growling stomach, screaming bladder and completely numb ass insisted on a stop. She found a nice pizza place for lunch and met a boy. A nice, safe, seven-year-old boy.

"What's your name?"

"Gwenn. What's yours?" Gwenn smiled at the innocence of youth; the safety in a gap-toothed smile.

"I'm Mat. I like school."

"What's your favorite thing about school?" Gwenn inquired.

"My favorite theeng is lunch, because theen I get a beet of play afta," smiled Mat.

Gwenn smiled wide and suppressed a titter. She was sure that *getting a bit of play* meant something quite different in the seven-year-old vernacular.

"Do you have a girlfriend?"

"Yeah, she likes to play on the monkey bars and I like to play een the sand peet, but sometimes I play on the monkey bars weeth her. My older brother plays rugby. But I didn't geet to watch the beeg game last night because my fatha wasn't home." Mat sounded quite disappointed.

"Oh, what does your father do?" Gwenn was really enjoying this blessed distraction.

"Today he's vomeeting cuz he drank too much rum!"

Soda actually came out of Gwenn's nose. Mat was thrilled. He ran off saying something about having to tell his mates, and Gwenn mopped the spray off her face and her pizza.

Gwenn thought about how comfortable Mat was is in his environment, so relaxed and free...that must be what it feels like to grow up in one place.

One time Gwenn's family had actually lived in a place long enough for her to make some friends and fall madly in love. It was their third northern Minnesota house.

She had an actual date with Eric Whitely. Sure it was just a baseball game and Eric's older brother had to drive them, but they held hands all the way there and back. Eric had walked her to the door and into the mudroom, when he dropped her off. Gwenn leaned in hopefully and was richly rewarded. It wasn't her first kiss, but it was the kiss she had been planning for two years.

Eric tasted delicious, like soda and salt and something indescribable. Gwenn imagined kissing him forever. There was just no way she could ever get tired of those lips.

The next day Ed and Shirley announced that god had told them to move to Dul-uth. Gwenn was more than a little pissed at god. On the cusp of womanhood, staring sophomore year in the face, Gwenn was dragged across Minnesota to the bleak harbor town of Dul-uth. Gwenn liked to emphasize the *Dull*. Looking back, she had to admit, that was the day she stopped believing good things could happen to her. She learned to value herself less and she didn't value her body at all. The only thing that kept her from total self-annihilation was the looming, Shirley-implanted specter of some supernatural being secretly watching her every move. What if some ominous, eternal tattletale was just waiting to show the movie of her secret life to all her friends and family?

She had heard the sermons twice a week for as long as she could remember, she had attended Sunday school every week. Eventually Pastor Ed and Shirley had added a weekly Bible study to the agenda. It was like brainwashing—subtle, slow and irresistible.

Gwenn had spent years trying to debrief herself, and she finally understood her aching need for freedom on a whole new level. She just wanted to lose herself in this place...to start over...to love herself, fearlessly.

Gwenn was looking for a beach when she saw the sign for a Kauri Tree Park—that sounded interesting.

She was immediately struck by the massive girth of the kauri trees. They reminded her of redwoods, but not as tall. The sign read "center growth 7.62 m," Gwenn attempted to convert metric to Imperial, but sadly, like most of her American compatriots she had only toyed with the metric system in school, not really taken it seriously.

"It would take ten or 12 people holding hands in a circle to make a ring around this thing." Gwenn patted the bark with admiration. Wouldn't it be nice if someone appreciated her natural talents instead of waiting for her to become a doctor or a lawyer? She patted the tree again, conspiratorially, "Nice job on the growing."

"Thanks Miss," said a disembodied voice.

Gwenn's eyes widened and she stepped back from the tree, and ran directly into John, the owner of the park.

"Oh, sorry, I thought—never mind—hello." Gwenn hurriedly tried to cover up her tree-hugging.

"There's a Bush Walk through the trees—just over there," pointed John.

"Thank you." Gwenn strode swiftly to the raised boardwalk that serpentined through the forest. The colors were rich and moist—it felt like a jungle. There were so many shades of green, so many textures and smells. Gwenn sat down on the boardwalk and looked up through the leaves of a silver fern tree. It was like looking into another world. She expected a tardy rabbit to hop hastily by at any moment.

Gwenn thought about the Henry debacle and her strange history with men. She leaned down, brushed some leaves off the walkway and lay down on her back. The sun was filtering through the canopy and illuminating drops of dew, scattered like tiny jewels across the underbrush. The quiet was mesmerizing. Time stood still. There was only Gwenn in the forest; the rest of the world had ceased to exist. She lay there for a long time, finding new joy in each frond, each leaf, each ray of sunshine. This was the most peaceful she had felt since she ran out of Dr. Watkins' office.

The magic was fractured—reality came rolling back, like an ugly thunderhead across the plains.

"Time to hit the road. Thanks for the moment," Gwenn spread her arms magnanimously to include the entire forest in her gratitude.

Gwenn continued to drive up the peninsula. She tried a couple of stops, but didn't even get out of the car. She drove through a few tiny towns and meandered along the coast.

The sun poked its head out from behind a cloud and lit up the bay like a sea of crushed diamonds. The tide was very low and lots of sand bars were poking through the shimmering surface.

"Yes." Gwenn immediately parked the car. Then she spent ten minutes slathering her lily-white, northern-Minnesota girl skin with SPF 100 sunscreen.

She ran down to the beach pulling her wrap around her waist. Gwenn struggled to remember the name; *sarong, sari, or what did they call it in Fiji? Was it a sulu?* She settled on, "Piece of fabric, possibly with an 'S' name," and felt it billowing out behind her as she moved.

When Gwenn reached the beach she hesitated and crouched down in amazement. There was no sand, well none to speak of. The beach was packed solid with shells—millions and millions of shells, as far as the eye could see. She waded out through the warm, ankle-deep water only to find that the *sandbars* were just huge mounds of shells. Gwenn grinned hungrily. She loved to collect shells.

She made a little basket by pulling the bottom of her shirt out and up, and filled it with treasures. The intricate shell mosaics reminded her of Native American sand paintings or Tibetan mandalas, she was consumed by the maze of beauty.

The sun was sinking behind her and a hearty growl from her stomach reminded her "woman cannot live by shells alone." Hours had passed and Gwenn had thought of nothing; nothing but the joy of shells. For a moment she had been free. She had to bring the shells home, she had to have a piece of this place—a connection to the freedom.

Gwenn went to the market to buy some dinner and find some containers to protect her shells on the long flight home.

Thirty-three

Todd was pleased to see Dawn's car disappearing around the corner as he approached Daniel's house. He was thrilled to see Frankie's car in the driveway. Todd pulled into the garage and got out of the BMW.

Frankie was standing beside his car in the driveway, in February, in nothing but swim trunks. Todd shook his head in disbelief as he noticed that not a single shiver dared to disturb Frankie's menacingly muscular frame.

Todd tried to imagine being the guy who threw the flying, leg-scissor into a heel-hook that put Frankie in the submission hold that had ended his career.

If Frankie had just tapped out—but Frankie didn't tap out and the cracking of his femur had sounded like a gunshot in the arena. His knee had also been dislocated, and there had been extreme ACL and MCL damage. The doctors told Frankie that eight to ten months of physical therapy could get him 50-60% usage. Of course, Frankie got 80-90% back in three months, but he would never be able to compete for the title. Instead of feeling sorry for himself, Frankie the Big Bang Anderson, capitalized on his notoriety and opened a gym in Minneapolis. It was an overnight success, and Frankie hired the cream of the crop in martial arts, weight lifting and yoga to run the place while he took on a very limited number of wealthy private clients. Frankie's private clients were like family and he helped them anyway, anytime.

"Frankie, thanks for coming. Can you please help me get Mr. Gregory out of the car and into the shower?" Todd gestured to the semi-conscious mass of humanity in the back seat.

"No sweat, you get the doors, I'll get the dude."

Todd opened the car door and Frankie grabbed Daniel, slid him out of the car and over his shoulder into a fireman's carry.

Even Todd was impressed. "Nicely done."

The odd little procession worked its way up to the master bath. Frankie stepped directly into the walk-in shower, turned on both showerheads, and placed Daniel squarely in the line of fire.

It is a testament to Frankie's loyalty and professionalism that he resisted the urge to heel-hook Daniel after an inebriated fist connected with Frankie's left eye.

"Todd, dude, you're gonna need to talk him down. He's all rock 'em sock 'em robots in here," chuckled Frankie.

"Mr. Gregory? Mr. Gregory? Can you hear me?"

"Todd zat you?" Daniel's eyes squinted painfully against the sun streaming through the skylight. "Nice hair," a drunken gurgle escaped Daniel's lips.

"Dude he's gonna chunder!" Unshakable Frankie sounded a bit quivery.

"Not to worry Frankie. I believe that was a laugh. You see Mr. Gregory is a professional, tragedy-induced, binge drinker. He rarely, as you say, chunders." Todd continued his efforts to contact the Daniel trapped within the drunk.

"Mr. Gregory," Todd peeked around the wall of the walk-in shower, "Mr. Gregory, I'm over here. I need you to cooperate with Frankie. I need you to wake up. I'm going to make you some coffee."

"Black, like I like my men!" more gurgling.

"Dude is he a fag?" Frankie was once again shaken by this unpredictable opponent.

"Not to worry Frankie, Mr. Gregory is a good old boy. Likes to bang chicks as much as the next guy." Todd hoped he had used the proper jargon. He knew it wasn't exactly true, but he also knew it would appease Frankie's homophobia.

"Cool." Frankie was emboldened by this latest piece of information. "Put out a robe or somethin', I'll bring him down in a few."

"We're not paying you enough Frankie."

"Dude, you so will. You so will." Frankie exclaimed.

Todd checked the work Dawn had performed, and when he was satisfied that the house was alcohol-free and the wine cellar was secured, he busied himself in the kitchen.

Todd was about to go back upstairs when Frankie emerged, supporting a soggy—but conscious—Daniel.

"Please sit down Mr. Gregory. Drink the water first and eat as much of the sandwich as possible." Todd confirmed that Daniel was cooperating and turned his attention to Frankie.

"You are a saint."

"Just helpin' a friend man," smiled Frankie.

"Of course, thank you. I know I don't have to say it, but none of this leaves the house. I can count on you, right?"

"Dude, you know my motto, 'what happens with Frankie, stays with Frankie.'" A huge grin spread across Frankie's face and he flexed his pecs to emphasize his tagline.

"Isn't that Las Vegas' motto?" Todd asked sarcastically.

"Whatever dude, I dig it."

"Regardless, thank you for the confidentiality Frankie. I'll call you tomorrow." Todd pointed to the puddle forming around Frankie's feet and gestured toward the door.

"Sorry dude, later," and Frankie was gone.

He was surprisingly quick and graceful. Todd marveled at the thought of Frankie blindsiding an opponent with a roundhouse to the head. He seemed so kind. Although, Todd had never had the occasion to piss him off—thank heaven for small favors.

"So sorry, really, so sorry," Daniel forced the words past the partially masticated turkey sandwich bits in his mouth.

"This is not a pity party Mr. Gregory. This is a confessional. Now I want you to tell me exactly what happened in New Zealand."

When Daniel described the moonlit scene on the bridge at the Botanical Gardens, Todd cringed. "I'm very sorry Mr. Gregory."

"Not a pity party...remember," Daniel forced a wistful half-smile.

"Do you think there is any possibility you misinterpreted things?"

"Todd don't patronize me, I saw them...lovers' embrace, intimate kisses...I saw it," Daniel's voice was hurt and angry.

"No, Mr. Gregory, I mean before, with Ms. Hutchinson."
Todd tried to be gentle.

Daniel forced himself to think back over the brief
moments he had shared with Gwenn. She had been
confused and preoccupied, but the spark was real. The
connection could not be trivialized.

"She was focused on different things, I felt a connection
Todd. There was something between us."

"Why this woman Mr. Gregory? There are plenty of
women in Minneapolis. Why are you obsessing about
this one?"

"I'm not obsessing."

"You flew to New Zealand. Do I need more proof?" Todd
was shaking his head.

"No."

"Then why? Why her? Why now?"

"When I look at her I see her, only her. There's not
even a hint of Angeline—no trace." Daniel's eyes begged
Todd to understand.

That was all Todd needed to hear. "Excuse me Mr.
Gregory I'm going to call Rachel, Ms. Hutchinson's sister.
We'll get to the bottom of this."

Todd came back a few moments later grinning like an
idiot. "It appears you missed the main event, Mr. Gregory."

"Todd, if what I saw was the warm-up act, the headliner
would've killed me."

"I doubt that. You see Mr. Gregory, apparently later that
same evening this Henry fellow, 'the bloody wanker' is the
term Rachel used, revealed to your Ms. Hutchinson that he
was a married man," Todd's sardonic smirk punctuated the
last line.

"I'll kill him," Daniel's voice was gravelly and menacing.

"Easy Jesse James. You're an artist not a fighter. Rachel's informed me that Gwenn is continuing her vacation solo and she will be home soon."

"How soon?" Daniel didn't bother to hide his eagerness.

"I suggest we focus on stabilizing your psyche and repairing your liver."

"I do seem to have a pattern," grinned Daniel, guiltily.

"Drink this." Todd handed Daniel a glass of slightly cloudy water.

"Hey, what's this?"

"This is my reward for being the best goddamn assistant in the known universe. Now drink." Todd shoved the glass at Daniel.

"When will I wake up?" Daniel stared at the glass nervously.

"When I've outlined an appropriate plan for continuing this single-minded pursuit of Ms. Hutchinson."

"Todd, if you were a woman I'd kiss you on the lips."

"Yes, and then drink yourself into oblivion upon my rejection. Better if we avoided that spiral."

Daniel took the glass and chugged the contents down. Ignoring the bitter taste of Todd's secret ingredient.

"All right, Step 4 complete, good. Now get up to bed. I've got to grab some things from my place and make a few calls. I'll be back in an hour or two."

Daniel's eyes inadvertently shot to the wet bar in the den.

"There is no alcohol in the house," Todd's voice was firm.

Daniel was helpless as his eyes flicked toward the basement and the wine cellar.

"Locked. I also have the spare key," added Todd smugly.

"I'm going to bed. The worst is over. I can manage."

"Mr. Gregory I plan to call Dr. Watkins for a referral. You have never bothered to take my advice before, but you cannot proceed with Ms. Hutchinson without benefit of a therapist. Binge drinking is not a healthy response to tragedy. Agreed?"

"Agreed." Daniel put his hand on his forehead, "I feel dizzy."

Todd was instantly by his side, arm around Daniel's waist. "Okay let me help you up to bed."

Thirty-four

Rachel couldn't be bothered with typing. She didn't give a crap about time zones or phone charges.

"Gwenny? Gwenny wake up! It's me, Rache."

"Rachel it's 6:00 p.m. here. I've been awake for hours. Why are you calling? I said e-mail—this Vodafone is so expensive."

"Screw e-mail, this news can't wait—"

"Let me guess, Danica's leaving her husband?"

"How rude! I took your advice and broke it off with her, anyway it's not about me—"

"Shocking."

"Fine, I won't tell you, brat."

"Sorry Rache, go ahead."

"Daniel saw you. He was at the Gardens, he saw you."

"I never saw him. Why didn't he say something?"

"Todd said it was an intimate moment, Daniel was hurt and angry."

"Intimate—what?" Gwenn searched her mind, unwilling to think back to that night. One time on the bridge...she had thought she heard footsteps... "Oh no."

"What? What did he see?"

"Right before Henry—the bloody wanker—broke my heart, things were pretty cozy, embracing, whispering, you know." Gwenn shuddered at the uncomfortable memory.

"And..."

"I thought I heard footsteps—if Daniel saw that—yikes!"

"Yeah, yikes. What are you gonna do?" Rachel was secretly rooting for Daniel.

"I'm not sure. I'll have a long plane ride to sort it all out."

"You're comin' home?" Rachel didn't even bother to hide her excitement.

"I'll find a pay phone at Bradley International, after I clear customs. Thanks Rache."

"I miss you Gwenny."

"I miss you, too. Bye. Rache."

Gwenn hung up the phone and pondered her options. Did she really want a man in her life? She couldn't deny the pleasure of spending time with Henry, before he became Henry the bloody wanker. But she was just finding herself and she didn't want this fragile New Gwenn to be swallowed up by a new relationship—or worse, beaten to death by bitter, fearful Old Gwenn.

Rachel threw her head back onto her pillows and kicked her smooth, toned legs in the air. Gwenny was coming home. Everything was going to be okay. She thought about her next move, but the choice was easy—she had to call Todd.

"Hey Todd, it's Rachel again."

"Rachel, I told you—"

"Gwenn's comin' back!" Rachel was too excited to wait for Todd's over-protective Daniel speech.

"When?" Todd was on high alert, his entire body tense and ready for action.

"She's getting on a plane today...which is tomorrow over there...so I think that means she'll be home tomorrow here...because that would be—"

"Yes Rachel, I am familiar with the machinations of the time space continuum."

"Pull the stick outta your ass Todd. I just thought you would wanna know, Daniel sounded a bit splintered."

"He's agreed to get some help, I was planning to make the call tomorrow...but now..." Todd's mind was racing through the variables on several separate scenarios.

"You want Dr. Mountainside, she's the best. Daniel would need to stay in Duluth, but she'll see him twice a day in the beginning and she's a totally straight shooter."

"Personal recommendation?" Todd casually inquired.

"Oh yeah! You see, Todd, I'm a lesbian and that doesn't get a lotta press in northern Minnesota," chuckled Rachel. "I could've moved to a big city to find a community, but I actually love it here, and I was miserable...you know denying reality and all."

"So you sought help?"

"No way, Gwenny made me go. I hated her for months, but after Dr. Mountainside finished blowing holes in my facade and helped me get in touch with the real Rachel—I can never repay Gwenny for gettin' me through that."

"I understand." Although Todd had never had someone care for him in that way, he knew the satisfaction of helping someone through dark days.

"I guess that's why I'm on Daniel's side. I want something good for her, something real. I get that he's got issues...everyone's got issues...but I think he loves her in a way that can't be manufactured." Rachel's voice was hopeful and insistent.

"I think you may be right, about several things," Todd couldn't resist adding, "except of course the time continuum thing."

"Ya know, you're a lot like the brother I never wanted—maybe we should have a DNA test." Rachel was impressed with Todd, once again. He was highly efficient and remarkably witty—maybe an android.

Rachel gave Todd the necessary information on Dr. Mountainside, including the cell number, for emergencies. She decided to get some sleep before the call of the dough forced her out of bed at 4:00 a.m. Why had she given Nathan the day off? Arghh.

Her dreams were full of dough-related disasters. There was a wedding cake that wouldn't rise and ended up looking like a stack of frosted pancakes—bride not happy. Then the bread dough wouldn't stop rising and flowed off the table and filled the entire bakery, the doors were locked and Rachel couldn't get out. Annie was on the outside of the door trying to break in, but the insatiable sourdough was smothering Rachel's screams.

Rachel woke up gasping for air 10 minutes before her alarm was supposed to go off. How rude!

Rachel couldn't help but eye the bread dough suspiciously as she left it to proof. She nearly burned the custard as she imagined Annie breaking down the door and giving her mouth-to-mouth, saving her from a doughy death.

The chocolate and blonde brownies were far more cooperative and the carrot cookies practically frosted themselves. By the time Mike arrived with the donut delivery all memory of the dough that ate Duluth was gone.

"Thanks, Mike. These look spectacular."

"No problem Miss Hutchinson."

"My sister's Miss Hutchinson, call me Rachel." Did that sound flirty? It wasn't meant to be flirty...certainly Mike knew...oh crap.

"Thanks, Rachel." Mike smiled, "Can I ask you something?"

Rachel decided it would be better to nip this in the bud. "Mike, I'm flattered, but I'm also gay." There, quick as lightning. He wouldn't even be embarrassed, she had spared him that much.

Mike's huge, belly laugh deeply confounded Saint Rachel.

"I was going to ask you why you don't just make your own donuts—is it a gay thing?" Mike continued laughing.

"Touché. I deserved that." Rachel bowed to the victor. "Sorry I jumped to...I didn't sleep too much last night. Does that excuse work for you?" Rachel smiled weakly.

"No sweat, it was funny." Mike smiled and shook his head, still chuckling under his breath. "But, seriously, why don't you just make the donuts?"

"I really hate donuts...and deep fryers. I love to bake, to make almost every imaginable delectable desert, but I just can't stand making donuts. The fat kid in me doesn't like to be reminded of the bad ol' days. I had a serious addiction," Rachel chuckled.

Mike just shrugged his shoulders.

"I know it's weird. If it was up to me I wouldn't even sell donuts, but old Mrs. Lindstrom insists," offered Rachel. "Thanks again." She turned to go.

"Thanks for the laugh," Mike waved. "I think it's fair to warn you I'll be repeating the story."

"I wouldn't have expected any less. To the victor go the spoils and all." Rachel waved and got back to work.

Thirty-five

Gwenn ate the last of her chicken Kiev with savory, mushroom rice and marveled at the shock of great tasting airplane food. The Pavlova with passion fruit sauce and whipped cream sounded divine. She decided on coffee with dessert, not just because they proudly served Starbucks, but also because she desperately needed to stay awake and organize her life.

The Pavlova did not disappoint. She must remember to tell Rachel about this desert. Rachel could probably—*Focus. Stop procrastinating and focus.* Easier said than done.

Gwenn dutifully extracted her notebook and her mind flashed to a picture of Pastor Ed reverently writing his sermon in his notebook. He made such an effort to appear pious and he made sure his family appeared equally holy.

As dark as her sinful doings were behind the scenes, Gwenn was a perfect preacher's daughter at church. She sang in the choir, she prayed fervently and she was in church twice every Sunday. The fact that there were several eligible boys at church was pure coincidence. After all, Shirley had always taught Gwenn that appearances were far more important than reality. Gwenn *appeared* to be a good Christian.

It was only after her father, Ed, had accepted the Associate Pastor position that he began harping on Gwenn to date "nice Christian boys."

Anyone who wanted to date Gwenn had to come to her house and be interviewed by her dad. It was embarrassing and made Gwenn feel completely unsure of her instincts—when it came to dating. So, she always pushed the limits, just to see if Pastor Ed would ever reject one of her suitors.

"So, Kent, where do your parents go to church?" Pastor Ed asked meaningfully.

"Um, I don't know my dad, he left when I was three. My mom has to work weekends," Kent answered honestly.

"How is your walk with the Lord?" Ed was eager to ask his favorite question.

"Okay, I guess," Kent looked confused.

"What are your intentions with Gwenn?" Ed leaned forward and gave his patented 'I can see your soul' look.

"Just a movie," Kent shrugged.

"Have her home by midnight Kent. And if you ever need to talk to anyone about your relationship with Jesus Christ, just give me a call," Ed smiled a pastorly smile.

"Okay, see ya," Kent walked out of the living room, shrugged his shoulders at Gwenn and they bolted out to his truck; the back of which was half full of smashed beer cans. Kent was an amazing kisser.

Those were the days, when rebellion consisted of the simple act of dating a known drug dealer from school. Now there wasn't really anyone to rebel against. The relationship playing field was littered with hidden emotional landmines and everyone came with so much damn baggage. What was the point?

Gwenn decided to take control of her tornado of a love life. She double-checked her astrological info: the moon was waning – good time to prepare for a new project; the moon was in Scorpio – good time for self-examination and getting rid of old things; and since she was kind of traveling back in time the moon would still be in Libra from Minnesota's perspective – a good sign for relationship issues. It was time to make a decision that was just for her—no pressure, no guilt and no limits. She drew two columns in her notepad, "Pros" in the left-hand column and "Cons" in the right-hand column. Pros and cons of what? How about Daniel? How about...no. Gwenn decided to start with the pros and cons of remaining single. The pros were easy.

No one to answer to—no one to compromise with—no one to limit freedoms—no one to clean up after. Gwenn wrote a few more, but as she looked over the list only one thing was clear. "No one!" That kind of sounded like a con.

Alone—lonely—no one to share old movies with—no one to share romantic dinners—no lingering kisses—no long embraces—no sex *(well, no great, toy-free sex)*—no long walks at Park Point—no canoeing in the Boundary Waters...

The cons were so plentiful that Gwenn had to admit she was writing things she wouldn't even do. Canoeing! Get a grip. She hadn't canoed since she was a kid at Gramma Carlson's in the summer. But the long walks at Park Point would be missed. Daniel's place was on Park Point—time for the next list. Heading "Daniel as Best Friend." Subheadings "Pros/Cons."

Gwenn decided to start with the cons. Blow this whole stupid idea out of the water and never even have to bother with pros. Good thinking Gwenn, she patted herself on the back.

Cons...her pen doodled of its own accord. Cons...he's too...hmmm...he's never...well, he isn't...come on. Gwenn couldn't really think of anything, but she chalked that up to hardly knowing him. Ah ha!

Cons—hardly know him.

Now she was grasping at straws. The entire point of a friendship was getting to know someone better. Gwenn angrily scraped a line through the con.

Fine, she looked toward the pros column.

His hair screams to be touched—his chest looks big and safe—his stomach is flat and probably toned (*maybe six-packish*).

She imagined what might lie beneath his shirt. She could almost feel his smooth, hard chest and the ripples of muscle as she slid her hand down his abdomen. With a flick of her thumb and finger she could release the button on the jeans...whoa!

She added *tingly* to the pros column and rang the attendant for some ice water.

Friends? What could it hurt? She owed it to herself to at least give Daniel a chance.

Thirty-six

He awoke slowly, his head felt tight and his brain felt like all the water had been squeezed out. Daniel looked at the clock on the nightstand, 2:23 a.m. He reached for the glass of water, undoubtedly left by Todd, to rehydrate his cerebral cortex. He imagined one of those gimmicky children's toys, something mysterious squeezed into a tiny capsule, and when it's dropped into hot water a three-inch dinosaur-shaped sponge magically emerges. Mostly though, he just thought *water good.*

Daniel didn't have to look to know that Todd was asleep in the next room. He knew that if he got up and made even the tiniest peep of noise Todd would instantly be at his side. It was hard to remember when Todd went from world's finest assistant to Daniel's best friend, but it was a fact that Daniel treasured. Todd refused to dispense with the formalities, Mr. Gregory, and all that crap. Daniel accepted it as a necessary eccentricity.

Todd heard the glass slide off the nightstand, before he even opened his eyes. He listened intently for Daniel to get up or go back to sleep. Todd cared for Daniel like a brother, but kept the formalities of their business relationship for one important reason; Personal Assistant Todd could say just about anything and his opinions were well respected. Todd was quite sure that a best friend or brother could be far more easily overruled.

When Todd heard Daniel rollover and settle in, he gave himself permission to go back to sleep for about five more hours. He would need to get up early to give himself time to run down to the Gallery and grab a few files before he packed Daniel's bags and made them both some breakfast.

The first thing he did when he got to the Gallery, was call Dr. Mountainside and make arrangements.

"Hello, Dr. Mountainside, how can I help?" Brenda Mountainside was a petite, firebrand of a woman. Her short, salt-and-pepper pixie haircut and her bright, sparkling eyes gave her a slightly elvish look—Tolkien's elves not Santa's. She shopped almost exclusively from the Spiegel catalog and she wore only two-inch heels, not one, not three...two, always two. She kept to a strictly neutral palette with the occasional brightly colored accent scarf or vintage bauble. From head to perfectly pedicured toe, Dr. Mountainside radiated professionalism. See no crap, hear no crap, speak no crap. Todd would've fallen at her feet in worship, if only he could have seen her through the phone.

"Good morning Dr. Mountainside, this is Mr. Gregory's assistant Todd. Rachel Hutchinson gave me this number, and we do have a rather urgent situation."

"Aah, Rachel, I'm glad she gave you my number. What is Mr. Gregory's situation Todd?" Brenda had dealt with assistants before; they seldom did more than make appointments for their wealthy patrons.

"I will summarize the current situation as briefly as possible and I will give you a few important emotional events from Mr. Gregory's past that will help give you perspective on the current debacle." Todd paused for permission to continue.

"I have 30 minutes until my first session, please begin." Brenda smiled; she may have under estimated Todd.

Todd described the situation with Gwenn, hitting all the high points. The strangers flirting at the bar, the potentially incestuous feelings at the first meeting and the results of the DNA test which allowed those feelings to blossom into the possibility of love, on Daniel's side. Then he outlined the pursuit to New Zealand and the ensuing tragic tryst witnessed by Mr. Gregory.

"Todd, is there really a Mr. Gregory or are you Mr. Gregory?" Brenda was suspicious of the emotional detail Todd was accessing.

"Dr. Mountainside, I am Mr. Gregory's personal assistant and the only family he has. I kept him afloat after the loss of his first wife Angeline, the love of his life, and I kept his head above the rim of the glass after his father passed away four years ago. Mr. Gregory is a gifted but tortured artist, Ms. Hutchinson is the first woman who has allowed him to let go, even temporarily, of the memory of Angeline. Will you or will you not take him on as a client?" Todd struggled to keep his tone all business, but the effort of keeping Daniel safe, again, was wearing on him.

"Todd I'd like to offer you a sincere apology. You are truly an amazing friend to Mr. Gregory, together we can get him through this."

"Thank you." Todd exhaled, swallowed and felt his shoulders relax an eighth of an inch, or so.

"You seem extraordinarily efficient Todd, but I must ask. Have you removed all alcohol from Mr. Gregory's home?"

"Those of us closest to Mr. Gregory know the drill, Dr. Mountainside. The housekeeper took care of that while I picked Mr. Gregory up from the airport."

"I am going to enjoy having you on the team, Todd. Mr. Gregory can sign a release so that I may inform you of any support he might need. Can we schedule something today?"

"Of course, I will pack his things and we will be at the Park Point property by noon." Todd was already forming a checklist in his mind.

"How does 2:00 p.m. sound, Todd?"

"We'll be there, and thank you Dr. Mountainside."

Todd tapped *End* and sprang into action.

Daniel had been sound asleep when Todd refilled his water glass and silently slipped from the house. So it was with much surprise and a little consternation that Todd found Daniel making breakfast when he returned.

"Morning Todd. I thought I'd make some pancakes," Daniel smiled.

"And you can actually make pancakes?"

"Todd, I manage to eat several meals each week without your supervision."

"No you don't." Todd's tone was matter-of-fact, but his eyes were smiling.

"Okay, but I can make pancakes."

"We'll soon find out." Todd busied himself with table setting and syrup warming—only looking over Daniel's shoulder twice to see that the pancake operation was proceeding successfully.

"After breakfast I'll get things packed up and we can drive up to Duluth." Todd was casually making sure that Daniel was still on board with the agreement of yesterday.

"What time is my appointment?"

"Two o'clock, sharp."

"You make it sound like I have a problem with timeliness, Todd."

"Well, you're no Old Faithful, if that's what you wanted to hear."

"I'm reliable..."

"There is a difference between doing what you say, and doing what you say *when* you say you will do it."

"That was a mouthful, Todd," laughed Daniel.

Todd smiled at the sound of Daniel's laugh. "We'll get through this, I think you'll really like Dr. Mountainside."

"How much did you tell her?" Daniel's tone became serious.

"I gave her the Little Golden Books version of everything." Todd met Daniel's gaze with steady, caring eyes.

"Good. Then we can jump right in." Daniel shoveled a forkful of pancakes into his mouth and grinned at Todd, "Pretty good, eh?"

"They're surprisingly delicious, a function of the extraordinary syrup warming I'd imagine." Todd was pleased to hear Daniel's muffled laugh filter through a mouthful of pancakes. "Alright Mr. Gregory you clean up the kitchen and I'll pack the bags. Will you need workout stuff? Do you want Frankie to come up?"

"I dreamed I took a shower with Frankie...weird, huh."

"That was not a dream Mr. Gregory, that was yesterday."

"So...then...I must've dreamed—did I punch him?"

"Squarely in the left eye. Fortunately, Frankie is a real, live saint and opted to let you live." Todd looked gravely at Daniel.

"Shit he could've massacred me." Daniel's eyes widened at the thought of an angry Frankie the Big Bang Anderson letting loose on him in the confines of a shower. Daniel swallowed hard, "Call 'em, Todd. I gotta apologize. Tell him I want him in Duluth for sessions on Tuesdays and Thursdays, he can stay at a hotel...on me...or he can drive back and forth. Whatever he wants, I owe him."

Todd had them packed, loaded in the car and backing out of the garage at 10:00 a.m. sharp.

Thirty-seven

Gwenn had been through the passport station and was waiting at the luggage carousel. She saw the drug dog sniffing people's bags and worried that her secret shells might be contraband. Suddenly the dog froze in front of a middle-aged man. The dog barked once and lunged for the man's crotch. Two additional DEA officers appeared out of nowhere and took the man into custody.

Gwenn chuckled to herself at the idiocy of smuggling a *fatty* in one's undershorts, and laughed even harder when she got her own joke.

Her colorful, beribboned bag appeared in the sea of black and blue suitcases, and Gwenn jockeyed for position. An incredibly rude man in a fancy suit would not budge an inch. Gwenn's bag was rapidly approaching, she felt panic welling up in her stomach. She was mumbling and exhaling as she searched for a weak link in the chain of carousel brigands. A little old woman, perfect.

"Harvey get the cart! I see it." The booming voice that issued from that small, unassuming woman, threw Gwenn off balance. She backed into Harvey and the luggage cart, falling squarely on her ass on top of the cart.

"Harvey! You're gonna miss it!" yelled scary old woman.

"I got some clumsy broad in my way!" Harvey hollered back. "Do ya mind, kid?" Harvey wiggled the cart impatiently.

A strong, feminine hand came out of nowhere. Gwenn reached for it in desperation. The hand pulled her free of Harvey's luggage cart just as scary old woman let out another bellow.

"Damn it Harvey! You missed it. You couldn't shoot fish in a barrel!"

Gwenn looked at her rescuer and was surprised to see a lovely mane of blond hair surrounding a scintillating set of almond-shaped eyes.

"I believe this is yours?" Asian, savior woman presented Gwenn's suitcase.

"Thanks. I thought I was a goner. The Boca Raton mafia is more dangerous than they look," Gwenn gestured toward the octogenarians.

"Yes, you could've ended up as Harvey's love slave!" They both cracked up laughing.

"I'm Gwenn, by the way."

"I'm Lucy."

"Thanks again Lucy. The carousels always freak me out. I think that if I don't get my bag on the first pass, they'll grab it and ship it off to lost luggage and—"

"I was going to ask if you wanted to grab a cup of coffee, but I may have to insist on decaf for you." Lucy's smile was broad and inviting; her teeth were perfect.

"I have to get over to the North by Northwest terminal, but thanks for the offer." Gwenn smiled, self-conscious of her slightly crooked bottom teeth and her less than pure-white chompers, she opted for a lips-together grin.

"Hey, me to. I'm on my way to Chicago, via Minneapolis, for some reason only my assistant could explain."

"Oh, I have to buy a ticket for Minneapolis, maybe I can get on your flight."

"Follow me Gwenn." Lucy pulled up the handle on her rolling case and walked confidently out of customs.

Gwenn admired Lucy's black, strappy sandals and khaki, capri pants. Gwenn remembered that Lucy had been surprisingly strong during the rescue. Her build was rather slight, almost waif-like, but those angular shoulders and slender arms had saved the day. Gwenn hurried after Lucy, who obviously knew exactly where she was going.

Lucy ended up switching her ticket to a direct to Chicago, and gave her seat on the sold-out Minneapolis flight to Gwenn.

"Are you sure I can't pay you something for switching the ticket?" Gwenn insisted.

"Don't worry about it Gwenn. My company will pick it up. They love me," laughed Lucy.

"What do you do?" Gwenn wondered what kind of employer could overlook several hundred dollars in airline tickets.

"I'm in International Relations for one of the largest pharmaceutical conglomerates in the world."

"Oh," Gwenn nodded, understanding completely. "At least let me buy you some lunch before my flight."

"I would love to have lunch with you Gwenn, but I'll pay."

"But..."

"Gwenn, I sold my soul to the devil for a fancy office, a company limousine on call, and an unlimited expense account. My random acts of kindness are just my little efforts to try to balance out my karma." Lucy shrugged her shoulders and smiled, "So, you'll be doing me a favor if you let me pay."

"Well, if your soul's at stake!" laughed Gwenn.

Lunch in the North by Northwest Captains Club was delicious. Lucy was fascinating and funny. Gwenn was unable to imagine how Lucy could be single.

"You're gorgeous, and smart and you've got a great job. How can you be single?"

"By choice."

"But, don't you get lonely?"

"I'm not a vestal virgin Gwenn, I'm just single," grinned Lucy.

"I...yeah I mean...I assumed," Gwenn paused to collect her thoughts. "Does it ever feel empty, not having someone there?"

"In my twenties I was desperate for a husband. I nearly got married three different times. Somehow I avoided disaster. Now I have a different perspective, I'm totally able to take care of myself. I'm financially independent and I'm surrounded by wonderful people...in my personal life, that is." Lucy was careful to differentiate between her private and work lives.

"Do you have a boyfriend?"

"There are a few men, in various parts of the world, that fill my need for romance and male companionship. But if I want to spend a month in Crete, all by myself...I don't have to get anyone's permission. I mean I have to take work off, but you get my point." Lucy smiled peacefully.

Gwenn took a moment to mull things over. She'd been denying herself the joy of being single. She had allowed Ed and Shirley to make her feel *less than* because she wasn't half of a couple—because she wasn't popping out grandkids. "What about children?" Gwenn blurted.

"I get that a lot," Lucy nodded knowingly. "Technically I have years to make that decision, but the reality is I'm not sure I'm ever going to be ready. I like my life. I mean, I like kids, I have nieces and nephews and I spoil them rotten and shower them with hugs and kisses, but I don't think I need to have my own child," Lucy paused, "I know it's unusual."

"No, I get it. I've always felt extra pressure because my sister's gay. I felt like I had to carry on the family tree." Gwenn stopped and chuckled, "The more I think about it, I might be doing the world a favor if I pruned this particular tree before Ed and Shirley's DNA pollute anymore branches."

"Your parents are unsupportive?"

"My parents are born-again Christians with a penchant for sitting in judgment over everyone and everything."

"Wow, I thought my mom was bad, when she didn't like my blonde hair," Lucy laughed conspiratorially.

"Oh, don't worry, my mom never liked my hair either, 'it's not my favorite...' which is her code for 'you look awful and I wouldn't be seen in public with you!'" Gwenn shook her finger at an imaginary daughter.

"Gwenn, you're hilarious. I'm so glad you fell on your ass," teased Lucy.

"Me too, my most fortuitous accident to date." Gwenn remembered her horoscope had mentioned something about a wonderful person who could change her life for the better.

Lucy tilted her head and looked at Gwenn, "Where do you work?"

"I'm *The Organizer*. I own my own business in Duluth. I organize stuff...people, homes, businesses...you know," Gwenn was self-deprecating.

"I've actually heard of you! Oh my god! One of the execs used you to organize her summer home on Lake Superior. Small world."

"I hope she was pleased..."

"She raved about you for ever," Lucy nodded approvingly. "I can't believe you're her...*The Organizer*."

"Yes, it's my burden to bear," Gwenn feigned modesty.

"You've got to transfer that name back to the company, if you ever want to have a life."

Gwenn was caught off-guard. "But I—what?"

"Sorry, it's in my nature to streamline operations. If *The Organizer* is associated with you specifically you can never really get away from the business. If you re-brand the business as *The Organizer, Inc.* or whatever, you can train your replacement and be free."

"Do I want to be free? I kinda like my job," Gwenn sounded more defensive than she intended.

"Gwenn, I didn't mean to offend you. I just think life is for living. I tack personal days on to every trip I take for the company. The experiences I've had and the people I've met...well, it makes my life satisfying, ya know?"

Gwenn was surprised to discover that she didn't know, she had just kept herself busy organizing everyone else, so she wouldn't have to look at the monstrous mess her own life had become. "I didn't ever think about things that way. Are you for real? Are you some fairy godmother or something?"

"Serendipity, Gwenn." Lucy smiled and looked at her watch, "You better get to the gate. It was an honor to meet you."

"If you're ever in Duluth…"

"If you ever decide to get out of Duluth…"

"Touché." Gwenn reached out to shake Lucy's hand.

"I feel we're at a point in our relationship where we can hug, Gwenn." Lucy laughed and embraced Gwenn with her shockingly strong arms.

Gwenn hugged back and already missed Lucy. "I'm going to think about what you said, you might not be completely insane."

"Insanity is the true beauty." Lucy maintained a serious expression, for about three seconds, which melted into an impish grin. "Have a great flight Gwenn."

"Yeah, you bet…you too."

***

Rachel was expecting a call from Gwenn, so when the phone rang she answered without thinking.

"Gwenny?"

"Rachel this is yer mother, I thought ya had the caller ID?"

Rachel mouthed a silent "shit" and braced herself. " Hey mom, what's up?"

"What's up, as ya so eloquently put it, is that I've been calling yer sister fer days and she is purposely ignoring my messages," Shirley's self-righteous tone was rising in pitch.

"She lost her phone mom." Rachel had always been blessed with a talent for highly believable lies.

"Oh fer goodness sake. Can't she get another one?" Shirley had been severely inconvenienced and it was important that everyone knew the degree of her suffering.

Rachel's practiced mind kicked into overdrive. "She had to order it online, they didn't have the right one at that tiny store in the mall. It should arrive before she gets back."

"Back? Back from where?" Shirley's tone had turned indignant at the thought of one of her offspring leaving town without her express blessing.

Shit. Shit. Shit. Rachel had allowed herself to get too caught up in the lie and had blended it with some truth. That truth would have to be immediately subverted.

"She had an out-of-town job, I think it was in Grand Rapids? I don't know, I wasn't really listening mom." When lying fails, go for stupidity, Shirley always believed that.

"Well, ya always have been easily distracted." Shirley exhaled one of her patented martyr sighs and continued, "If ya can remember ta tell her I called, I would appreciate it Rachel."

"I'll try, mom. Bye." Rachel hung up before Shirley could release any more venom.

***

Where the hell was Gwenn? She called Gwenn's lost phone in frustration. When Rachel's phone beeped for call-waiting she freaked.

"Hello?"

"Rache, sorry, I got totally sidetracked at LAX. In a good way...I'll fill you in when I get home."

"Gwenny? I was just calling you on the other line," Rachel was still a bit confused.

"Calling me on what? I threw my old phone in the trash...well the trash in my apartment...so I can probably just get it when I get home...but—"

"Never mind freak. When do you get into Minneapolis?"

"Around 10:30 p.m., but then I have to find a flight to Duluth."

"Screw that! I'm pickin' you up. I'll drive around Arrivals till I see you. Wear a big hat."

"I will not!"

"I know, but I like to get you riled up."

"They're calling my flight, Rache, I gotta go."

"See ya in the Mini-apple."

"Um, the airport is actually in St. Paul. Love ya, Rache." Gwenn hung up the pay phone and ran to the gate. She looked back hoping to catch sight of Lucy—but the crabby attendant interrupted her crowd scan.

"Miss, are you boarding or not?" Snotty Voice asked.

Gwenn stifled the sarcastic response forming in her thoughts and managed an, "Umm...I...here," and thrust her boarding pass at Snotty Voice.

Gwenn grabbed a pillow and a blanket from the overhead compartment. Exhaustion was pulling at her like quicksand.

The flight was a blessed blur. Distant snotty voices pedaled soda and coffee but Gwenn just floated blissfully out of reach. She was following a trail of shells that kept winding and winding. Each time she thought she could see the end of the trail, she would come upon another twist or turn. The image abruptly evaporated when the landing gear slammed onto the runway. Gwenn imagined she could already smell the Minnesota air—she remembered who was waiting, Rachel. A small grin pushed at the corners of Gwenn's mouth.

Thirty-eight

The office had lovely lighting. The mournful cry of the harbor foghorn drew Daniel's attention to the windows. The view of the Duluth Harbor would have been nothing short of spectacular, had it not been enshrouded by a thick, pasty fog. Daniel paced nervously in front of the windows as he waited for Dr. Mountainside to finish her current session—he was growing impatient, and no one was coming out of the room.

"Mr. Gregory, you can go in now." The young receptionist was efficient and shy, never actually making eye contact.

Daniel stopped, puzzled, and abruptly proceeded through the door that the receptionist had indicated. As he entered he noticed a second door on the side of the doctor's office, for what he assumed would be his covert exit.

"Mr. Gregory, please come in."

She was older than Daniel had imagined, and yet strangely powerful. Her camel colored dress, punctuated by an eggplant, cashmere scarf, caught the artist's eye. He noticed how the gray pixie-cut hair added energy and movement to her face, while the simple lines of her clothing complemented the calm of the room. The light filtering in through the blinds cast a peaceful glow all around her shoulders. '*Serenity*, oil on canvas' Daniel smiled and sat down.

"Any trouble finding the office, Mr. Gregory?" Dr. Mountainside noticed the lack of response, "Mr. Gregory?"

"No trouble...Todd...fine." Daniel was distracted by the play of light across a small fountain in the corner of her office.

"Mr. Gregory, is something wrong." Dr. Mountainside couldn't read Daniel's expression, but he seemed far away.

"Sorry, I'm just—hey, can you call me Daniel?"

"Of course. Would you prefer to call me Brenda?"

"Yeah, actually I would. Thanks Brenda." Daniel stretched his arms and leaned back into the chair.

"You're welcome, Daniel. Have you done any previous work with a therapist?"

"No, I did some AA meetings for awhile, Todd forced me, but it turns out I'm not an alcoholic. It seems that alcohol is just my chosen anesthetic during intense emotional pain. Todd says it's because I refuse to face the pain and move through it. He's probably right...he's always right," Daniel chuckled.

Brenda made a few quick notes. "Todd seems like more than an assistant? Are you two involved?"

"What? Oh...no, no...I mean I support people having the choice or whatever. It's just not my choice." Daniel's eyes darted around the room as he struggled to make his, "hey I'm straight," point without sounding like a bigot. "Todd's like a brother, a best friend and business partner...mostly a brother..." Daniel looked Brenda squarely in her blue-green eyes, "That's the one thing you can never tell him."

"I understand." Brenda made another quick entry on her notepad. "Daniel, why are you here?"

"Mostly because of this whole situation with Gwenn, I guess." Daniel shrugged his shoulders helplessly.

"Tell me about Gwenn," Brenda smiled encouragingly. Brenda could've listened to Daniel's story all day. He painted pictures with his words. She could see the outfit Gwenn wore at the bar and imagine the way the strobing lights played tricks on Daniel's eyes, making Gwenn seem much younger than her actual years. Brenda felt Daniel's awe when he saw Gwenn at his doorstep and her beauty took his breath away. Brenda experienced his longing for a sister...and his loss after the DNA test.

"Daniel, when did you decide you loved Gwenn, as more than a sister?"

"When I opened my front door. I was crushed when I thought she might be my sister. I mean I longed for family, but my feelings for her were already way down the road in the other direction. I felt pretty uncomfortable."

"Did you tell Gwenn how you felt?" Brenda's eyes searched Daniel's face.

He looked away, "I couldn't." Daniel shook his head, "She wanted the test results to be positive, she wanted a new family more than anything."

"And when the test results came back?"

"She ran away, just disappeared. I couldn't take it. I had to find her, I was so worried." Daniel looked at Brenda, "Todd says I obsessed."

"In a manner of speaking," smiled Brenda. "So you flew off to New Zealand to find Gwenn," Brenda waited for Daniel's confirmation. "What did you plan to say to her?"

"I didn't plan to say anything." Daniel's eyes drifted off to a faraway place. "I just planned to hold her while she cried—to stroke her velvety, auburn hair and kiss her porcelain forehead. I just wanted to be the reason she stopped crying...I wanted..."

"You wanted her to love you." Brenda's voice was filled with compassion.

"Is that wrong?" Daniel's eyes begged for absolution.

"No Daniel, it's not wrong. The issue isn't about right or wrong, the issue is finding a common ground. You and Gwenn are in very different emotional spaces. She has lost a father that she has dreamed of for decades. You have lost a lover that you never knew you needed."

"What do you mean common ground?"

"In order for Gwenn to see you as a potential partner, she has to stop seeing you as a brother, or rather a representation of the family she should've had. Do you understand?"

Daniel nodded, "But how do I do that?"

"You can't. Gwenn has to do it for herself."

Daniel's shoulders slumped in discouragement and he put his head in his hands.

"Daniel, this is a wonderful opportunity for you to get to know Gwenn." Brenda smiled at Daniel, "Bring her into your world, allow her to get to know the real Daniel Gregory. In time the new experiences she has will replace the old images she had created and she will be able to see you for who you truly are, a caring, compassionate man," Brenda paused, "who happens to be in love with her."

"Sounds easy enough." Daniel's tone was a bit sarcastic, "So, what do I owe you?"

"Daniel, I would like to continue seeing you, working through the process together."

"No, it's okay. I get it, take it slow, don't push her...it's pretty straightforward." Daniel slid toward the edge of the chair, preparing to leave.

"I'd like to see you tomorrow at 10:00 a.m." Brenda's penetrating gaze gave Daniel pause.

"Seriously, I think we covered it all." Daniel hoped his voice sounded more confident than he felt.

"Daniel, I would really like to hear about Angeline tomorrow." Brenda looked deeply into Daniel's eyes. One blue, one brown...interesting. "If you're willing to share that with me."

Daniel collapsed back into the chair, the soft leather made a small creaking sound, "Boy, Todd didn't leave out anything...did he?"

"Todd is an exceptionally observant individual. Will I see you tomorrow?"

"Yeah, Todd will make sure I'm here." Daniel shook his head; he knew when he'd been beaten.

"Thank you Daniel," Brenda extended her hand.

"Thanks Doc," Daniel grinned sheepishly and shook Brenda's hand.

Thirty-nine

Gwenn didn't have a big hat, so she took one of her sarong/sari/sulu things out of her bag, folded it a couple of times and held it up like a flag. Nothing. Five more minutes—nothing. Maybe Rachel was running late or got lost—two things that were not outside the realm of possibilities. Gwenn's arm was getting tired; she folded up the fabric and put it back into her luggage.

Screeching brakes and flashing lights caught Gwenn's attention. Rachel was slicing through traffic like a NASCAR driver. Her fellow motorists were less than pleased. Rachel ran one tire up on the curb, slammed the shifter in park and jumped out of the van—leaving the door open.

"Gwenny!" Rachel's arms squeezed the air out of Gwenn's lungs.

"Rache...air...need air."

"Let me grab your stuff, uh oh here comes the parking cop." Rachel grabbed a bag. "Hurry Gwenny."

In seconds they were squealing away from the curb and darting through the airport traffic.

Gwenn's knuckles were white. "So you brought the delivery van?"

"Yeah, I couldn't find my keys, so ya know..."

Oh yes, Gwenn knew. Rachel had learned to hotwire cars in the eleventh grade because she was so adept at losing keys. Of course, modern autos were not so easily accessed, hence the van.

"Okay, tell me everything," grinned Rachel.

"There's not that much to tell Rachel, I just went to a tree park and got some shells."

"Not that, freak. I wanna hear about how perfect little organized Gwenny, took up with Henry the bloody wanker and had a sordid affair!"

"Honestly Rache." Gwenn was turning several shades of red.

"Was it good? The sex?"

Gwenn exhaled, "All right, christ god! Do I really have to relive these painful memories?"

"Oh, was it not good? How bad was he?"

"Rache, you're gay. Why do you even want to hear about my breeder sex?"

"Nice word Gwenny, you learn that on the interwebs?" Rachel cracked herself up. "You're a corker Gwenny Hutchinson, quite a corker," Rachel laughed louder. "Gwenny sex is sex. Was it hot and steamy or not?"

Gwenn was forced to feed Rachel all the embarrassing details of her *sordid affair*. Time flew by, and Gwenn was surprised to see the Tobies on the horizon. "Can we stop for donuts?"

"I hate donuts! Don't even get me started. We can stop for chili and coffee—"

"Now who's the freak?" Gwenn smacked Rachel on the arm, just like when they were kids.

"I'm tellin'!" Rachel yelled in her best baby voice. They both laughed so hard they cried. It was good to be back.

Gwenn got to hear all about Danica over coffee. "Sounds pretty hot," she admitted.

"See Gwenn, sex is sex," Rachel winked.

Gwenn finished her caramel roll, reached across the table with her spoon and stole some of Rachel's chili. "What's Daniel up to?"

The topic of Daniel occupied the remainder of the drive to Duluth. Gwenn was surprised to hear he was apparently going to counseling.

"You should go see Dr. Mountainside yourself, Gwenn."

"No thanks." Gwenn was quite firm.

"Gwenn you lost your dream, you have to face the fact that Ed and Shirley actually are your biological parents."

"No I don't. I could've been switched at birth." Gwenn laughed.

"You know what Gwenn? Screw you!" Rachel's eyes spilled over with angry tears.

"Rache...I—"

"Screw you! I have to deal with the fact that they're my parents every day. They don't even know I'm gay," Rachel sobbed. "The only two people in the world who don't know I'm gay."

Gwenn reached out to put a hand on Rachel's shoulder but Rachel furiously swatted the hand away.

"You have everything. You're smart, you can get married and have kids and they'll just love you even more. Don't you understand Gwenn, I can never have that, I can never make them happy. I'm the eternal damned disappointment."

"Rachel don't be stupid. I don't make them happy, and I never will. I don't want to get married. I don't want to have kids. I don't want to be organized. I gave up all my dreams to be the good girl...and look where it got me. Alone. All alone." Gwenn threw her hands up in the air. "They drove the one man I loved out of my life. You're a selfish idiot Rachel, you always think of yourself first. No one could possibly be in as much pain as poor Rachel." Gwenn felt the words forming in her throat and she knew she wanted to stop, but the rage just took over, "You're just like mom."

Rachel's eyes widened like an actual knife was plunging into her back. She looked at Gwenn with pain and malice in her eyes, "You bitch."

The rest of the drive was tense. Gwenn fumed. Rachel alternated between crying and fuming. The van stopped abruptly in front of Gwenn's apartment. Gwenn got out, in silence, and opened the sliding door; she had to duck as Rachel threw a small bag to the curb. Gwenn grabbed her large suitcase and barely cleared the door before Rachel sped away. Gwenn turned to pick up her other bag and she heard the brakes screech...for a split second she thought Rachel may be coming back to apologize. She heard the sliding door slam shut, with a deafening metallic crunch.

Gwenn opened the door to her apartment and felt the relief, and foreboding, of being home. She opened her bag to see if her shells had survived Rachel's wrath. The little plastic containers and toilet paper stuffing had done their job.

She looked at the swirling lines and felt a sense of freedom creeping up her spine. There had been freedom, hours of it. Now, she was back in her cage, but steps could be taken. Gwenn decided to take a handful of the shells to the office tomorrow, to remind her of that amazing moment on the beach in New Zealand.

Gwenn put some of the shells on her nightstand and crawled into bed. Then she calculated how long it had been since her last shower and climbed right back out. The hot water washed some of the tension away. Gwenn grabbed a fresh T-shirt from the drawer and noticed her phone in the trash bin. She plucked it out of the bin and plugged it into the charger. Wow! Two hundred and seventeen messages... jeez, Rachel must've been freaked out.

First unheard message:

"Hey Gwenny, it's me. I've gotta tell you about last night. She was amazing! Call me as soon as you get this."

Next unheard message:

"Gwenny, where are you? I gotta talk to you."

Next unheard message:

"Gwenny, how rude! I had a hot one-night stand and I can't even gloat. Call me!"

Gwenn hurled the phone right back in the trash. "Selfish bitch."

Her dreams were filled with images of adoption centers and orphanages where Ed and Shirley were forcing her to pick out a sister. She kept seeing Rachel's eager face but purposely choosing someone else.

Forty

Gwenn dressed quickly for the office and pulled her hair into a low ponytail. She was anxious to throw herself back into a routine and forget about all the uneasy questions that had come up on her trip. Normalcy, that was just what the doctor ordered.

Flora nearly sprinted across the room to hug Gwenn. "I was so worried. Daniel said it was a matter of life and death—I was so worried." Flora hugged Gwenn again.

"I just needed some time to myself. I think Mr. Gregory may have blown things out of proportion, a bit." Gwenn kept an even tone. This Daniel Gregory was going to get a serious tongue lashing next time he crossed paths with Gwenn.

"Do you want the update?" Flora was eager to please.

"I live for your updates, Flora. Let me grab some coffee and we can get right to the Hit List." Gwenn marveled at the perfection of her office. No stacks. Flora had filed everything. The furniture had all been straightened and the plants looked freshly pruned. Flora had definitely been worried.

Flora began with project status updates and continued with new accounts.

"Thea has been busy," Gwenn nodded approvingly.

"Umm, actually two of those new accounts are mine," corrected Flora timidly.

"Flora, what have you been up to?" Gwenn was pleased with Flora's initiative.

"Thea was out of the office and the job sounded simple, I thought it would be okay—"

"It's more than okay, I'm proud of you. This is what we were talking about before I left."

"Unfortunately the Linder project got cancelled. Dean and Diane are getting a divorce," gushed Flora.

"No great surprise there—the lecher," mumbled Gwenn.

"I told him his fifty percent deposit would be forfeited though, because materials had already been purchased and it was too late to get the subcontractors on other projects. Was that okay?" Flora waited for some kind of acknowledgement from Gwenn.

Gwenn was struck with an inspiration. She could almost see Lucy's bright, almond-shaped eyes smiling at her.

"Flora, what do you think of my office."

"It's very nice Miss Hutchinson. I hope it's okay that I cleaned up a bit...did I..." Flora's face was flittering with befuddlement.

"How would you like it to be your office?" Gwenn felt a little lump in her throat.

"Oh, I like my desk Miss Hutchinson, I mean..." Flora was confused and nervous.

"Find someone else to sit in your desk Flora. You're gonna run this place." Gwenn stood up and walked toward Flora.

"Miss Hutchinson, you have jet lag, you're…"

Gwenn gave Flora a congratulatory hug. "My decision is made…unless you're refusing?"

"Refusing what?"

"You are the new General Manager of The Organizer!" Gwenn beamed like a proud mother.

"But…you are The Organizer," stammered Flora.

"No, Flora, this company is The Organizer, Inc. We need to re-establish that brand. We are a team." Gwenn hugged Flora and placed one hand on each shoulder, "Find your replacement."

"Thank you, Gwenn." Flora's eyes filled with joy and trepidation, but her mind never missed a beat. "Will we need a new photo, for the billboards, you know…of the whole team?"

"Yes, Miss Manager. I think you're going to need a whole new ad campaign," Gwenn smiled.

"What about Thea?" Flora suddenly worried about the paradigm shift for her coworker, now employee.

"She lives for commissions. More sales equals more commissions," Gwenn nodded in Thea's direction, "I'll handle Thea."

Forty-one

Daniel's second session with Dr. Mountainside delved into the deeply buried memories of Angeline.

"She was my world and then," Daniel closed his eyes and swallowed, "then my world went black. Everything disappeared. No future. Nothing."

"Daniel, how did Angeline die?" Brenda wasn't sure if Daniel could tell her but it was important to try.

"She was on assignment in Rwanda with Doctors Without Borders. She was headstrong and independent." Daniel paused and his eyes drifted back in time. "I got the call at 3:00 a.m. Angeline had refused to leave the Displaced Persons camp in Kibeho with the other doctors. There was a woman in labor, the baby was breech... Angeline couldn't have children...so babies..." Daniel closed his eyes and took a ragged breath. "Angeline had a special place in her heart for babies."

Brenda nodded, "Can you continue?" She wanted to make some notes but she felt it was more important to maintain eye contact with Daniel during this difficult story.

"Sometime during the night the camp was raided by some of the Interahamwe militia. They killed everyone... everyone...," Daniel's voice was a painful whisper, "they burned the camp to the ground."

"I'm so sorry Daniel." Brenda wiped the tears from her eyes. What could she possibly say to this man?

"The United Nations wasn't able to get a team into the camp for nearly a month, the area was too hot." Daniel looked down at his feet. "I hoped...for...hoped...for a miracle...maybe because she was a doctor...when they told me they found the remains of a Caucasian female clutching the remains of a Tutsi infant, I knew...I knew before they even said that a partially melted stethoscope was found on the body."

"Oh Daniel, that must've been horrible."

"I ask them to send everything back, the infant, the melted stethoscope...all of it. The Doctors Without Borders had to pull some strings...but I just thought...you know... she gave her life trying to save that little child. They should be buried together." A silent sob shook Daniel's body.

"I'm so sorry for your loss. Angeline was incredibly brave Daniel." Even Brenda had to admit, those words could hardly fill the void Daniel must've felt when he got that phone call.

"But I wasn't brave," Daniel looked away and his voice turned cold and distant.

"What do you mean?" Brenda leaned forward.

"She wanted me to go with her. I made up all kinds of excuses about unclean water, my hatred of *roughing it*...just a bunch of lies. The truth is that I was scared shitless to go into some war-torn country to help sick people. I thought she'd be okay...I thought that doctors would be safe." Daniel clenched his fists and his knuckles turned white. "I would've made her leave, if I'd been there...I could've...if—"

"Daniel there's nothing you could've done. You already stated that Angeline was headstrong and independent."

"But I didn't even try, I didn't even go after her and try to stop her from going to Rwanda. I just let it happen."

Brenda saw a thread that connected to the current Gwenn situation—but that would have to be explored on another day. "Daniel I want you to tell me three things you loved about Angeline."

Daniel rubbed his forehead trying to erase the images of Rwanda from his mind. He focused on Angeline's face, she was beautiful, but that was just a bonus. Daniel had fallen for Angeline's character, the beauty had just been icing on the cake.

"I loved her sense of right, she always wanted to help the underdog. She was so confident it was breathtaking. She just knew what she wanted and she knew she could do it. She was fearless. I loved the way her face would light up when she would tell me about how she trekked through some hostile country to bring medicine to some helpless villagers. She never thought of herself, she just thought about the people who needed her help." Daniel's face was filled with admiration.

"Daniel, if you had forbidden Angeline from going to Rwanda, would she have stayed home?" Brenda leaned back and made a quick note.

Daniel's laugh was loud and bitter. "She would've left me, and never looked back."

"Daniel, I think you need to stop blaming yourself for Angeline's death. She was yours to love, but she wasn't yours to keep in a cage. You loved her fierce independence and she loved that you set her free." Brenda gazed at Daniel's troubled face. She could almost see the wheels turning, the arguments back and forth.

Daniel looked up at Brenda, clouds clearing from his eyes, "Do you think she suffered?"

"Daniel, I think Angeline died doing what she believed in. No matter what happened in that camp, I think it's safe to say that her last breath was spent thanking you for loving her for who she really was." Brenda smiled serenely at Daniel, "Not many people have the privilege of being truly, deeply loved. You gave Angeline more in the few years you had together than some people get in a lifetime."

"Thank you...thank you, Brenda." Daniel looked out over the snowy harbor and imagined he could see Angeline's spirit floating freely, finally released, finally at peace. For the first time Daniel thought about loving her memory instead of hating her death.

Forty-two

Rachel was furious at Gwenn. Rachel had never been selfish, that was ridiculous. It wasn't her fault if her stories were more interesting than anyone else's. Was she just supposed to sit by and listen to someone blather on about the stock market when she had talked her way out of a speeding ticket by flirting with a female cop that turned out to be gay? Rachel wasn't selfish; she was concerned about everyone having a good time. Gwenn was a pompous, prudish bitch.

Rachel punched down the bread dough with zeal. She was winding up for seconds when a knock at the back door of the bakery broke her concentration. "Oh, I hope this is Gwenn." Rachel pounded her fist into the palm of her other hand and grinned menacingly.

The overly sarcastic, "Whaddya want?" was out before the door was open. "Annie?" Rachel froze.

"Hi, can I come in. I kinda need to talk to you." Annie shifted her weight nervously.

Rachel didn't move right away. She was drinking in the sweetness of Annie. The wild, spiky blond hair, now streaked with red, the adorable baby tee and the low-rise black pants. Rachel smiled at the Doc Martens she had bought for Annie.

"Did you leave something at the loft?" Rachel wasn't eager to let Annie open old wounds.

"Yeah, my best friend." Annie looked into Rachel's eyes and let the tears fall.

Rachel threw her flour-covered arms around Annie and squeezed her like a favorite stuffed animal.

"Can't...breathe," giggled Annie.

Rachel pulled back a few inches and kissed Annie gently on her perfectly-plump, naturally-soft lips.

Annie kissed back, hungrily, apologetically. "Rachel are you going to let me in or what?"

"I'm making bread...I gotta—well, we open in an hour." Rachel stepped back and let Annie into the kitchen.

"I can help ya know. What do you want me to do?"

"First I want to know why you're back, then you can help me make mini sweet rolls for the singles mixer at my parents' church tonight," laughed Rachel.

"I freaked out. I was a serial woman-ogamist before I met you, Rachel. I just kept moving, never getting serious. Then I met you," Annie was pacing around the kitchen. "I was feeling like half of a couple instead of like a whole me and I freaked. I needed space."

"So the loft...why did you want to buy property with me?" Rachel looked confused.

"I thought if I had more physical space I could keep myself separate from you...remain an individual. But I kept slipping deeper into the relationship. So I sabotaged it the only way I knew how...I cheated."

"I know," Rachel looked hurt.

"I know, and I hated myself for hurting you. Once I had gone that far it was easy to convince myself you'd be better off without me." Annie's words were racing out of her mouth, "I thought I was doing you a favor."

"Gee thanks." Rachel clapped flour off her hands and shook her head.

"Was I right?" Annie's eyes crinkled with worry as she waited for the answer. "Were you better off?"

"No, you stupid dyke. I was miserable."

"Me to!" Annie rushed over and hugged Rachel. There were several floury handprints on Annie's back and even one on her black jeans, right over the back pocket.

Rachel felt warm all over, it was just so right to have Annie back. It was perfect. Everything was perfect, except, "The loft sold last week—"

"Great! We'll use the money to buy this bakery from that decrepit Swedish woman and I'll move back into the apartment." Annie brushed a strand of hair from Rachel's forehead. "I don't need space, I need you...the closer the better." Annie nuzzled into Rachel's neck.

Rachel squealed with ticklish laughter, "Annie! Stop it that tickles!" But Rachel didn't pull away.

Annie whispered in Rachel's ear, "Maybe we should go up to the apartment right now."

"I have to open in less than an hour." Rachel was panicked. "The bread is not finished, the cookies aren't frosted, the brownies..."

"Just tell me what to do, honey." Annie was like a soldier awaiting orders.

"Wash your hands. Grab an apron..."

Annie turned to follow orders.

"And wipe that hand print off your ass!" Rachel laughed.

The rest of the day went by like molasses in January. There were lots of stolen kisses and even more passionate glances. Rachel did feel like half of a couple—and she loved it.

Forty-three

Gwenn was miserable. She'd given away her title *The Organizer*. She had been positively wicked to Rachel and she hated herself for even thinking about Daniel. Maybe she could borrow a copy of Rachel's latest bible, *The Tao of Pooh*, and learn about non-action. She knew she didn't feel like taking any action except possibly rolling over and going back to sleep.

She sought comfort in a game of "What difference would it make?". She had invented the game in an effort to squelch her religious guilt in high school. The idea being, once you had sinned a little, "What difference would it make?" if you sinned a little more. So when a boy would slide his hand across her breast and attempt to go under the sweater, she would protest a little. He would continue to slide the hand and Gwenn would say to herself, "He already felt my boob, what difference would it make if he feels it a little more thoroughly." The game had worked rather well until Eric Hudson had taken advantage of the system and slid his hand below the border. Then Gwenn understood it did make a difference if the finger was *on top of* or *inside of*. She still got tingly remembering that difference.

Back to the game at hand. She was already thinking about Daniel, so what difference would it make if she just left him a voicemail—

"Hello?"

"Daniel is that you?" Gwenn wasn't sure.

"No, I'm afraid Mr. Gregory is indisposed. This is Todd, his assistant, can I give Mr. Gregory a message?"

"Oh umm...I...umm...sure. Just tell him Gwenn Hutchinson called." Gwenn's first instinct had been to hang up, but the thought of caller ID prevented her from embarrassing herself.

"Just a moment Ms. Hutchinson." Todd wasn't sure if he was doing the right thing, but he knew the consequences if he did the wrong thing.

Gwenn heard mumbling, followed by louder voices. There appeared to be a struggle or something. Someone dropped the phone...finally Gwenn's patience was rewarded.

"Gwenn? Is it really you?" Daniel's velvety voice caressed Gwenn's ear.

"I got back last night. I heard you might be in town—"

"I'd invite you over, but my babysitter is here." Daniel glanced at Todd.

"My place is a perfect disaster." The words spilled out before Gwenn imagined the implication.

"How about Perkins on London?" Daniel exerted great effort to keep his voice even. "Coffee and pie?"

"Make it malts and French fries and you're on." The angel on Gwenn's right shoulder was shouting warnings in her ear. Fortunately, the devil on Gwenn's left shoulder was cheering her on loudly enough to drown out the pathetic do-gooder.

"Thirty minutes?" Daniel's heart was pounding like a kettle drum at the Metropolitan Opera.

"If you don't mind no makeup and a ponytail?" Gwenn tried to make a joke to hide her anxiety.

"Do you mean on me or you?" Daniel laughed nervously.

Gwenn laughed louder than necessary, "See ya in 30." Gwenn hung up before she could say anything more ridiculous.

Gwenn threw on blush, lip-gloss and mascara—she wasn't as brave as she had sounded. There was no way around the ponytail though; her hair was embarrassing. Snugly fitting jeans, a long sleeved tee and her cozy blue sweater completed her ensemble.

***

Todd was fuming. Daniel was pacing like a caged tiger.

"Just keep it casual Mr. Gregory."

"Todd, relax it's Perkins okay, not a bar. I'm not going to get her drunk and have my way with her." Daniel's eyes turned sultry, "Although..."

"Mr. Gregory, please, just friends. You don't know what she's been through. Just friends. Let her control the pace." Todd could feel things slipping out of his control and he didn't like it. "At least let me drop you off and—"

"Todd, keys." Daniel drew himself up to his full 6'3" and held his hand insistently in front of Todd

"Fine. But I'll not—"

"Todd, I'll be okay." Daniel grinned like a spoiled child as he snatched the keys from Todd's hand.

"Famous last words," mumbled Todd as he shut the door.

Daniel arrived at Perkins before Gwenn, so he chose a table that was in full view of the front door and practiced molding his features into the portrait of nonchalance.

Gwenn walked through the door an agonizing ten minutes later. He saw her first and drank in every curve of her body. He barely had time to reorganize his face before Gwenn caught sight of him.

She gave a casual, friendly wave and walked toward the table. Daniel worried that the wave was too casual; maybe she really did just want to be friends.

Gwenn hoped her eagerness had been masked by the casual wave. She had forgotten how handsome Daniel was and how his smile was so disarming. She forced herself to walk slowly, to appear calm and to give herself time to look at him.

He seemed so much younger. It was funny how much gray she had imagined in his hair when she had tried to make him fit an image of a father. Now, as a friend his caramel-brown hair looked youthful and luxuriant. His oxford shirt and brown leather jacket could not conceal the strong chest beneath. The walk was interminable.

How could she walk so slowly? Daniel's mask of casual patience was cracking. Was she worried? Was she going to turn and run? Daniel imagined chasing after her and catching her in a tender embrace. More cracks formed in the mask.

Finally the table, Gwenn thought she would die. "Oh hi, have you been waiting long?"

Daniel wanted to scream, "I've grown two years older just waiting for you to cross the blasted restaurant!" In the end he chose a simple, "Oh, I don't know...a few minutes, maybe."

The aged, polyester-clad waitress arrived seconds after Gwenn slid into the booth.

"What can I getcha dear?" Polyester rocked back and forth in her comfortable, black-soled, grease-resistant shoes.

Gwenn smiled, "Chocolate malt and an order of French fries, and can I get some sour cream on the side?"

Daniel raised an eyebrow.

"You betcha sweetie. Ya want some water or coffee?" Polyester asked the question as though the two liquids were interchangeable.

"A water would be great. Thanks," Gwenn smiled, again.

"And what would you like young man?" Polyester flashed what would've passed as a flirtatious grin 30 years earlier.

"Well, I'd like to adopt you for starters." Daniel flashed a heartbreakingly innocent smile at Polyester.

She giggled and flushed, "Oh, pshaw." Polyester was glowing.

"I'm old enough to be your brother," Daniel snuck a peek at Polyester's nametag, "Adele. I'll have what my friend is having." Daniel gestured toward Gwenn, "I'm intrigued by the odd pairing."

Adele jotted down a few notes, "I'll bring yer waters right out."

As soon as the coast was clear Gwenn hissed, "What's with the flirting with your grandmother?"

"Jealous?" Daniel's eyes twinkled.

"No...that's not..." she exhaled in frustration.

"Listen, someday you'll be an older woman and, god forbid, you have to work a crappy waitressing job, wouldn't you like it if a young, handsome," Daniel emphasized the last word, "man flirted with you?"

"Fine, but you're going to break her heart and all the ladies at bingo night will curse the day you were born." Gwenn smirked.

"What about you?" Daniel pointed an accusing finger.

"I wasn't flirting!" Gwenn was shocked.

"No, the malt with fries and sour cream? Who orders that?" Daniel feigned disgust.

"For your information, Don Juan, French fries are potatoes and sour cream is quite tasty on potatoes."

"Okay, I'll give you that one...but the malt?"

"I like ice cream...okay? Don't judge me." Gwenn crossed her arms like a pouting child.

"I don't think that's having the effect you hoped for Gwenn. You're rather sexy when you pout." Daniel grinned.

The hair on the back of Gwenn's neck was buzzing, and all the blood in her entire body charged simultaneously to her pouting little cheeks. Gwenn attempted a haughty tone, "How do you know what effect I intended?"

They both laughed and Gwenn felt her whole body relax. Daniel was fun, he was intelligent and witty and compassionate. Mustn't forget mouthwatering. Gwenn forced herself to look out the window at an imaginary passerby, "Easy girl," she told herself. She decided to stick with superficial questions. "Daniel, what month and day were you born?"

"I'm a Libra. Did you seriously just ask me my sign?" Daniel smirked.

"Well, no...I mean, yes...it's just a thing I do. I just always look at astrological influences in business and relationships—"

"How's that been working out?" Daniel laughed.

"Hey, that was mean!" Gwenn was a little offended but mostly because the truth stings a bit.

"I am just the pot calling the kettle black over here. It's not like I have some amazing history in either of those areas."

"In my childhood I always heard the 'speck in your neighbors eye...log in your own' analogy. Same thing, I know what you mean." Gwenn couldn't stay mad at that gorgeous face. "It's just a habit. I don't know I guess it's really just something to hide behind."

"Gwenn, I have a bad habit of pretending like I'm fine, like I can handle everything even when the exact opposite is true. Do I have your permission to base our friendship on complete honesty?"

Gwenn suddenly met Daniel's piercing gaze and swallowed hard. Here it comes, the bitch session for running out of Dr. Watkins' office, the protestations of eternal love. Shit. "Umm, yeah I guess."

"Great. First off, I owe you a huge apology."

"Why? For the astrology thing?" Gwenn wasn't expecting this tack.

"No, I learned something about myself today. I don't know if it's okay for me to know it, I mean my therapist didn't actually say it—but I connected the dots." Daniel took a deep breath; good she didn't flip out at the word therapist. "I wasn't able to save my late wife, Angeline, and I was unable to save my dad...so, I guess...when you took off, so upset...I put all of those feelings of inadequacy into your situation. I convinced myself that if I could rescue you it would somehow make up for Angeline and my dad." Daniel paused, Gwenn said nothing. "Kinda stupid, huh?"

Adele arrived with waters and malts. "Here ya go kids. Fries'll be right up."

Gwenn smiled impulsively and Daniel winked. Adele blushed and scurried off, her shoes making a slight hum against the carpet.

"Daniel I don't know what to say, I mean, I don't know anything about you—I would never judge your actions." Gwenn was trying to process the pain and loss Daniel had endured, twice. "Do you want to tell me what happened, I mean before?" Gwenn's eyes were full of sympathy.

"Some other time, I just lived through one telling today... I don't think I can do it again. Besides I'd really like to talk about us, I just wanted you to know why I became a freak-show stalker...frame of reference and all that bullshit."

Daniel's laugh was like a favorite shirt, soothing and comforting.

"I actually liked the stalker thing, a real turn on, you know—I'm glad you didn't find me." Gwenn's pupils dilated with the panic of stepping on her own tongue. "I mean...or didn't say anything...or...shit. Talk now, Daniel."

"I guess you must've heard what happened at the Botanical Gardens?"

"Yeah, sorry. If it's any consolation I got my comeuppance about ten seconds after you bailed."

"It's not. I mean, I derive no pleasure from your pain." Daniel smacked his fist against his palm. "I would, however, derive great pleasure from inflicting some pain on Henry the bloody wanker."

"Rachel! That bitch." Gwenn looked at Daniel and rolled her eyes. "I guess my sister was trying to play Cupid for me."

"I think she was playing for me. I must've sounded pretty desperate."

Gwenn felt incredibly uncomfortable, the booth seemed to be shrinking and she imagined she was being pushed toward Daniel. "I never meant to—1 didn't even know—we just met," managed Gwenn.

"Keeping with the honesty policy," Daniel looked at Gwenn's face and changed his mind. "I think we should get to know each other better. Why did you start your own company?"

"Honestly?"

Daniel nodded, "Preferably."

"It is very easy for me to organize other people's shit. I cram my days full of assessing, planning and executing. By the time I drag myself out of the office I don't have the energy to think about the chaos in my own life. It's an over-functioning coping mechanism I learned in my happy childhood." Gwenn finished with a small slap of her hand on the table, just as Adele returned with the fries.

"Here we are." Adele looked nervously between Gwenn and Daniel, hoping there was a disagreement she could gossip about back in the kitchen.

"Thank you, Adele." Daniel smiled, no wink though.

Adele high-tailed it back to the kitchen to prevaricate on the sequence of events at table 25.

"Okay, your turn. Why did you start painting?"

"I was always creative, different. I mean look at me, pretty athletic right?" Daniel's grin dared Gwenn to inspect his physique.

Gwenn nodded, in what she hoped was innocent agreement.

"Wrong, never played a day of organized sports in my life. I was always drawing stuff and writing poetry. I'm sure plenty of guys thought I was gay, but no one was brave enough to say it to my face—"

"Ahem, this isn't a 'feel free to brag needlessly' question—why?"

"Am I that transparent?" Daniel chuckled. "I wanted to impress my dad. I wanted him to notice me and include me in his world."

"Did he?"

"He would encourage me occasionally, I had some pretty good stuff. Not museum quality, but good. It was after Angeline died that something shifted. I guess I just sunk so low; I kind of had to rebuild myself. That's when I found the real artist inside of me—that's when my dad noticed."

"Do you miss him?"

"Hell yeah. We were so close those last few years...he had stopped painting, mostly, and he was just building up the Gallery and turning me into a superstar. I got pretty full of myself."

"You don't say," snickered Gwenn.

"Hey, you asked, Miss smarty-pants. All right, back to you. What happened in New Zealand?" Daniel's eyes were full of concern.

"I can't explain it...I just...some part of me changed. I found a way to be okay with me. I don't need a mother ship or a fantasy family. I'm enough." Gwenn met Daniel's gaze and smiled confidently. "I make my own life, based on what I want. I feel totally free...like a clean slate."

"Wow, I think I went to the wrong New Zealand."

"I think you're wrong. I think it changed you, too. Your eyes are peaceful." Gwenn looked deeply into Daniel's eyes and before she could stop herself, her hand slid across the table and grasped his.

Daniel raised one eyebrow and looked from the hands back to Gwenn's eyes.

"Honestly? I don't know," Gwenn fumbled for the words, "I want you in my new life, I'm just not sure how or how much. Is that okay?"

"It's more than I expected. It's enough...for now."

"Don't be greedy," scolded Gwenn.

"When it comes to you I'm a glutton...I just hope it's not a glutton for punishment!" Daniel teased.

Daniel dunked one of his fries in the sour cream and held it out for Gwenn to sample. She leaned in and swallowed the whole fry. Her lips brushing Daniel's fingers as she completed the steal. Sparks shot up her spine.

"That seemed a bit greedy Ms. Hutchinson."

Gwenn grinned playfully and grabbed her purse. She thought she had the jump on him, but Daniel's money hit the counter, next to the cash register, before Gwenn even opened her purse.

"Nice try, Gwenn."

Gwenn pretended to pout.

Daniel brought his lips within millimeters of her ear. "You're pushing your luck."

The dangerous whisper ignited Gwenn's entire body. She quickly shifted her weight to hide the fact that her knees were collapsing. Oh, she was playing with fire. The problem was that she was pretty sure she would enjoy a good searing.

They exited the Perkins in silence and Daniel walked Gwenn to her car.

Gwenn turned as she dug for her keys. "Thanks Daniel, that was fun."

"Gwenn, would you be interested in a small experiment?"

"Maybe..." her heart was picking up speed.

"May I kiss you goodbye?"

Gwenn was certain everyone inside the Perkins could hear her heart thumping in her chest. "Where's the experiment?"

"If you don't like it then we'll know were just BFFs." Daniel leaned in so that Gwenn could feel his breath on her skin. "If you like it then I'll come over to your house for—"

Gwenn felt something inside her explode. Before Daniel could finish his sentence she caught his lower lip with hers and explored the rich, lavish textures of his lips.

Daniel was thrown off his game by losing the initial strike, but he quickly recovered and returned Gwenn's kisses with the heat of his own.

The kiss touched Gwenn's soul and she lost track of time and temperature.

It was Daniel who finally came up for air, "So, you like?"

Gwenn was breathing so hard she could barely speak, "Get...in." She waved to the passenger door.

Forty-four

Todd was pacing and checking his phone every two seconds. He would give Daniel 30 more minutes before taking action.

"Okay time's up." Todd announced to the empty cabin. He grabbed his coat and drove to the Perkins. When he saw Daniel's car in the parking lot he was completely embarrassed.

"Oh my God! I'm an old woman...a worrywart. I need to get a life." Todd admonished himself relentlessly, but he parked the car and surreptitiously sneaked into the restaurant, just to be sure.

There were only six tables of people in the restaurant. Three men, each alone, a table of young girls all giggling, and two tables of teenage boys playing it cool.

The sirens in Todd's head were deafening. Todd scanned the neighboring establishments in search of a bar. None in sight, but—

"Can I help you sweetie?"

"I was meeting a friend, tall guy, longish brown hair, probably wearing—"

"Oh, that handsome young man with the blue and brown eyes?" Adele had a great memory for faces, that's why her regulars tipped her so well.

"Yes, that's him." Todd looked around. "His car's in the parking lot, but I don't see him. Are there any bars—?"

"Oh, he left with that plain girl in the sweatshirt." Adele was quite certain that the *plain* girl couldn't have held a candle to her back in the day.

"Oh...oh." Todd thanked the helpful waitress and hurried back to the car. He toyed with the idea of calling, but couldn't make up his mind. He hated to give up, but calling Daniel could be overstepping, even the generous bounds Todd had established. Todd didn't know where Gwenn lived and it was far too late to call Flora or Rachel. The best plan would be to get a good night's sleep and put Frankie on notice for a possible rescue mission tomorrow. C'est la vie.

***

Daniel opened his eyes and looked at the unfamiliar ceiling. A delectable shiver caressed his body. For once his head was clear and his memories were sharp. His hands felt the thrill of Gwenn's soft, fragile body. His mouth tasted the salty sweetness of her skin—he rolled over to look at the object of his desire.

Gwenn's soft hazel eyes peeked open. "Again?" she giggled.

"I don't know what you're talking about." Daniel played innocent.

Gwenn stuck her bottom lip out as far as she could and attempted to pout.

"I believe I warned you about that." Daniel slid his arm under Gwenn and scooped her up and on top of him before she could even squeal.

Gwenn looked down into Daniel's welcoming face, "So BFFs, huh?"

"Best friends forever, or at least as long as you'll have me." Daniel placed his hands gently on each side of Gwenn's face and pulled her into a long deep kiss.

The morning lovemaking was slow and easy, compared to the hungry wildness of last night. Gwenn liked both. She was bursting with adrenaline last night, eager to feel the weight of Daniel—she was like a hungry beast, she never thought she would feel sated. This morning she felt content, she just wanted to touch him, to listen to his heartbeat, to kiss him slowly and enjoy every curve of his lips. She wanted this morning to last forever, but as she lost herself in the moment and kissed him more forcefully—forever came sooner than anticipated.

Forty-five

Annie was watching Rachel sleep. Rachel's wild mane of carmine-streaked, ebony hair was splayed out across the pillow. Her small ruby lips were stretched into a sleepy smile. At that moment Annie knew that Rachel was the one. The always one. Even when Annie had convinced herself to leave, to claim that it was over, there had been a part of her that just covered its ears and refused to hear the announcement.

Rachel rubbed her eyes and blinked at the late morning sun. Before she could even wonder if she'd been dreaming Annie's lips were on hers. Rachel's heart flipped somersaults of joy. "I thought it was a dream."

"It was." Annie traced the curve of Rachel's cheek. "A dream that came true."

Rachel squirmed away from the intense emotions. "Ooooh, saccharine alert." She rolled out of bed and flung the covers over Annie's head.

Rachel ran for the shower, hoping that she wouldn't be alone for long. Annie did not disappoint.

Standing there, with nothing between them but a sheet of water, the tears finally came for Rachel. The tough, take-no-shit girl melted in the warm water flowing over her, and the tears flowed freely. "I thought I lost you—I was so hurt."

"I'm so sorry I hurt you, I thought I was doing us both a favor." Annie's eyes were glistening with un-shed tears. "I thought I would fuck up and disappoint you in the end—I didn't trust myself. I thought you'd be better off without me screwing up your life."

"I wasn't...I was miserable." Rachel's conscience got the better of her, "I had an affair, with a married woman."

"Wow, things must've been bad if you stooped to recruiting." Annie's laugh was gentle and forgiving.

"Oh, shut up freak. It wasn't like that." Rachel's voice was defensive.

"I gotta be honest with ya Rache, I don't think I want to know what it was like. We both made mistakes, in the past... let's just leave 'em there." Annie put her hand out for a handshake, "Deal?"

Rachel grabbed Annie's hand and put it on her left breast, "Cross my heart and hope to die," Rachel leaned in and kissed Annie intensely, "in your arms, when I'm 103."

"Okay, deal. Now get busy, we're wasting water."

"You're such a granola girl!" Rachel grabbed the shampoo and hastily got down to business.

Forty-six

Todd had not slept much and he was anxious for the light of day to signal an *all clear* to call Flora. He had come up with the Flora plan as a way around Daniel and Gwenn.

"Good morning Flora, it's Todd."

"Oh no, did someone run away again?" Flora's tone was only half jesting. She was still quite concerned about Gwenn's recent behavior.

"I'm not entirely sure...umm...what have you heard."

"I haven't had time to check up on Miss Hutchinson, Todd. Yesterday she promoted me to General Manager and decided to re-brand the company...and she wants new billboards and—"

"How can I help?" Todd was eager to find something to occupy his time.

"What do you mean?"

"I mean I came up here to babysit Mr. Gregory and I have a feeling he's taken up with Ms. Hutchinson, and I'm not interested in sitting here twiddling my thumbs." Todd sounded exasperated.

"Taken up with Miss Hutchinson, do you mean—?"

"Let's not dwell on the unsavory details, Flora. I've got skills—you've got a crisis. I'll be there in 30 minutes." Todd hung up without waiting for Flora's response. He was desperate for a distraction.

Todd arrived 27 minutes later. His blond hair was short and professional. He was wearing a loose, but pressed, pair of chinos and a button-down white oxford shirt.

Flora blushed before she even said hello. "You must be Todd." Her smile was nervous and self-conscious.

"Pleased to meet you Flora." Todd smiled and nodded appreciatively at Flora's smart pantsuit and understated necklace. "Thanks again for all your help with the New Zealand nonsense."

"Oh, sure. You bet." Flora could not stop blushing. "No problem."

"Okay, give me the timeline and we'll work backwards. First we'll set up the milestones and then we'll assign responsibilities." Todd smiled, "Is it just you and I?"

"I'm supposed to hire an assistant and put all of us in a new team photo for the billboards...but I—"

"First things first. Timeline."

"Miss Hutchinson wanted the new billboards up in two weeks, but the outdoor company—" Flora was exasperated.

"Limitations are for amateurs, not for pros like us. Having said that, I want to find you the best assistant in northern Minnesota, so we're going to push the deadline out to one month from now."

"But Miss Hutchinson—"

"I think when she sees your proposal, she'll be so elated, she'll faint when you tell her you can do it in one month," grinned Todd.

"Okay, where do we start?"

"We will have to have a grand re-opening. Exclusive guest list, wristbands, velvet rope...the whole works." Todd was already planning the menu.

"But this is Duluth, not Minneapolis." Flora could not imagine a swanky, exclusive party in Dul-uth.

"We are raising the bar Flora. Now, call the best temp agency in town and tell them you want a personal assistant with excellent typing skills and a reputation for confidentiality."

"But the assistant is for the office—" stammered Flora.

"No, the assistant is for you. She or he," Todd emphasized he, "will work in the office but their first priority will be seeing to your sublime happiness." Todd scanned through an invisible checklist and continued, "Next call the college and find one or two students in the business, marketing or advertising programs that want to earn some class credit for assisting with a launch party."

"You're amazing."

"I am." Todd grabbed some paper and scribbled some notes. "Okay launch party in 30 days, and that's a Saturday night...perfect. I want new billboards up one week before. And we'll want a feature story in the paper on Wednesday and an item in the entertainment section on Friday. Save-the-date cards will go out to our exclusive list ASAP, and invites two weeks prior." Todd was tapping his pen and calculating.

Flora liked the way he bit his lip when he was concentrating. "Oh, we can use Rachel for the catering," Flora was pleased to help.

"We'll have to sample her work...this has to be very top-notch."

"She's the best. Everyone says so," Flora was a little defensive.

"Okay, call her and set up a tasting. Tell her exotic, unusual...the kind of menu that people will drool over just reading about it in the paper." Todd got that warm, geniusy feeling in his frontal lobe, "I will arrange for some of Mr. Gregory's work to be displayed in the office during the event. That will get media attention of a potentially national level."

"Do you think Mr. Gregory would mind? I mean it's not his usual venue?"

"I'm impressed Flora, do you follow Mr. Gregory's work?"

"Just lately," Flora didn't want to mention it was only since the first time she had talked to Todd.

"Besides, I think it's safe to say that Mr. Gregory would do just about anything for Ms. Hutchinson, right now."

Forty-seven

Daniel kissed Gwenn's stomach and her cheek and her neck. He whispered hotly into her ear, "Is there anything else I can do for you Ms. Hutchinson?"

Gwenn's breathing was fast and she struggled to keep her voice even, "No, that will be all Mr. Gregory." She giggled as Daniel bit her earlobe and ran his tongue down her neck. "Daniel, I have to eat something, I'm dying."

Daniel rolled out of bed and, with the excitement of a child, yelled, "Oooh, I can make pancakes!"

Gwenn stared longingly at the graceful, muscular body silhouetted by the midday light. In what world had she imagined this gorgeous man was in his 60s? Ageless, like a statue of a Greek god, the way his abdomen tapered into... Mount Olympus...that's where the Greek gods lived, right? Gwenn forced herself to recite more useless facts about Greek mythology. "Ummm pancakes, yes I—"

Daniel followed Gwenn's gaze and grinned, "Maybe you're feeling a bit carnivorous?"

Gwenn flushed a near perfect shade of magenta. "I think I better carbo-load on some pancakes if I'm going to keep up with you."

"Excuses, excuses," Daniel laughed and grabbed his boxers off the floor. "Pancakes it is."

Gwenn heard the cupboard doors opening and closing in the kitchen. She grabbed her bathrobe and shuffled out to the couch. She felt like she had run a marathon—except more tingly and less incontinent.

"Bowls are in the bottom cupboard on the far left. Spoons are in the drawer next to the stove. Dry goods are on the third shelf of the large, pantry cupboard. Milk and eggs are in the fridge on the middle shelf."

"Jeez! You are The Organizer."

"No I'm not!" Gwenn stomped her foot into the couch pillow. "I just promoted Flora to manager yesterday and I'm re-branding the company as The Organizer, Inc.," announced Gwenn defiantly.

"Good for you!" Daniel clapped, "Sounds like a lot of work, I should get Todd—shit—Todd." Daniel realized the severe abuse of friendship he'd committed by disappearing last night. "I gotta call him—" Daniel ran to find his pants and the phone he hoped was in the pocket.

"If I'd known you had a boyfriend I never would've brought you home," yelled Gwenn. She took full advantage of this opportunity to go on a brief cleaning spree—madly throwing a bunch of crap in the trash, grabbing all loose articles of clothing, including a stray pair of underwear, and stuffing them into the hall closet.

"Not funny—okay kinda funny, but I really should've called Todd last night. He worries." Daniel was already dialing in the phone.

"Mr. Gregory, are you sober?" Todd's tone was curt.

"Sober as a judge." Daniel lowered his voice, like a teenager trying to make plans to sneak out, "I'm at Gwenn's."

Todd couldn't help but notice the elated tone in Daniel's whisper. "Everything okay?"

"Couldn't be better, man." Daniel could feel the face-splitting grin spread across his cheeks. "I'm making pancakes."

Todd laughed, "Oh, the lucky girl." At the word girl, Flora looked nervously at Todd. He shook his head and tried to make a gesture that everything was just fine. Flora looked relieved and returned to her phone calls.

"I'm the lucky one, Todd. Seriously..." Daniel swallowed a lump that had suddenly formed in his throat. "While I've got you on the phone, I was wondering if you could help Gwenn with a re-branding thing? I mean we're up here for awhile, and you only need to check in on the Gallery maybe once a week—"

"Just a moment Mr. Gregory," Todd turned to Flora. "Flora, let's schedule that interview for 2:00 p.m. and bring the interns in at 3:00 p.m." Todd turned back to the phone. "You were saying."

"Once again, Todd if you were a woman I'd—"

"And I'd sue you for sexual harassment! Flora and I have everything under control. You have an appointment with Dr. Mountainside at 2:30. I rescheduled your 10:00 a.m. when you went AWOL last night."

"Thanks and...well, thanks. I'll be there at 2:30...sharp," Daniel chuckled.

"Sharp," Todd emphasized as he hung up.

Daniel dropped his phone and turned to face Gwenn.

Her eyes were full of concern and guilt. "Did I get you in trouble?"

"Nothing serious. I'm sure Todd prefers this situation, to picking me up off a barroom floor."

"Alcoholic?" Gwenn tried to sound casual.

"No, my therapist tells me I'm a drama king," laughed Daniel. "I just use alcohol to get attention, because it works. If I had tried X or crack the first time, I guess I'd have taken a different path." Daniel shrugged his shoulders. "So we're working on getting comfortable with speaking the truth and asking for what I need, ya now...so I don't have to get blind drunk to tell people what I really want."

"I can relate, New Zealand was way over-dramatic for me." Gwenn smiled slyly at Daniel, "But last night definitely showed me the value of honesty."

"Here, here," Daniel raised his batter-coated, wooden spoon in a sloppy toast to Gwenn's proclamation.

The pancakes were delicious and when Daniel leaned over and kissed the syrup off her lips, Gwenn was sure she'd be equally pleased with dessert.

Forty-eight

Annie and Rachel were enjoying scrambled eggs, bacon, day-old scones and fresh coffee. Annie put her hand on Rachel's. Annie's long beautifully-callused fingers tenderly rubbed the back of Rachel's hand.

"Rachel, there's something I've got to say. Don't be mad, but I think it's really important." Annie's big, green eyes begged for mercy.

"I'm not cutting my hair!" Rachel was adamant.

"I love your hair...you can do anything you want with your hair." Annie's face clouded over, "I want you to tell your parents."

Rachel pulled her hand free. "What the hell are you thinking? Are you crazy?"

"Rache, you have to...it's the last step."

"You are out of your fucking mind."

"Maybe, but I feel like we're hiding. Like you are somehow ashamed of me, and I don't like it."

"They'll freak out. They won't ever speak to me again." Rachel could feel the panic rising.

"Rachel, if your bitter, judgmental, condescending mother never spoke to you again—how would that be a bad thing?"

"But my dad—it would kill him."

"I think your dad's a lot stronger than you think. He's not gonna do cartwheels or whatever, but I think he may surprise you...eventually."

"I can't, I just can't," Rachel said obstinately. "You know the Hutchinson rule; if you don't talk about it, it's not happening."

"Rachel that's ridiculous, and it undermines everything we're fighting for in this community. How can we expect to be equal if we don't act equal? Would you introduce me if I was your BOY-friend?"

"That's different."

"That's the problem."

"Will you come with me, Annie?"

"I would be honored."

"I've gotta talk to Gwenn first," said Rachel, hesitantly.

"Can't you ever make a decision without your sister's approval?" Annie had always felt a little threatened by Gwenn's influence on Rachel's life.

"I had a huge fight with her, it was awful. We haven't spoken for days."

"Oh, sorry." Annie recognized the gravity of the situation. Days? Annie couldn't remember a single day passing without Rachel calling Gwenn. "You should call her. I'm sure she feels as bad as you do."

"She should, bitch compared me to my mom!" Rachel pounded her fist on the table as she hurled the words out.

"That was cold. Musta been some fight."

"Maybe I should wait for her to call me?" Rachel toyed with the idea of playing the martyr, but immediately grabbed the phone when she realized that was something her mother would do. She dialed Gwenn's home phone, hoping she would get off by just leaving a vague message after the beep.

"Gwenny, it's Rachel, I was—"

Gwenn lunged for the phone, nearly socking Daniel in the eye. "Rache, hold on..." Gwenn slithered off of Daniel and searched for her robe.

As she bent to fetch the robe Daniel accidentally blurted one of his titles out loud. "*Secret Pleasures*, limited edition giclee."

Gwenn turned and gave him a silent shushing.

"Gwenny, is someone there?" Rachel grew suspicious, "Gwenny?"

"I'm here Rache I just had to—never mind. I'm so sorry about the other day. I had no right to say you were like mom. That was the worst—"

"I'm sorry I called you a bitch," Rachel sniffled.

"You always call me a bitch," Gwenn laughed through her tears.

"But that time I really meant it, I'm so sorry."

"Me too. It wasn't fair of me to trivialize your situation." Gwenn sniffed, "I was so tired and emotional—"

"Yeah, and I hadn't seen you for days and I was missing Annie and—"

"I'm really sorry about Annie, she was the best."

Rachel paused, "Umm...the thing is...see, Annie came back—"

"Oh, that's awesome. I'm so glad. It is awesome, right? So why do you sound so worried?"

"She wants me to tell mom and dad," Rachel was crying in earnest.

"You mean tell them, tell them...about the gayness?"

"Yeah, the gayness," Rachel laughed through her tears.

"Do you want me to go with you?"

Rachel's heart burst with love for this wonderful sister who would volunteer to face a firing squad. "No, you take cover. If that's who I think it is at your apartment—you're going to have your own people-come-to-Jesus meeting soon enough." Rachel snuffled, "I mean an artist Gwenny, what will people say?"

The sisters laughed and cried and laughed some more. Just the comfort of knowing their connection reached through the phone and into each other's hearts was enough to bring a sense of peace to both their minds.

"I'm gonna do it Gwenny, I'm gonna set myself free. I guess it's the non-action, Tao thing. I didn't plan this, it just feels like what I need to do."

"I'm so proud I'm going to burst. Call me the second it's over. I want all the details." Gwenn quickly added, "Try to watch your tongue Rache. You tend to swear like a truck driver when you're nervous or angry. I don't think foul language will help your case much."

"I'll try," promised Rachel.

"I love you."

"I love you too, Gwenny. Bye."

Rachel dreaded the next call she had to make and she really dreaded the thought of Shirley actually answering.

Forty-nine

Shirley was anxious to find out exactly where Gwendolyn had been. She was indignant that her messages had been ignored, so she drove downtown and marched into Gwendolyn's office.

Todd heard the steps and sensed the threat on the air. He instinctively moved in front of Flora. Protect the primary... the assistants' code.

Shirley rounded the corner like a jungle cat closing on her prey. She would soon have some answers from Gwendolyn. Her world was rapidly capsized when she saw a handsome, young man blocking her ingress. Shirley changed masks with the skill of an ancient Chinese face-changing artist. Her sing-song voice rang out, "Oh, who do we have here?"

"Good morning, I'm Todd, Mr. Gregory's assistant. And you are?" Todd kept his tone professional, even though he felt the woman might not deserve that gesture.

"I'm Shirley, Gwendolyn's mother, young man. Yer gonna have ta learn the chain of command, if ya want ta last around here," Shirley's voice was territorial and patronizing.

Todd did not tolerate patronizing. "I wasn't aware that you worked here, Mrs. Hutchinson," Todd smiled blandly.

Shirley was thrown off balance by this young man who seemed immune to her pretense of charm. "I'm Gwendolyn's mother, Shirley," she repeated, her tone softening, "I'm sorry I didn't quite catch yer title."

"I don't work here Mrs. Hutchinson. I'm Daniel Gregory's assistant, I'm here on a joint venture." Todd enjoyed a good yarn as much as the next guy. He was quite unprepared for the strange reaction his story garnered.

"What does Daniel Gregory have ta do with my Gwendolyn?" Buried emotions were bubbling to the surface and Shirley looked panicked. It took her a good ten seconds to erase the unwelcome, and unacceptable, emotions from her façade.

"I'm sure Ms. Hutchinson will bring you up to speed when she is ready." Todd wasn't sure but he felt that Gwenn would not want her mother to know anything about the re-branding project.

"Is he still painting?" Shirley's voice had gone quite meek.

"Yes ma'am, he is," the sudden drop in energy confused Todd. Shirley looked as though someone had washed the starch right out of her.

"I used to know him, in Minneapolis...," Shirley's eyes clouded over, "decades ago." Shirley looked around for the door.

Todd was suddenly struck by the idea that Gwenn might not be the only one with false information about her parentage and the Daniels. "I believe you must be referring to the older Mr. Gregory. He has a son, also named Daniel Gregory, no junior or second or anything. The elder Mr. Gregory passed away a little over four years ago. Were you close?" Todd couldn't resist.

Shirley's face raced through a montage of emotions before she was able to hit the brakes and stick with calm disinterest. "Oh, I hardly knew him, ya know. Just met once or twice, he had a kinda small studio in Minneapolis." Shirley was trying to get the upper hand in this greased pig of a conversation. "I'm sorry fer yer loss. I hope he was right with God before he passed, ya know."

Todd's jaw tightened, "Yes, I am sure God and Mr. Gregory had made arrangements." His tone was sarcastic but frosted with just the right amount of piety—reminiscent of Shirley's own special blend.

"Oh fer goodness sakes, what is Daniel Jr. doin' with my Gwendolyn."

Todd's mathematical brain spit out at least two hundred delightful responses, but his conscience would not let him spill Mr. Gregory's beans to this poisonous adder of a woman. "I'm sure Ms. Hutchinson will be happy to fill you in on the details. Would you like to wait in her office?" Todd chuckled to himself at the thought of Shirley, caged up in the office, waiting for a daughter that was currently ravishing his boss.

"Sure, you betcha, I'll wait in Gwendolyn's office," Shirley was regaining most of her self-importance.

"Can I get you some coffee?"

Shirley looked at Todd as though he had offered her chilled monkey brains. "Oh my, I don't drink anything that pollutes the temple of the Holy Spirit," Shirley shook her head in dismay.

"So, that's a 'no, thank you' on the coffee," Todd despised poor manners—especially when they were combined with proselytizing. Todd led Shirley into Gwenn's office, got her some water—which he had not turned into wine—and closed the door firmly behind himself as he exited.

Flora was beaming at Todd like he was a superhero. "No one can handle her like that."

"Piece of cake. I'm wearing my bullshit-proof vest under this shirt," Todd tugged jokingly at his collar.

Flora giggled like a schoolgirl, "Thanks for taking one for the team."

"My pleasure. Now where were we before we were so rudely interrupted?" Todd put his hand on Flora's shoulder. He meant it as a conspiratorial *team* gesture, but when he felt his face get hot and saw Flora's cheeks flush he instantly put both hands in his pockets.

Fifty

Gwenn was dropping Daniel off at his car in the Perkins parking lot—they were brazenly sucking face next to his open car door. The cool autumn breeze was blowing Gwenn's hair like a model on a photo shoot. Daniel twirled his fingers in the loose strands.

"I hope somebody in there is taking notes for Adele," laughed Daniel.

"I'm sure by the time the story reaches the night shift you'll have had me splayed across the hood of the car."

"I'm not one to disappoint the fans," Daniel picked Gwenn up and made for the hood.

"Daniel! Daniel!" Gwenn was protesting with nervous laughter. She was incredibly turned on by the raw power in his arms and the dangerous look in his eye—but she was utterly mortified by all the rest.

Daniel set her gently on the fender, "I'll settle for one last kiss, but you better make it good or there'll be consequences." Daniel squeezed between her knees and slowly leaned her back.

Gwenn lunged up and threw her arms around his neck. Her tongue licked the edge of his lip before plunging into his mouth. She wickedly bit his bottom lip and softly kissed his top lip. One final open-mouthed, passionate display and she eased back onto the hood.

"Well, now you're just showing off," Daniel lifted Gwenn off the car and kissed the tip of her nose. "Okay, I really have to go. Todd will crucify me if I'm late for my appointment."

"When can I see you again?" Gwenn was feeling the high slipping away and the old doubts were creeping in. What if he was busy tonight?

"My appointment with Dr. Mountainside ends at 3:30 and I think I can make the drive in under 15 minutes..." Daniel pretended to do a complicated math calculation in his head. "How does 3:45 sound?"

Gwenn just cracked up, "We're pathetic you know."

"That's what I love about us," grinned Daniel.

Daniel slipped into the driver's seat and Gwenn kissed his cheek and closed the door. She spun to walk back over to her car. The sound of his car window sliding open caused her to turn.

Daniel was waving a small envelope at her, "Hey, Gwenn you left these photos at my place."

"You keep them. It's your dad's work, it'll mean more to you," Gwenn was proud of her new grown-up attitude.

"That's the thing, there's one photo in there that's not my dad's stuff."

Gwenn walked back toward his car. "What do you mean?"

Daniel opened the package and slid out the odd photo. "See this one...it's a wall mural, totally different than my dad's style. Plus, look at the date on the border..." Daniel turned it so Gwenn could read the date. "It's one month earlier than the others."

"What the hell was Shirley up to?" Gwenn was furious to think that her mom had been fooling around on Ed and treating him like shit ever since—maybe that made it *okay* in Shirley's mind? If Ed was worthless...maybe that's how Shirley justified her indiscretions. Gwenn was sick of this woman.

Daniel felt Gwenn tug the photos out of his hand. "Gwenn don't do anything you'll regret—"

"You know what I regret? I regret living half a life. I regret giving up on my dreams and watching my father be beaten into submission by that insidious woman. She would never let up, she always called him a dreamer. She was always criticizing him for not making more money. She just made him feel small...and he took it...because he thought she was some perfect, Virgin Queen." Gwenn was getting a full head of steam, "It's about time someone pointed to the Empress and told her she had no clothes."

"Gwenn?" Daniel could see a storm was brewing.

Gwenn took a deep breath, "I'm okay, honestly. I just need to do this for myself, and for Rachel. We've lived in fear of the legend of 'Shirley the Pure' for way too long."

"Is 'good luck' the right thing to say to someone who is about to open the family closet and turn on a million-watt bulb?"

"Thanks Daniel. Good luck to you, too. See you at 3:45—if I make it out alive," smiled Gwenn.

Daniel wiggled his finger in a little "come here" gesture and planted one more kiss on Gwenn's beautiful, but slightly chapped, lips. "You may need some Chapstick before 3:45 miss."

"Point taken," Gwenn smiled and walked to her car.

Daniel heard her squeal out of the parking lot and felt a sudden sense of pity for Ed and Shirley.

Fifty-one

"Shirley! Shirley?" Gwenn was on the rampage. When she threw open the study door and saw Pastor Ed sipping some decaffeinated tea and reviewing his sermon, the words spilled out before she had time to self edit, "Where the hell is Shirley?"

Ed raised his eyebrows and slipped off his drugstore reading glasses, "She's not home, Gwenny. What's gotten inta ya kiddo?"

Gwenn's rage was at the boil and if Shirley wasn't here to get tarred and feathered then somebody else was going down. Gwenn flung the photos onto the shabby desk that Ed always insisted on keeping, "Did you know about this?"

Ed sorted through the photos nodding as he remembered the paintings of Daniel Gregory. When he came to the wall mural he stopped, and Gwenn thought she saw tears well up in his eyes.

"I knew it! That bit—" Gwenn stopped herself this time, collapsed into a chair and heard it squeak in protest to the force of her descent. "Why didn't you call her on it? Why did you let her treat you like dirt and cut down all your dreams?" Gwenn put her head in her hands, "I can't believe you...dad." She felt the significance of calling him *dad*. She had called him Ed for so many years, years of hoping he wasn't her dad...but now she felt compassion. He was a victim of Shirley's wickedness, just like Gwenn. She felt camaraderie with the man. She could finally call him dad, and not regret it.

"Gwenny, I think there's somethin' ya should know," Ed paused and looked at the photo of the mural.

"I know dad, I already know. I tracked down the guy's son; he admits his dad was a bit of a womanizer. Shirley was young...whatever...but the other artist, I don't know about the wall mural guy...maybe she was seeing him, too."

"Yeah, she was," smiled Ed.

How could he be happy about this? "Dad, you knew?" Gwenn cried bitterly. "How could you stand it?"

"Gwenny yer mom was married ta the mural guy."

Gwenn still wasn't getting it. "But when did she meet you?"

Ed laughed a low, tired rumble, "Let me start at the beginning, Trixie."

Gwenn nodded. She was so eager to hear the tale of Shirley's infidelities that she ignored the Trixie-ism.

"I painted this mural. It was a gift ta yer mom. See the eyes and the lips," Ed pointed at the features of a beautiful woman in the midst of the psychedelic swirls.

"You paint?" Gwenn was shocked. "But if you—"

"Yer mom thought it was real good. She had met this Gregory fella at a protest rally or concert; anyway she thought he could get me into the art circles. Ya know how Shirley always wants the best fer people."

"What—?" Gwenn knew no such thing and she was growing concerned for Ed's sanity.

"We met with him, I took some pictures of his work, I thought it was pretty good stuff, ya know. He said he liked my mural, wanted me to do more...he asked Shirley ta bring him some prints of the photos I took at his studio." Ed chuckled, "Turns out he was much more interested in that there Shirley than my murals."

"So she cheated on you?" Gwenn was desperately trying to salvage some sordid outcome.

"She punched him square in the face and marched out," Ed's face glowed with pride. "She's got a helluva right hook."

Gwenn's head was spinning like Nancy Kerrigan, before the incident. Shirley was Ed's hero—and Ed had just used a partial swearword. Had she slipped and hit her head? Gwenn was trapped in Bizarro World. "She was trying to promote you? She wanted you to paint?"

"She's changed a lot over the years Gwenny. We've had money troubles and God's asked us ta give a lot ta the church." Pastor Ed put on his thoughtful, pious face, "But my relationship with God and my relationship with yer mother are still the two most important things in my life. Ya don't quit when things get tough... 'Let no man put asunder,'" Pastor Ed nodded his Sunday morning prayer nod.

Gwenn smiled, *and we're back*, she thought. Everything was right with the world. Ed stayed with Shirley because God had joined them, blah, blah. Gwenn was shocked to learn that Shirley had ever been a generous champion of Ed's, but Gwenn was relieved to hear that even Ed could see that things had changed over the years.

"Ya really worked yerself into a lather, Gwenny. How long have ya been stewing over this?" Ed leaned in and gave Gwenn the caring pastor look.

Gwenn didn't have the heart to tell him the whole truth. "Oh, I just found those pictures a little while ago—thanks for setting me straight, dad."

"We'd like ta see ya at church Gwenny."

All trace of relatability was gone and Gwenn grinned as Pastor Hutchinson hit his stride. "I'd like to see you paint again, Ed."

Gwenn grabbed the photo of his mural off the table, looked at Ed and walked out of the house. That should make him go easier on Rachel, she hoped, as she drove slowly back to her apartment.

Fifty-two

Annie was holding the phone in front of Rachel and Rachel was spitting out excuses.

"Just call them," insisted Annie.

"I'll do it tomorrow, first thing tomorrow," Rachel was begging.

"Rachel, just get it over with." Annie pushed the phone closer, "It's not gonna be any easier tomorrow."

"Fine! Gimme the fucking phone!" Rachel grabbed the phone from Annie and hastily dialed. The anger would only stave off the fear for a few seconds.

"No swearing," cajoled Annie.

Rachel stuck her tongue out and thumbed her nose at Annie. "Hi dad, it's Rachel."

"Well, today is my lucky day. Gwenny just left. How's my baby girl?"

Rachel was curious about Gwenn's visit but thought it would be best to strike before she lost her nerve. "Dad I need to talk to you and mom...tonight," Rachel stuck her tongue out at Annie for a second time, "I'm bringing a friend."

"Why don'tcha come fer dinner, ya know how yer mother loves ta entertain," Ed was thrilled that Rachel had finally found a nice boy. He just hoped the boy was right with God.

"No, we have dinner plans," Rachel easily lied. "We'll just come by around 7:30 or 8:00...okay?"

"I'll tell yer mother the good news, kiddo. Can't wait ta meet yer friend," Ed was bubbling with good cheer.

Rachel felt a little sick. "Bye dad."

***

Shirley was fed up with this nonsense. She emerged from the seclusion of Gwenn's office, "I have things ta do, please tell Gwendolyn I stopped by." Shirley fixed Todd with a condescending stare, "Can ya help me with my coat?"

Todd chuckled at the two-syllable *coe-utt*. "Certainly Mrs. Hutchinson it was a pleasure to meet you," Todd took great pride in his ability to keep a civil tone.

Shirley drove home in huff. She could not believe the nerve of that Todd person. She would have a word with Gwendolyn about him.

***

Shirley allowed the door to slam behind her. "Ed? Ed? Did Gwendolyn call? I've been ta her office and she's not there. I thought I raised her better—not returning her own mother's calls. I mean fer goodness sake!"

Shirley was surprised that Ed hadn't thrown in a supportive response. "Ed, where are ya?" Shirley nearly fainted when she rounded the corner and saw what Ed was holding. "What are ya doin' with the good china?"

"Great news! Rachel's bringing a friend over. I thought ya'd want ta make pie or something." Ed was humming a little Battle Hymn of the Republic under his breath.

Shirley forgot all about her ungrateful daughter Gwendolyn and swung into action. "Give me those plates Ed, ya don't use dinner plates fer dessert," Shirley was offended at the mere thought.

Ed obediently handed over the plates. He was completely out of his element in the kitchen.

"Ed go ta the Piggly Wiggly and get a bucket of vanilla ice cream and some cool whip fer the pie," Shirley was looking in the refrigerator, "and get s'more caffeine-free pop, too."

Ed dutifully got the keys and headed out the door.

Shirley was frantically straightening the living room. She turned and ran for the vacuum. The house was immaculate by the time Ed returned. Even the silk plants had been dusted.

Shirley had heated up some leftover tuna hot dish for dinner. "Do ya want some fresh potato chips crumbled on yers Ed?" Shirley called from the kitchen.

"Whatever's best, there dear."

Shirley brought the plates to the table. "Well, of course fresh is best Ed. The old ones there get soggy in the fridge. Ya'd think after 35 years ya would've figured that out."

Ed just smiled and took his plate. "Rachel will be here at 7:30 or 8:00, did I tell ya?"

"No ya did not tell me. Now I'm gonna get indigestion from eatin' too fast," Shirley shook her head in defeat. All these years she'd tried to train Ed, but it was too great a task. It was just her burden to bear. God would see the sacrifices she'd made.

The pie was on the cooling rack when the doorbell rang.

Ed was surprised to see a pretty, blonde girl with Rachel. He smiled warmly, assuming Rachel was bringing a lost soul into the flock. Maybe Rachel was getting more out of those singles' nights than he thought.

"Hi dad," Rachel hugged Ed, "this is Annie." Rachel opted to save the *girlfriend* bomb for later.

Shirley was not as quick to hide her disappointment. "Oh, Rachel yer father said ya were bringing a boy over," Shirley just shook her head.

"I said friend, Shirley," Ed offered up, in his defense, but no one was listening.

"I'm Annie, nice to meet you Mrs. Hutchinson," Annie shook Shirley's hand vigorously.

"Aren't you a strong little girl," Shirley eyed Annie suspiciously. "Who wants apple pie?"

Rachel froze in horror, remembering her thirteenth-birthday disaster. Shirley had made the *Mock Apple Pie* recipe on the back of the cracker box and Rachel's friends had teased her for months.

"Oh, don'tcha look at me like that Rachel—it's real apple pie."

"I'd love a piece Mrs. Hutchinson," Annie thought she might be slightly allergic to apples, but at this point dying of anaphylactic shock seemed like a great option.

"I'll have some too, mom."

"Count me in, honey," Ed was looking forward to bringing another lamb to God's fold. "Extra ice cream, too."

"Honestly Ed, think about yer health," admonished Shirley. "Who, besides Ed here, wants ice cream?"

"We'll all have ice cream, mom," Rachel was growing impatient.

When Shirley served the pie, Rachel scooped her ice cream onto Ed's plate. He smiled up at her as though the Savior himself had bestowed the loaves and fishes upon him.

"Oh, Rachel. Really," Shirley shook her head.

The foursome ate the remainder of their pie in silence. Ed finished first, "Must be good, no one's talking."

"Yes, the pie is delicious Mrs. Hutchinson. I see where Rachel gets her flair for baking," Annie hated the sound of her own voice. "Suck up a little more Annie. I don't think she's going to give a shit about your lame compliments once she finds out you're actually eating her daughter's pie," Annie silently scolded herself.

Shirley collected the plates and an uncomfortable quiet settled on the front room.

Ed sensed Rachel's hesitancy and hoped to ease Annie's journey to the Lord. "Rachel, honey, is there somethin' ya wanted ta tell us about Annie, here?"

Rachel took a deep breath and reached for Annie's hand, "Annie is my girlfriend." Rachel forced the tears back into the ducts, "I'm gay." She squeezed Annie's hand so hard she thought she may be crushing actual bones, but she couldn't let go.

Shirley was a quick study and was the first to find her tongue, "Rachel Hutchinson I'm not havin' this nonsense. If you two are gettin' married er havin' a commitment ceremony, er whatever you people call it. I will not be there." Shirley stood up and narrowed her eyes on Rachel, "And if anyone asks why I'm not there, ya know, ya can tell 'em I'm dead."

Shirley marched from the room and slammed the bedroom door.

Ed's face was a mask of pain. He just couldn't accept the image of his baby girl burning in hell for all eternity.

"Dad, say something," tears were spilling from the corners of Rachel's eyes.

"I'm sure it's just a phase yer going through, kiddo. Ya just haven't met the right man, ya know."

Annie felt invisible. Rachel hadn't exaggerated one bit; this was one creepy freak show. Her own mother had been very supportive when Annie broke the news. She had never known her dad, but she assumed he would have coped.

Rachel knew there was no turning back; better toss all the cards on the table right now. "Dad, I've been gay forever. I mean I didn't know what to call it when I was 13 or 14 but I've been openly gay for over 10 years. Everyone else knows."

Ed shook his head in disbelief, "But ya dated that nice Christian boy, Matt er was it Alan?"

"Yeah, we had a great arrangement, until he met Eric and they started going steady. Alan was gay, dad."

Ed couldn't deal with all this information. He reacted in the only way he knew how, "I'll pray fer ya, Rachel. It's never too late ta come back ta God."

Rachel took her dad's hand and looked into his confused, misty eyes, "I'll pray for you too, dad. We are all equal in His eyes."

Fifty-three

Rachel and Annie rode home in silence. Annie drove and Rachel sat on the middle console with her arm around Annie's neck and her head on Annie's shoulder.

Annie held her arm tightly around Rachel's waist as they walked up the stairs to the apartment. She grabbed the wine and Rachel flopped onto the couch.

"Annie?"

"Be right there..."

"I gotta call Gwenn, okay?" Rachel knew Annie was sensitive about Gwenn, but Rachel really needed to hear Gwenn's voice.

"It's fine, I'm fine...whatever you need." Annie sat down on the couch and put her hand on Rachel's cheek, "Thank you," a tear trickled down Annie's face.

"I'm sorry it took me so long. You deserve better," Rachel looked away, ashamed.

"You're the best. That was a nightmare. I mean, I thought you were always exaggerating about your parents. You were a rock star in there. And I would know."

Rachel laughed and hugged Annie.

"That line you threw down, on Ed—that was bad ass," Annie nodded her head. She was so proud of Rachel. "All right call your sis. I'm gonna start on the wine."

"Pour me some, too. I can multi-task." Rachel was wiggling with anticipation as the phone rang.

Gwenn grabbed her phone, anxious for news from her sister. "Rache, did you do it?"

"Done."

"Did everyone make it out alive?" Gwenn rolled out of Daniel's arms and searched the floor for her underwear.

Daniel grinned lasciviously and whispered, "I'm not done with you."

Gwenn giggled and mouthed, "Shut up."

"Gwenny, you nympho! Is Daniel still there?" Rachel was glad, for once, for the distraction from her story.

"Not still...more like again," Gwenn winked at Daniel as she left the bedroom. "Did you really tell them... everything?"

"I even outed Alan Peterson. That probably wasn't cool, but he's been out with his parents for years, so I think it's okay."

"Did Shirley totally freak?"

"Not to worry, she's dead."

"What?" Gwenn screeched so loudly Daniel was forced to peek around the corner. Gwenn waved him away.

Rachel recounted the story of the pie, the silence, the announcement and Shirley's instantaneous death.

"Wow, that's cold. Are you okay?"

"It's weird Gwenny, I actually feel kind of free. Like I was carrying all the burden of the secret and now it's just gone. I'm actually a little happy," Rachel smiled at Annie.

"How about Pastor Ed, did he try to 'lay hands' on you and Annie to exorcise the demons?"

"Oh shit, that's right. I forgot tell you that he thought I was bringing Annie home to be saved," they both screamed and laugh.

"Did he rebuke you?"

"No Gwenn, he's going to pray for me."

"Oh, sorry," Gwenn knew the frustration of parents who refused to accept their child's choices, parents who thought they could pray their own will onto their children.

"Actually, it was cool. I had the perfect comeback," Rachel recited the line about everyone being equal.

"Rache, that was inspired. Ed might come around, give him time," Gwenn thought about the glimpse of her real father that she had seen in the study. There might be some hope of finding a dad she could relate to, somewhere in there—someday.

"Yeah maybe. Hey what were you doing over at the house? Dad said something about seeing both his girls today."

"This is your day Rache. That story can wait."

"My day my way!" Rachel giggled. "Right now I'm gonna drink some wine and make out with my girlfriend!"

"Good for you!" Gwenn cheered.

"I want to meet Daniel though. Do you think you could *drag* him to the Big Gay Halloween party next month? No pun intended. I mean, can you keep your tongue out of his mouth long enough to talk?" Rachel teased.

"Barely," Gwenn laughed. "Can we just sneak in and sit in a corner, in like regular clothes?"

"No costumes? Are you serious?"

"Rache, I hardly know him—"

"Oh, you hardly know him? You've been romping him raw for 24 hours and you hardly know him?" Rachel cracked up.

"Shut up freak!"

"I think we know who the freak is...freak," Rachel laughed. "Go big or go home. That is the dress code. So you find him a sexy costume and parade him around. Because you love me sooooo much!"

"Apparently, polyester is all the rage."

"Not happening Gwenn. So, we can all grab breakfast or dinner before then—but you guys have to go. It's my official coming out party! I love you...bye."

"I love you too, Rache...bye."

Gwenn hung up the phone and ran back to the bedroom. Daniel had carefully draped the sheet across his lower half, making a nice tent.

"I'm glad you found a way to amuse yourself while I was on the phone," Gwenn tried to be stern.

"I don't know what happened?" Daniel opened his eyes wide. "I was just laying here innocently, thinking about you bent over looking for your panties—"

Gwenn slipped her panties off, turned around and bent over, "You mean like this?"

The speed at which Daniel flew off the bed and slipped into position behind Gwenn was breathtaking.

"Exactly," Daniel pulled Gwenn closer and thrilled as she moaned softly.

Daniel pressed Gwenn up against the wall and nipped teasingly at the nape of her neck. He pushed into her slowly, deeply—like he had all the time in the world.

Gwenn felt the heat of Daniel's breath on her neck and she arched her back and sank onto him. His hands lingered on her breasts and finally she felt his fingers interlocking with her own.

Daniel turned her around and her legs immediately wrapped around his flexing hips. His lips moved across her face kissing her cheekbone, her eyelid and finally her expectant mouth.

Gwenn lurched and momentarily lost her rhythm as her entire being enjoyed Daniel's tongue exploring her lips. She could feel her tea-kettle coming to a boil and she dug her fingers into Daniel's shoulders to increase her pace.

Daniel got the message and met her speed with a power all his own.

Gwenn was so high and the sensations so unbelievable she was certain she would lose consciousness. Thankfully Daniel bit into her neck just hard enough to keep her lucid.

Morning found Gwenn spread across Daniel's chest, her hair tickling his nose. Daniel pushed the auburn-streaked tresses off his face and ran his fingers through Gwenn's hair. It was unexpectedly tangled and Gwenn awoke with a start.

"Ow! Are you torturing me now?" Gwenn rubbed the sleep from her eyes.

"You started it. With the hot, sexy breath on my chest and stuff."

"What am I going to do with you, Daniel?"

"Honestly, what are you going to do with me?" Daniel's multi-hued eyes fixed Gwenn with a soul-penetrating gaze.

"Honestly? I just want things to be easy." Gwenn glanced at the spiral shells on her nightstand, took a deep breath and forged ahead. "I don't want to *work* on a relationship. I just want it to be natural. If you feel like being here, great! If you have to be at the Gallery in Minneapolis, okay. If you have to travel to Europe—"

"You'll come with me! Great!" Daniel jumped in.

"If I have time, and if you let me pay my own way."

"Okay, if you let me treat you any time I choose, along the way."

"I don't love you for your money Daniel."

"But it's a nice bonus, don't ya think?"

"Sure, but it's not the reason—"

"Wait, did you say you loved me?" Daniel raised an eyebrow.

"I meant...it's just that...did I?"

"Did you?"

"If love is feeling happy and free, and just hanging out with your best friend...then yes, I said it. I love you Daniel."

"I love you, too Gwenn," Daniel kissed Gwenn's cheek. "Easy, free, no pressure. BFFs," Daniel smiled and nodded.

"BFFs." Gwenn laid her head back on Daniel's chest and smiled as she listened to the strong, steady rhythm of his heartbeat. "And no pressure, except that you have to escort me to the Big Gay Halloween party with Rachel and Annie. And, apparently you have to wear a sexy costume." Gwenn barely had time to squeal before Daniel engulfed her, rolled her over and descended.

Epilogue

Gwenn and Daniel found their way through the labyrinth of skyways to the Curling Club, took a deep breath, walked through the doors and into the Silver Broom banquet facility.

"Holy frickin' moley!" Gwenn exhaled. The flashing lights, the crazy costumes and the pounding music hit her like an icy snowball. She felt ultra self-conscious. Her decision to risk a *couples* costume for herself and Daniel was immediately regrettable. She put up the hood on her little red cape and tugged her skirt down in a fruitless attempt to hide her face and cover her thigh-high fishnet stockings. She tried to hold her wicker basket lower to cover her shame...too late.

"GOD DAMN! Gwendolyn Hutchinson you beautiful WHORE!" Rachel came screaming over in her see-thru genie costume, crossed her arms over her chest and nodded her head at Gwenn. "Poof! You're all kinds of sexy, master."

"Shut up! You little bitch! I can't believe you talked me into this—"

Rachel put her hand up in front of Gwenn's face and wagged her other finger at Daniel. "Oh, this little wolf thing is workin' for you. I mean, obviously you painted the crazy awesome wolf on your own face, but who found the fur chaps? There are some boys that are gonna go home crying their little gay eyes out!"

"Why thank you Rachel." Daniel bowed his ear-clad mane and flourished a furry paw to Rachel. "I personally think that Gwenn found the chaps first and used this ridiculous 'you gotta go over-the-top for a gay party' excuse to get me in them." Daniel and Rachel shared a hearty laugh at Gwenn's expense.

Gwenn's face was nearly as red as her cape, but it got redder when Daniel howled and whispered in Gwenn's ear some nonsense about eating a *cookie* later.

Rachel's eyes sparkled and Gwenn noticed the crispness of the sparkle. "Hey, are you really doing the sober season thing?" Gwenn asked, unable to keep the disbelief from her voice.

"Yeah, that's my Satan's Eve resolution to Annie. No drinking until Valentine's Day." Rachel rolled her eyes and shrugged. "No drowning my sorrows—you know honesty and sharing my feelings and a bunch of other shit."

And right on queue, Annie rounded the corner, barely able to walk in her genie's bottle costume. "Hey, you guys need to get your name on a team. The curling competition starts at 10 p.m."

"Wait, we are actually going to curl?" Daniel raised both paws in alarm. "I thought having the party here was just a crazy gimmick."

"Uh, yeah, it is a gimmick. It's the curling gimmick, los lobos." Annie looked at Daniel like he was the crazy one, and continued, "FYI don't sign up on the drag queen team. It's a blast to watch them sliding around in eight-inch platforms, but they play like crap."

Rachel grabbed Annie and planted a huge kiss on her silvery blue face. Annie stumbled and nearly tripped on her bottle. "Just making sure I passed the breathalyzer—and I'll be getting' back IN you later." Rachel winked at Annie, in case the reference was too subtle, and strutted off.

Gwenn reached out a hand to stabilize Annie. "She's almost more obnoxious sober!"

Annie laughed and unexpectedly hugged Gwenn. "Thanks for not talkin' shit about me when I flaked. She's the best thing that ever happened to me and it's pretty awesome that you let her trust me again."

"Annie, I...Rachel makes her...she was—"

"She worships the ground you fuckin' walk on. If you would have pushed her to ditch me, she would have dropped me like a—" Annie searched for the right word.

"A donut!" Annie and Gwenn screamed it in unison.

"Don't mean to break up this Dali-esque portrait, but I don't know a goddamn thing about curling and I am a tiny bit competitive. Shall we retire to the ice lane...thing?" Daniel gestured to the curling pits.

"It is so hard to take you seriously with paws," Gwenn hugged her wolfie and took several courageous steps toward the ice before she was blindsided by a seven-foot drag queen.

"Oh, sorry miss sweetness. You are lookin' fierce in that Li'l Red get-up!"

Gwenn glanced way up at the huge pink wig, feather eyelashes and hairy chest, "Alan?"

"Gwenny? Is that you underneath at that sha-bam?"

"It is I, Gwenn Hutchinson out sinning with the best of them. So what have you been up to since you so rudely dumped my sister for that Eric stud-muffin?"

"OMG, I can't believe you remember his name! I didn't! But who has time for the past, when there is a present to open. Who is this precious doggie?"

"I'm Daniel, and I am sorry to report that I am the property of this little girl, from head to tail." Daniel spun his backside around to show-off his tail, forgetting he wore chaps.

Alan clutched his stuffed breast and gasped, "I am gonna need a Cosmo to cry into—STAT!" He spun on his silver platform heels and strutted into the crowd.

"Daniel, how thoughtless!" Gwenn giggled and cuddled up next to him, letting her hand slowly drift down to his nearly exposed haunch. She squeezed, "We better run you through some drills wolfie, Li'l Red doesn't like to lose.

Acknowledgments

It is a terrifyingly beautiful moment to reach this acknowledgments page. Despite the solitary nature of my childhood, there have been some amazing people in my life. It is a wonderful honor to be able to thank them for their support.

A huge hug to my grandmother, Rita [pronounced *Right-a*]. She gave me the greatest gift I could ever receive—laughter.

I am overjoyed to thank the people who willingly listened to my ramblings as I worked my way toward completing this novel: David, Jamie, Anne, Joy, Cindy, Katherine, Carolyn, Tiffany, Topher, Jim, Natalia, Kristi and Roy. Thank you DVRD—you know why!

Thank you to my first readers, who gave me invaluable insights and encouragement: Anne, David, Sterling, Tracy and Scott. *(More than once!)*

This book would not have been possible with out the endless support of my partner, Scott and the indulgence of my two sons. I also want to thank my sister for showing me the depth of our bond—on too many occasions to count.

I love reading, and the tale of the Hutchinson sisters owes a thanks to Juliet Marillier, Michael Chabon and Marian Keyes, just to name a few. Finally, thank *you* for spending a little time with Rachel and Gwenn.

Photo by Michele Bradley

RUE graduated from Pepperdine University with a degree in Journalism. Her intimate knowledge of the Midwest, the inordinate amount of time she spent in its churches' pews and her unique parentage make her an expert on life after religion. Having moved 17 times by the time she graduated from high school Rue has seen more than her share of the Great Plains. She never stayed in one place long enough to make human friends. Her best friends were all characters from her beloved books; and the love of reading led to a lifelong passion for writing.

www.ruescorner.com

Made in the USA
Lexington, KY
21 June 2014